M000278773

# GREAT EXPECTATIONS

*A Novel*

# VINSON CUNNINGHAM

HOGARTH

LONDON / NEW YORK

*Great Expectations* is a work of fiction. Names, characters, places, and incidents are the products of the author's imagination or are used fictitiously. Any resemblance to actual events, locales, or persons, living or dead, is entirely coincidental.

Copyright © 2024 by Vinson Cunningham

All rights reserved.

Published in the United States by Hogarth, an imprint of Random House, a division of Penguin Random House LLC, New York.

HOGARTH is a trademark of the Random House Group Limited, and the H colophon is a trademark of Penguin Random House LLC.

Library of Congress Cataloging-in-Publication Data
Names: Cunningham, Vinson, author.
Title: Great expectations: a novel / by Vinson Cunningham.
Description: First edition. | London; New York: Hogarth, 2024.
Identifiers: LCCN 2023041470 (print) | LCCN 2023041471 (ebook) |
ISBN 9780593448236 (hardcover) | ISBN 9780593448243 (ebook)
Subjects: LCGFT: Political fiction. | Novels.
Classification: LCC PS3603.U68 G74 2024 (print) |
LCC PS3603.U68 (ebook) | DDC 813/.6—dc23/eng/20231023
LC record available at lccn.loc.gov/2023041470
LC ebook record available at lccn.loc.gov/2023041471

Printed in the United States of America on acid-free paper

randomhousebooks.com

2 4 6 8 9 7 5 3 1

First Edition

*Book design by Susan Turner*

*For Renée.*
*I hope you can hear me.*

*I'm Nobody! Who are you?*

—EMILY DICKINSON

I

# 1

I'D SEEN THE SENATOR SPEAK A FEW TIMES BEFORE MY LIFE GOT caught up, however distantly, with his, but the first time I can remember paying real attention was when he delivered the speech announcing his run for the presidency. He spoke before the pillars of the Illinois statehouse, where, something like a century and a half earlier, Abraham Lincoln had performed the same ritual. The Senator brought his elegant wife and young daughters onstage when he made his entrance. A song by U2 played as they waved. All four wore long coats and breathed ghosts of visible vapor into the cold February morning. It was as frigid and sunny out there in Springfield as it was almost a thousand miles away, where I sat alone, hollering distance from the northern woods of Central Park, watching the Senator on TV.

"Giving all praise and honor to God for bringing us together here today," he began. I recognized that black-pulpit touch immediately, and felt almost flattered by the feeling—new to me—of being pandered to so directly by someone who so nakedly wanted something in return. It was later reported that he had spent the moments before the address praying in a circle with his family and certain friends, including the light-skinned stentor who was his pastor in Chicago. Perhaps the churchy greeting was a case of spillover from the sound of the pastor's prayer. Or—and from the vantage of several years, this seems by far the likelier answer—the Senator had begun, even then, at the outset of his campaign, to understand his supporters, however small their number at that point, as congregants, as members of a mystical body, their bonds invisible but real. They waved and stretched their arms toward the stage; some lifted red, white, and blue signs emblazoned with his name in a sleek sans serif. The whole thing seemed aimed at making you cry.

I wonder now (this, again, with all the benefit and distortion of hindsight) whether these first words of the campaign and their hungry reception by the crowd were the sharpest harbinger— more than demography or conscious strategy—of the victory to come. Toward the end of the speech, during a stream of steadily intensifying clauses whose final pooling was a plea to join him in the work of renewal, he wondered "if you"—the assembled— "feel destiny calling." In bidding goodbye, he said, "Thank you," and then, more curiously, "I love you."

Despite his references, overt and otherwise, to Lincoln— and, more gingerly, to King—his closer resemblance was to John Winthrop making phrases on the ship *Arbella*, assuring his fellow travelers that the religion by whose light they'd left Europe in 1630 could cross spheres, from the personally salvific to the civic and concrete. If you could love God and love your neighbor, Winthrop promised, you could build a city, too, and that city could be a great monument to the Beloved. That swift motion—God to *polis* and back up, shiningly, to God—made Winthrop an unintentional paganizer. His attempt to subjugate politics to sacred things had only, over time, made the holy more worldly, more easily used by the likes of the Senator. I was only freewheelingly guessing; feeling bright, disconnected, and experimental; trying to bring a few loose intimations into closer communion with one another—but I thought I sensed a quality similar to Winthrop's in the Senator. Or maybe, I thought, doubling back as I've always done, he was the well-developed melody of which Winthrop was the earliest theme. The Senator had invoked God at the top of his text, a numbingly common move in these settings, and sounded comfortable, even natural, doing it, which was becoming somewhat more rare. He seemed to have resolved an older generation's jittery and overscrupulous tension about church and state. He'd figured out how to say aloud and with good cheer and without seeming to be some nationalist-imperialist pervert what had been implicit for too long: that now we had a country that could more or less plausibly claim—as much by dint of its world-shredding misdeeds as by its misty glories—not to serve God but to *be* God. Render unto Caesar and rest your conscience. Without any off-putting intensity, the Senator insisted, above all, on faith. "In my heart I know you didn't just come here for me," he said. "You came here because you *believe* in what this country can be."

"Your Love Keeps Lifting Me" played him off the stage. The campaign, just beginning, was still a scarcely glimpsed frontier. I can't say that I thought he would win.

I REALIZE ONLY NOW, TOO late for it to matter much, that the Senator reminded me of my pastor, who had died not long before the beginning of the campaign and, in those days, was often on my mind. Both men were tall and skinny, both hooked their thumbs slightly and used their other outstretched fingers as scythes cutting syntax into the air. Both had the complexion of a cardboard box left out to bleach in the sun. The pastor wore glasses, like I did, but the Senator didn't. Both had smooth, flexible voices that could sound rough in a pinch. Their similarities aside, though, that enigmatic word—*destiny*—must have put me in mind of my pastor, too. I can remember one Friday night, many years earlier—I must have been twelve—at a Bible-study session in the former Elks lodge in Harlem where our church held its services. My pastor had slowly paced the two long aisles of the church. Wearing a zip-up sweater and soft slacks instead of his Sunday robes, he gave a long disquisition on a topic he loved: the many ways in which the future belonged to God. We believed in predestination, he said, not in destiny; the latter word, despite what it shared in etymology with the former, contained no implication of an Author, and had therefore been co-opted by the squishy New Age. As he talked, he held the microphone loosely but securely, like how good tennis players hold the racket. He looked around the room, catching gazes and letting them drop, smiling prettily even as he unfolded mysteries that terrified me. The truth, he said, was that your life—and *this* was freedom—was a gesture minutely choreographed by God. To seek salvation required free will, but the one who had planted, and could count, the hairs on your head had also engineered your mechanisms of choice. Your heart could open only if He'd given it a hinge. He chose you before you chose Him, and so it was with every other eventuality, no matter how hidden or seemingly accidental. You are not *lucky*, my mother often said, you are *blessed*.

DESPITE MYSELF, AND NOT WITHOUT some reservations, I find that I do believe in luck, in flukes, in the meaningless harmony of certain sequences. Take the one whereby I landed on the Senator's campaign, only a month or so after watching his big speech. I'd flunked out of college after learning, aged twenty, that I would soon become a father and, after a year of occasional classes at the City University and weekends spent staring at my little daughter, found a wintertime job as a private tutor. My first and only student was a kid of thirteen or fourteen named Thadd Whitlock, whose mother, Beverly Whitlock, had once appeared on the cover of *Black Enterprise* magazine; she also—and here was the luck—served on the board of my high school, where people still vaguely remembered and liked me. Somebody who knew that I was back home and had strayed from the path had passed along my name. Thadd was sweet and gangly, with an indecisive almost-Afro, ashy elbows, and a mouth crowded with braces and spit. His parents had divorced when he was very young; from the beginning he expressed to me a mild, unsecret dislike for them both.

Once a week, we worked on what Beverly called his "opportunities for improvement," English and math. Thadd's problem, such that he had one at all, seemed to be a simple, sometimes willful indolence. Often, after settling himself at the table in Beverly's long, sparsely decorated living room, he would fold his thin forearms, skin to tabletop, forming a cushion on which he finally, with a flop, rested a cheek. In this naptime position, he'd say, "I had a long day. I don't know how much I'm gonna be able to focus." He'd take a look at the short stories I'd photocopied (Hawthorne, Jackson) and shrug. "I mean, that looks like a *lot*." Soon I started bringing sections of the newspaper— sports, politics, reviews of movies he'd seen—and having him read those instead. This was better: he laughed as he read, or nodded his agreement, or got surprisingly mad, and afterward I'd make him tell me, aloud or in writing, why. When he had math homework, I'd watch him scrawl his way through equations, then point out his errors, usually born of inattention. I assumed, but never said, that he had ADD.

I didn't see Beverly much. She was usually still at work when I got to her building, just south of Central Park. A doorman let me go up to the apartment, where Thadd was home alone. I sent weekly emails to Beverly about his progress.

This week, Thadd and I focused on the Writing/Reading side of our studies more heavily than the Math. I wanted to steer us a little away from the newspaper articles we had been reading previously and back toward some literature. After trying to get through a bit of Thornton Wilder's *Our Town*, I decided that the play might be a little dense and slow-moving for Thadd's taste. I wanted to stick with drama, though, because 1) it's much faster to read than prose fiction, and 2) Thadd has shared with me his interest in acting. I decided that the next play would be Lorraine Hansberry's *Raisin in the Sun*. It was a little difficult to start; for some reason, Thadd decided before reading the play that it just wasn't something he'd like. I told him that there was no way to know whether he'd like it or not unless he tried. After a scene or two, he seemed to warm up. Toward the end of last week's session I tried something with Thadd that I haven't before: I gave him small sections of the reading to do on his own, along with some questions to answer. The reading went fine; I could tell that he had read what had been assigned to him. The questions I gave him were another story—he'd forgotten about them. We also read a few poems (Ginsberg, Hughes, Brooks) this week and Thadd did some writing comparing them and mining them for their central themes. He did a generally good job, although he needs to make sure that he's writing in complete sentences at all times. He should also work hard to make his handwriting as legible as possible.

Beverly overpaid me, as far as I could tell. At the end of my sessions with Thadd, she'd show up in a long coat, flecked gray with a velvety black collar, and stick a plain white envelope into my hand. Two uncreased hundreds for two hours' work. Her hair was often tied back into a loose, glossy bun. Her brows were full, almost bushy, and her dark, sparkling eyes almost always looked wet. At rest, her plush lips sat slightly open, showing her perfectly even teeth. She always looked ready to smile or to talk. She had a firm, quick way of asking how things had gone—was Thadd cooperating, did he seem to me hostile or sad—and, no matter my answer, allowed no hint of worry to mar her beech-colored face. I'd promise my weekly report and quickly leave. Sometimes, when Beverly was away at meetings or out of the country, the doorman would slip me the envelope on my way out.

One day, the doorman didn't have my envelope. "Says she's sorry," he said, "but she forgot to leave the money. Says to call her." The doorman's big, close-set eyes funneled into a straight, sharp wedge of a nose and, below, a mustache that looked like the fur lining of a coat. He smirked nicely, and I took this—it was the first time I'd seen him approximate a smile—as an expression of our mutual status as inconvenienced employees. "Thanks," I said, wondering, not for the first time, about the doorman's ethnicity. He spoke with an unplaceable accent.

"Fucking euro's killing me," Beverly said when I called, in a way that intimated, mistakenly, that exchange rates played an irritating role, any role, in my life, too. "When I'm back I'll pay you double, I promise; I left in a rush—but listen, I wanted to ask you something else."

She was part of a loosely organized group of former midwesterners, now geographically diffuse, all known names in their various fields, who were patrons of—and proselytizers on behalf of—the young junior Senator from Illinois. "I've been a supporter since he ran for *state* senate, right?" Beverly said. Now he was running for president, and his campaign had asked if she knew anybody young and competent. (The thought that, by asking Beverly, they had also been implicitly seeking somebody *black* swung athletically through my mind.) Had I heard of him? "I know you talk lots of politics with Thadd, right?" She said *right* a lot. Sometimes it was a question punctuating her phrases. Sometimes she said, "Right, right, right" as a complete sentence, very briskly, a way to answer something you'd said without producing a real response. Either way, it made you feel in the know, on her wavelength.

Yes, right, I'd heard of him, I said. Within a week I had an interview. After another week I started.

EXILED FROM SCHOOL, I NOW lived back at home with my mother, just south of Columbia University, in those blocks between 100th and 110th where the Upper West Side starts its softening into Morningside Heights. Mom and I were close. Sometimes she sprayed me with the battery of sighs (comic) and stares (insinuating her insight) that had been her weapons when I was a kid. She was short, with smooth, dark skin and a prosecutor's ersatz innocence in her eyes.

When I told her about this job that had arrived from nowhere, she tucked her small mouth into a pretty purse and worked her eyebrows into glyphs. "Davey," she said, unprompted and without the consolation of any answer from me. "Davey!" Just as she'd acted, prophetically, in the months before I'd admitted to her, in a letter from school, that my girlfriend was pregnant. "Davey, tell me again how you know this woman? Bethany?" She purposely botched people's names when she was working up some prescient dislike. "She's just giving out jobs?"

To pacify her, I showed her the ten-year-old *Black Enterprise* cover: "Beverly Whitlock Seals $175 Million Deal," went the exuberant headline. In the picture, Beverly stood with her arms crossed, with the skyline—the old skyline, the one with both towers, still lively and pert like a pair of Dobermans—behind her, river water sparkling at the bottom of the photograph. "Mmm-hmm," said my mom. "Deal with who?"

Back then, Beverly had started one of the first black-owned investment banks. But to make it go big—thus went capital in America—she'd cut a deal with an even bigger white-owned outfit. She wasn't *owned*, I said, just *helped*. But I could see my mother forming a judgment and letting it harden.


I WAS EXPECTING THE KIND of place you see in movies about politics—a run-down storefront with concrete-colored carpeting studded with bits of crud and loose paper, and signs

and posters all over the walls. But the campaign finance office was an undercover operation, and we fundraisers were,
I quickly learned, apostles to the rich. The office was on an
upper floor of a building, on the corner of Fifty-ninth Street
and Park Avenue, whose deco façade was black and shining
gold. A wood-paneled wine shop occupied the storefront.
Ours was a suite of three small offices and a spacious front
room, all rented from a boutique hedge fund across the hall.
On the walls hung primary-color World War II–era cartoons
of smiling businessmen in boxy suits and secretaries in skirts
and pumps—each illustration was six or seven feet tall and
emblazoned with graphic logos about the rewards of plain
hard work. AVOID THE LOAFER!, one blared. I assumed that the
posters were the punchline to some subtle joke whose prem-
ise I couldn't quite get. It wasn't an art-world thing—making
fun of advertising with its harsh grammar and lurid images;
scrambling its nefarious formulas until they added up to a
critique—and neither could I imagine that the hedge fund
owner, whose name sounded formidable and vaguely British,
didn't earnestly believe in the sacrament of effort, at the very
least his own. Maybe the posters were funny just because they
were old and because, after their dated fashion, they put forward an unassailable message in a straightforward way. The
name of the Senator was nowhere—not so much as a sign on
the suite's front door.

My boss, the office's director, with whom I'd had my brisk,
friendly interview over the phone, was Jill Hunter. She had
been an entry-level staffer on his campaign for the Senate only
a few years earlier and now was responsible for his fundraising
in New Jersey, Connecticut, and, most importantly, New York.
(This was his world-famous opponent's home state, therefore

a rich symbolic field tilled by Jill, and now, in a small way, by
me. Every dollar harvested here would be fragrant with special
meaning.) Over the phone she'd pointedly emphasized the ve-
locity of her advancement as a way to say: *This could be you!* She
was older than me, but not yet thirty. She walked me through
the office with the vintage propaganda, showing me the room
where she sat with her two deputies, Hannah and Ashley, and
the smaller room that I'd share with another assistant hired
only a week before, a pale kid with curly reddish hair who went
by Howland, although his first name was James. Howland
waved to me casually as I passed, wearing a grin that looked
instinctual and sincere—*Homo americanus affabilis*—and made a
grand flourish toward the desk that was now mine.

Jill had a softened southern accent: she'd grown up in
North Carolina but had her professional sanding-down in political Chicago and on the transcontinental campaign circuit
whose transient heart was in the gentrified neighborhoods of
northwest Washington, D.C. She spoke in blunt, short, conspiratorial syllables that made you feel in on a joke. Total reverence she saved for the Senator—she called him that, "the
Senator"—alone. She had a flat, diligently pretty face spattered
with freckles. Her short nails were coated with clear polish. She
wore dark blue heels and bare legs. As she led me through the
office on that first day, both of her outer calves were ovals of
hot, bright red, the color of a mortified or sunburnt face—
evidence of hours of businesslike crossing at the knee. Everybody here dressed like a banker or a lawyer. I'd worn my boxy
black suit with a slight shine at the elbows.

Jill sat at the desk, between me and Howland, and started
to tell me about the way our work went. Spreadsheets, lists of
potential donors to call, detailed schedules of soon-coming

events. The whole fast-moving day was a recruitment into the
tedium behind the show.

"It's got its own kind of rhythm," Jill said in an abstract,
airy way that let me know that she'd given this a lot of rhap-
sodic thought. "A lot of building and tending and plain old
keeping up. Then, all of a sudden, a big show."

Her description matched patterns I already knew: rehearsal
and performance, observation and drawing, study and speech.

"I get it," I said. "That makes a lot of sense to me."

TWO WEEKS LATER, THE SENATOR was in town for a reception at
a music producer's apartment, only a block north of the office.
This was the first time I saw him in person—Jill and I stood
waiting for him on the sidewalk outside a building with a high,
stony, undecorated entryway. A black SUV pulled up, and he
stepped out of a backseat, moving to button his black suit even
before both of his feet had settled on the ground. He was tall
and skinny with a graceful, Roman bearing: almost exactly
how he looked on TV. His face, at rest, looked just a touch less
calm. Behind him was a tall man with a buffed bald head who
wordlessly and without much movement passed the Senator
something that looked like a mint.

As the Senator walked into the lobby of the building, Jill fell
into step with him and told him my name. He smiled and, for
the first time since he'd left the car, stopped moving. His height
was helped by an incredibly erect posture that looked almost
practiced, the kind of talismanic maneuver meant to send forth
subliminal messages about confidence and power. In the same
way, and engendering the same effect, he held his chin at a high
angle, aimed not directly ahead but at a point on the ceiling

several yards ahead. Proximity to the Senator made me feel slightly shabby. Unconsciously, I straightened out, too. Without looking down, I could count the dull, stressed-out spots on the dress shoes I'd only ever really worn to church before then.

"David!" he said peppily, repeating after Jill. He took my hand to shake it. Soft hands, tight enough grip. "Where you from?"

"Here," I said, pointing vaguely uptown, behind my head.

"Huh. Real New Yorker. I liked living here."

He went to Columbia, I knew, right near my mom's place. Whenever he set foot in Manhattan, one magazine or another made sure to run an old picture of him sitting on a park bench with a small Afro, wearing a tight bomber jacket.

"Well, welcome to it," the Senator said. "Glad to have you here. It's gonna be a ride."

Before I could come up with something else to say, he moved on. Soon he disappeared into an elevator, flanked by Jill and the bald aide. Jill had opened a folder she'd shown me an hour earlier, full of information about the producer and his guests, and was pointing down at it as the elevator doors slid shut. I stayed downstairs in the lobby beside a huge marble Last Supper–looking table, checking the names of incoming guests off a spreadsheet. They all looked happy to be where they were. The conversations I overheard had largely to do with polling data. From those who hadn't paid yet I collected checks. The freshly signed checks, casual and restrained in muted mints and grays, were all made out for twenty-three hundred dollars—the most you could donate without breaking the law. Before long I had more money sitting beside me than I'd earned in my entire working life. On the table was a big, smooth ceramic bowl, and sticking out of the bowl were several sheaves of nude, leafless vegetation.

After all the guests had come and the outstanding money had been gathered, I went upstairs, where the Senator was already talking to the crowd. The place was lit by candles and dimmed lamps. The audience of seventy-five or so was largely black. Two incredibly famous recording artists, he a rapper and she a singer, both given an extravisual glow by their renown, stood near the front of the throng. The men at the gathering (I watched them closely, searching for a way to be) had dutifully brushed hair and, I noticed, startlingly well-maintained cuticles. Understated signet pinkie rings abounded. The younger guys had sharp, rectilinear hairlines like mine. The older ones— those, that is, who hadn't shaved it all off—let their widow's peaks crag freely across their foreheads. Their suits were deep gray and midnight blue; cuff links peeked out over the rims of their sleeves. The women wore efficient cocktail dresses that cut closely under the folds of their armpits and tended to fall just above the darkening mounds of their knees. Their calves shone glossily. They had presses and perms that stretched to graze their shoulders and the tender places between their shoulder blades. Everybody looked less fancy than I had expected, and somehow this made them seem—to me, at least—more impressively rich. The room smelled like lotion and subtle cologne.

The televisual calm had crept back over the candidate's face. He spoke from a corner, behind a polished grand piano. The crowd had their backs to the window that was the living room wall. Over their heads you could see the East River slowly churning. The speech the candidate gave was a toned-down, smartened-up version of what he said on the stump in the early states: his same bright hope but for an in crowd; graduate-level electoral inspiration. He made in-jokes about the superstar couple—how he had them both on his iPod. He made lots of jokes, and organized his cadences around the crowd's laughs in the way he usually handled earnest cheers. He praised his host, the producer, exaggeratedly, called him everything short of a civic hero. The guy, cannonball bald with black plastic glasses, couldn't stop smiling. When things opened up for questions, only one person asked anything remotely challenging. It was a fairly famous writer, liberal cable-news pundit, and sometime journalist who spoke very quickly and loudly, with a nasal edge, and had the only Afro in the room. "Obviously everybody here loves you," he said. "But how are you gonna *win*?"

THE NEXT DAY, AT MY new desk, with the same black suit jacket slung over the chair behind me, I picked up two calls. One was from the producer. He wanted to talk to Jill, but she was gone. (Everybody, I soon learned, knew that she had a long history with the candidate—they imagined she had special access—and so nobody wanted to talk to anyone but her.) "Just let her know that last night was perfect," he said, "and tell her that I want to talk to the Senator for, like, five minutes. There's a bunch of money in Atlanta you guys need to pick up."

The next call was from Beverly. She didn't want Jill. "Congrats," she said. "They were right to hire you." Then she asked about who had been at the producer's house the night before and how much money I thought the event had brought in. I gave her all the names I could remember from the list, plus the ones I knew from TV. After a bit of crude math I offered a number, just a guess.

A high-dollar fundraiser for a presidential campaign is a glorified party planner, I soon discovered. The culminating accomplishment of the job, its chief evidentiary milestone, is an

~~event~~ at somebody's house, or at some art gallery or concert
hall, or in a big hotel auditorium. Rich people find you, or
you find them, and, after a heavy-petting period of tenuous
courtship, some of them offer up their places as venues for the
candidate to visit. Say you can fit a hundred fifty people, total,
in your townhouse—a hundred paying a thousand dollars, and
fifty more at twenty-three hundred, which, in those days, was
the max contribution for the primary campaign. The twenty-
threes would get admission to a small pre-party conversation,
plus a photo with the Senator. The whole group gets a short,
intimate-seeming speech at the zenith of the cocktail party,
plus a question-and-answer session. This brings in $215,000
for the campaign, at the expense of an hour, give or take, of the
candidate's time. That math was endlessly expansive, like a nation on the move. A thousand at a big Marriott for $500 each
was a neat half million, and even less handshake-dense for the
"principal," as a candidate was sometimes called.

Everybody thought of primary campaigns in terms of
the places where votes were cast first—Iowa, New Hampshire, Michigan, Nevada, South Carolina—but they were *built*,
as Jill liked to say, on phone calls with the people she called
"prospects," in New York, Los Angeles, San Francisco, Chicago, Boston, and Dallas: the big cities where lawyers, people
in "finance," and the rest of the pedestrian rich tend to cluster. These were the kinds of people who dreamed of political appointments and ambassadorships, invitations from the
president to state dinners and holiday parties. At the very least,
you'd have a story about how you knew him *when*. Our candidate wasn't a favorite to win; people were just starting to know
his name. All the more reward, then, for his earliest and most

intense supporters in the event that chance—or fate or a brush-
stroke by God—won him the race.

There were rules. Twenty-three hundred per person, not a
penny more. You could give another twenty-three, to be tucked
away for the general election, but the campaign had to promise
not to spend it until such a time came. The money had to come
from your personal account; no company cards or checks: cor-
porations couldn't contribute. If you were hosting a campaign
event at your home, you could spend only a couple thousand
on food or a sound system. Anything above that would have to
be tallied as a donation, and would start to count against your
twenty-three hundred. Rules for staffers were less byzantine
and, in fact, all came down to a single commandment: never
talk to the press.

The candidate's time was currency. He would alight on a
city for a few hours or, greater miracle, an entire day, and the
job of that town's fundraisers was to fill his time with parties
yielding checks. He had just "done" a million in a day in L.A.,
we'd hear on our weekly conference call with headquarters;
what did we think was possible in New York? Jill would make
an ambitious proposal—we could do a million too, but we'd
need time for four events—and we'd be gifted with the time.
We'd plan a big, semi-populist affair for the evening—a ballroom at the Hyatt with space for hundreds, tickets starting at
fifty a pop—and fill the rest of the day with stops at private
homes in the city or the suburbs.


IN EARLY SPRING, DURING THAT pregnant time when the city's
deep, salty musk begins to rise and its colors start to fizz—

greens greening; flowers in yellow and purple imported by
neighborhood associations and planted in the shallow square
beds around the trees—a publisher hosted the candidate at her
brownstone in Brooklyn Heights. The sidewalks outside the
place were lopsided and occasionally broken; there were huge,
lividly fertile tree roots bursting sexually through the concrete.
Overhead, the trees' branches hosannaed, casting inconsistent
patches of shade. Birds tattled. The neighborhood had a crumbling glamour I couldn't quite name.

Inside, on a wall near a staircase, was a skinny, vertical
LED screen; vaguely poetic sentences in red letters flowed
downward on it. The publisher, a white woman in soft clothes,
had slightly overbooked the event (fine for us; stressful for her),
and the dying afternoon was hot, and the walls of her half-
octagonal living room were slick with condensation. The air
smelled of allergenic grasses, and sneezes sounded at arrhyth-
mic intervals. I stood by the door holding a clipboard, pen-
ciling check marks next to the names of late arrivals, looking
over at the red letters on the screen—I found myself pleasantly
fixated on the artwork without really knowing why. None of
the phrases would stay still in my head, but as they scrolled
on, appearing out of and dissolving into some void beyond the
borders of the screen, they seemed fraught with deep meaning. Here came a snippet of a sentence: SWEET BREATH AND I
SHOW YOU THIS NOW AND KEEP IT FOR LATER MY ROOM HAS FOUR
DOORS NOT ALL CLOSED THE ROOM HAS THREE WINDOWS SHUT AND
A BLIND CLOSET HERE IS RUSTY WATER TO CLEAN ME. I wanted
to know about the room, and whose sweet breath, and whose
soon-clean body, poisonous with rust. And: Show you what?

The Senator stood on a rented platform, his back to the

high windows, his head a foot or so above the eye level of the rest of the crowd. He looked, I thought, like a drawing room orator out of Henry James. ("A voice, a human voice, is what we want," somebody pleads in *The Bostonians*.) He held a microphone and, after a quick exposition of his themes, fielded questions. "What *precisely* do you mean," asked a white woman wearing chunky glasses and dangling earrings in abstract shapes, friendly skepticism in her voice, "when you say that you're inspired by your relationship with God?"

In his college days—he told me this directly, after the event, just outside the brownstone, both of us negotiating a topsy-turvy slab of street—he'd sometimes haunted these Brooklyn streets so close to the bridge. Could we leave him alone while he headed to the car? "Could you guys let me walk ahead?" is what he actually said. I realized, looking around, that although he'd used the plural, I was the only person to whom the request could plausibly apply. Jill and Howland were already a few paces behind us, poking away at their BlackBerry phones with their thumbs. I'd instinctively followed close behind him, like a child caught up in his mother's skirt at the grocery store, warned in advance not to wander. I must've seemed like some presumptuous kid, intent on chatting his way up the rungs of the ladder.

"Of—no, of course, I'm sorry," I said, grimacing in a way I hoped he could see.

"You guys booked this thing tight," he said. (*You guys* again. Cloaking his authority in informal diction.) Before the publisher there'd been a thing up on Central Park West—another host, another party, another series of questions—then a private meeting with some tawdry-looking local politicians wearing

suits almost as shapeless as mine. His complaint almost flattered me; he seemed to think—that plural—that I'd had something do with the planning of the day.

Before I stepped back, I ventured a last bit of conversation.
"Did you like it? I mean, living here?" Casual, I hoped.

He laughed. "I think most people who come here do. The
young ones, at least." Then, pressing the issue: "Now I don't
get to walk around alone so much."

"That must be—" I said, regretting already having started
to say something else. "Yeah, yes."

I slowed down, and soon he was half a block ahead. At
the record producer's he'd carried his body with a controlled,
respectable cool: black man on the move. Since that day I'd
been conscious of my own shoulders, kept trying to ease them
backward. Now, though, perhaps under the influence of the
publisher and her friends, and of his own post-adolescent memories, he walked with a bohemian lilt, looser in the spine and
at the knees, Whitman over Brooklyn's "ample hills." After a
while, he came to a curve in the street and suddenly stopped,
having noticed a break between brownstones. Past a short gate,
painted black in chipped impasto, was an immediate drop; thin
trees grew from below and shadowed the sidewalk like an aw-
ning. Beyond was the highway, then the river and a snippet of
the skyline, Easter-colored and blurry-edged in the sunset. The
rest of us stood watching as the Senator leaned against the gate
and looked out at the water for a minute. When we reached
midtown, forty-five minutes later, he took a few steps toward
his hotel, then, after appearing to engage in some quiet delib-
eration, glared back at Jill and spoke tensely, with little of the
forbearance that had seemed to quiet and impress the crowd in

Brooklyn. Three events was too many, he said; he was losing his voice. He poked the air with his phone for effect.

That night I tried to figure out who had made the LED screen. The artist had to be famous, I figured. Otherwise the publisher wouldn't have put it in such a prominent spot. Into a search bar I wrote "LED artist," then "screen word artist," then "LED words screen visual art." Eventually I found an old review of a show by the artist, Jenny Holzer. "The use of language, especially writing, in works of art," the critic wrote, "is often thought to dilute the power of one medium by borrowing energy from another." The critic's name was Gary Indiana. He went on to make some fine points. But that opening salvo stuck with me for months. It made obvious sense to me, this idea that words could override and even hijack another—any other—medium. (Maybe I was uncommonly vulnerable to a generalism like this: I'd been preached to, or at, and mostly liked it, all my life. My interest in the visual arts often came down to meaning, which, for me, mostly came down to words.) And, sure, I thought, the pleasure I'd experienced in the brownstone was probably the product of one kingdom of language rubbing up hotly against another. The Senator against the artist. Formal politics against aesthetic politics. Establishment against avant-garde. Both could be bought and pedestaled in somebody's home.

I SOON LEARNED I WAS good at these kinds of things. I could talk to people and put them at ease; I could figure out what they wanted to hear and then say it. I learned fairly early on how to ask for money while seeming to flatter the person I was asking. I had always liked following. I got no special thrill from making

decisions, or issuing orders, or choosing sides. I could understand many ways of thinking without committing to anything
in particular. I admired surrender. Phenomena floated past me.
This was mostly unhelpful in everyday life, but as equipment
for a career in fundraising, it wasn't so bad.

I wasn't much good, though, at the basics of my work as
an assistant. The spreadsheets over which I had dominion—
the volunteer list, RSVP sheets for various events—were maintained only in sporadic drifts. I was slow to reply to emails and
slow to check voicemails. Before leaving for events I often forgot to print out check-in lists, and ended up asking the hosts
if they had a printer I could use. I often passed the time at
my desk reading articles on the internet. One of my favorite
political magazines had given front-page blogs to five or so of
its best writers. I read them compulsively, following the links
each writer offered, watching the political press convince itself
that the Senator could win. When, after our first full fundraising quarter, it turned out that we'd outraised our front-running
opponent, I could sense new sympathies in the bloggers' prose.
I couldn't figure out how to spend my energies in a more bal-
anced way.

LATER IN THE SPRING, WE brought the candidate to Harlem for a
speech at the Apollo. My name and email address were on the
flyer, and during the week before the event, RSVPs darkened
my inbox, arriving minutes apart, in clusters of six or seven,
like a blanket of locusts from the sky. Sooner or later, I copied
and pasted the names onto a lengthening list. There had, by
now, been several promising polls out of Iowa and New Hampshire, and our fundraising numbers—spurred more, propor-

tionally, by ordinary internet donors than our more glamorous high-dollar names—had begun to convince some of the political press that we could win. Outside the theater, a line of nervously happy, mostly black attendees began under the famous marquee and stretched along 125th Street, then around the corner onto Eighth Avenue. I walked up and down the line, checking its length and shouting reminders to be ready to walk through metal detectors. "Airplane rules," I kept saying, having come to enjoy the economy of the command.

Backstage, I met Cornel West, who had accepted our invitation to introduce the Senator. He wore a dully black three-piece suit, and an irregular Afro reached up and outward from his gray temples. Warmth radiated from the large gap between his front teeth. When I introduced myself, he made an ostentatious bow that ended with his torso perfectly parallel to the ground. "It's an honor to meet you, Brother David," he said, "and I can't even *begin* to express"—here his face glowed with something almost paternal—"how good it is to see *you* here." I'd heard variations on this construction for most of my life, and it had never lost its power to make me feel a mixture of pride and slight abashment. Once, during rehearsals of Verdi's *Requiem* for a Glee Club concert, in a big yellow auditorium at Riverside Church, a pretty soloist—black and heavyset, her soprano all high spikes and trembling swoops—pulled me aside and made the phrase, adding this tag: "Because you don't often see *us* in spaces like these." It was in part, or even mostly, a complaint, the deepest implication being that to be black and outnumbered—a fly sidestroking through milk, and therefore comically visible, as Ellison once put it—was a lonely thing. Funny, surely, but also sometimes sad. But, for me, the commiseration quickly turned into joy. Here, after all, was some-

one—an utter stranger, a singer or scholar—who was sincerely
glad to see me, who, unbidden, had expressed a kind of love. I
wondered if that ever happened to white people, and I counted
it—have *always* counted it, I realize now—as an advantage. In
this way, ethnicity was very much like grace, and very much
unlike most other American things: it existed apart from the
notion, the mere appearance, of merit. You could belong without a fee.

"It's good to see you too," I said to the professor, projecting, I hoped, a restrained but real admiration. I'd seen him
lecture once. In the year between my kid's birth and the beginning of the campaign, my custom—monthly, maybe—was
to visit friends at school. My friend Paul wrestled and studied
languages and literature "in New Jersey," as he called it. Everybody knew immediately, in spite of—indeed, *because* of—his
embarrassed euphemism, that he meant Princeton, but, still,
it made him feel better not to have to say the name. Paul's
opinions were always definite in the moment, if changeable
month to month. He liked to have his way, and appreciated
that I never seemed to care. I admired his confidence and took
real pleasure in doing whatever he wanted to do around campus. Paul woke me one morning—he lived in a suite with a kid
he didn't like; I'd slept on the pull-out couch in the common
room—and said I should come with him to class. "This guy's
amazing," he said. "I can't let you miss it." We watched from
the slack-jawed balcony of a wood-paneled hall.

The referential web of West's lecture made it like and
unlike—placed it in some bizarre reality just across from, but
somehow subsidiary to—the church preaching I'd known.
Here, he posited joyfully, was how *this* verse in the Bible was
like *that* passage from *Song of Solomon*, and *this* verse of *that* song

by "Brother Marvin," and how all three, and more, if you wanted, came together to help explain the antediluvian situation in New Orleans. Politics and literature and metaphysics all flowed from the same human-energetic deposit, and so, for him, they were one. Part of his performance—wild waves, arched eyebrows, stuttering chuckles, subtle movements of his long, thin fingers—was to make his connections seem complex (and, thereby, to make his listeners feel smart for following along), but the deeper effect of the lecture was the perception of an attractive simplicity at work in the world. Behind the veil of unscrutinized appearances was a grand, comprehensible unity. At bottom, all times were the present and all people the same. None of the shit he mentioned was even on the syllabus, Paul said, beaming. Papers were assigned and graded by teaching assistants, and nobody got anything but an A. I bought *Race Matters* after class and finished it before my time in New Jersey was up.

When, three years after I met him at the Apollo, the relationship between West and the Senator fell apart, I felt slightly depressed. Maybe the rift was inevitable. West was committed to the highest ideals—anti-capitalism and Christ—which made him quick to point out the many ways in which the Senator had failed to satisfy the special debt he owed to black people. But there was a personal dimension, too—soon after election night, the story goes, the Senator stopped returning West's calls, and when the inauguration came, the professor couldn't even score a ticket. He stood in the backmost regions of the Mall, behind the reflecting pool, wearing his mortician's costume and, on his face, a smoldering mask. In the early years of the presidency, he occasionally mentioned the snub—mentioned it often enough, in fact, to cause several of his fellow intellectuals to dismiss

his apparently principled arguments against the administration as being rooted, ultimately, in low emotions—pettiness
or jilted love. But when I think of the equalizing style of that
Friday-morning talk on the campus in New Jersey, I suspect
that personal loyalty is simply, for West, a swatch of the moral
quilt into which political economy and foreign policy are also
woven. Maybe the Senator's rudeness was a tip of the spear, a
hint of things to come.

After our greeting backstage, West walked out and delivered
his exhortatory—and, as was his custom, largely improvised—
introduction, explaining to the assembled how this candidacy
was a rare instance of "radical love" made real. When he was
done, the Senator joined him onstage. The men met in a half
embrace and waved to the crowd, their dark suits like shadows
against the Apollo's blood-red curtain.


I STILL LIVED IN MY old room, at my mother's, on the Upper
West Side—when my daughter was with me, she slept in a
small bed in primary colors, perpendicular to mine, our heads
pointing toward each other. She stayed here once or twice a
week, chattering volubly and clacking her hair clips together
in a constant swish. She liked to hear me talk, so as I dressed
I narrated my motions. In the mornings, I often splurged on
cabs to the campaign office on the East Side. Even when I
was running late, I asked the cabbie to go a handful of blocks
north, very much out of the way, so that we could enter the
park at its crown and ride down Park Drive. I looked out at the
fields of cupped leaves, still holding the past night's mist, then
emerged on Central Park South, feeling fresh. At lunchtime I
sometimes walked east, past the old Bloomingdale's building

and into an open-air rotunda where two curved buildings faced each other, creating a pair of glassy parentheses. Between the buildings was a circular driveway where nicely dressed people were dropped off to go to work, or to the comically expensive restaurant at the bottom of the building. I'd stand off to the side of the driveway, looking through the glass at the diners or up at the spot in the sky where the buildings seemed almost to meet.

One day, Jill took me to coffee and asked if I was interested in keeping my job through the end of the primary. Every assignment I was given I finished late, she pointed out; the lists I kept were never up to date; and I didn't try particularly hard to hide my internet habit. Everything she said was true. Still, she added, people liked me. "That matters," she said. But I'd have to get my shit together if I wanted to stick around.

# 2

I FIRST SAW TERRY BLACKSHEAR WHEN HE CRUTCHED UNBIDDEN into our office. Of all the aspects of his appearance, I remember the crutch best. Long, thin, made of light-looking hospital-grade metal, a gummy cushion at the underarm, its matte surface giving off a muffled sliver of reflected light. We learned later that he'd been tossed off a Jet Ski on vacation, off the coast of Antigua, and ripped his femur cleanly in two. That day, wearing a baseball cap and a rain-wet trench coat, a pillowy New Balance on his good foot, he'd offered himself up as an intern.

"I hope you don't mind my showing up like this," I overheard him saying to Jill. "But I believe in what you're doing. I really like everything he has to say, and I want to help in any way I can."

We almost never got uninvited guests; the address wasn't listed. Jill delivered the spiel we normally gave over the phone, about how this was a fundraising office; it wasn't the kind of place where people sat around waiting to go knock on doors or pass out signs. "I can make calls," Terry said, interrupting. "I'm very good on the phone." Jill finished the script: We mostly planned events—dinners and receptions, in private homes and hotel ballrooms. Sometimes we needed volunteers—"our assistant David keeps a list," she said, pointing to me—to show up on the night of one of these parties, check names off lists of RSVPs, collect the odd check, and help keep reporters away. "I can do that, too," Terry said. Before he left, he handed me a tan folder and said, "David, was it? Could you add me to your list?" I opened the folder, saw the résumé inside, and closed it without much more than a glance.

He showed up once or twice a week after that first visit, undeterred by the sameness of Jill's gentle dismissals. That kind of determination was alien to me. Everything that happened in my life, good or bad, seemed to be an accident; I couldn't imagine believing, like this kid Terry so evidently did, in a world pliant, over time, to my own exertions of control. "Nothing for you just yet," Jill said every time with a nice-nasty sunniness, meeting him smilingly at the door and letting him venture little farther. "Early days, but David's got you on our list." Here she always pointed with a thumb, over her shoulder, not even looking, at me. In truth I didn't have him on the list, but Jill didn't know it; I'd let a pile of names, including Terry's, on cards and CVs and in emails, accrue. On the list, an Excel sheet with a mustard-yellow heading row, were about fifty names, mostly younger relatives and bored spouses of early donors. When I finished my additions—tomorrow, I thought daily—there'd be about a hundred more. I thought of Terry's visits as pleasant interruptions to the week.

When he didn't show up in the flesh, he called, although nobody could remember having given him the number. "Hey, Dave," he said once, abbreviating my name through the receiver as if he'd known me for years. We were already, weirdly, sort of friends. "Any events coming up? Whenever you need me, I'm there." We had different ideas about effort, but we both, I could tell, found life in its unfolding mostly funny. Or we wanted to.

But Terry's irony wasn't really perceptible in how he held his body. He had a perfectly upright carriage—not unlike the Senator's, I noticed. He spoke coolly but forcibly, always, even in his position of abject asking, seeming to expect to be listened to and heard. He was urgent but never worked up. He always wore the trench. A campaign is a magnet for maniacs, we knew. At each of the small receptions we'd put on since the announcement speech in Illinois, impromptu encampments of fans, ranters, and ostensibly issueless picketers had assembled outside on the sidewalk. Just a week before Terry's first appearance, on Central Park West at Eighty-third, a bearded, stone-eyed man had grabbed me by the shoulder, drawn my face close to his, and told me that a black president, even the threat of one, was a sign of soon-coming apocalypse. "And, lest we forget," the man said, settling the matter, "the man sucked every dick at Harvard to get on the *Law Review*, and soon the whole world's gonna know."

Terry's résumé said Dartmouth. He'd been in lots of plays, apparently, and majored in history. We'd graduated from high school the same year. After a month or so of his visits, Howland thought to google him. His father was the leader of a firm whose specialty was trading in commodities. Earnest Blackshear was, in fact, one of the country's most prominent commodity traders—maybe the most accomplished, depending on whom you asked. (I did my own search while Howland shuffled through his results. I'd never heard of commodities trading—

I only barely knew what a standard-issue investment banker did, even though I was, by then, meeting a new one every day— and felt somewhat awed by the idea. Wheat and soybeans, rare gems and steel: real *stuff*, not just numbers on a screen, all brought to heel and, in their fluctuating movements, made to aim at, as if it were a destiny, making men like Blackshear very rich. It seemed to me more elemental and more honest than the other kinds of "finance" I was hearing more and more about. In his choice of profession, Mr. Blackshear acknowledged the true source of all wealth—the actual Earth!—and juiced it for goods like some kind of god. Thinking about it made me go silent as Howland talked.) Terry's mother, Paula, ran a marketing firm and taught business at NYU. Neither Mr. or Mrs. Blackshear had given much money to politicians or to parties—this kind of thing is easy to ascertain online; search engine light made Howland's red hair shine—but both sat on boards, this museum, that orchestra, and made philanthropic noises. There were dozens of photographs of them at galas and awards ceremonies, clad in midnight colors, always angled invitingly toward the camera, his left and her right shoulder forming the open mouth of a V.

Jill's face softened, I saw, at the discovery of the Blackshears' prominence and obvious wealth. She asked me for Terry's number and called him early the next morning, and although the headquarters in Chicago wouldn't give her the budget to make a new hire, she offered him a makeshift title, "head intern." Soon he had a schedule—Monday, Wednesday, Friday—and a loaned laptop on my sleek wooden desk. When I asked Terry, years later, about those first few weeks of bizarre persistence, he said, "My father was always talking about how you get what you want."

Not long after Terry started work, Beverly called the office. "I heard Earnest Blackshear's son's in your office now," she said. "That true?" It was, I said. "Is Blackshear trying to raise money?" she asked, sounding idly interested. I didn't know. "Okay," she said, more to herself than to me. "I mean, he should. I know some people who know him. Maybe we can figure that out."

I had no idea what she might mean, but in a week she called back, saying that she'd talked to Terry's dad. He'd agreed to host an event at his house, if we could promise some of the Senator's time. Beverly and Blackshear would work together to gather a crowd. When I told Jill, she looked at me as if we'd won a sweepstakes together. We got the time. Mr. Blackshear called the office the next Tuesday and, when Howland answered, asked for me. Nobody'd done that but Beverly.

"I hear you're my guy," he said. Earnest's voice, through the phone at least, was deeper but more nasal than Terry's. A big mountain with sharp ridges. The *y* at the end of the word *guy* tilted downward, velvet in texture, from playful baritone to basso profundo.

"I guess I am," I said, trying to match his mood of unsurprise. We were happy to have him; we thanked him so much for inviting us—for inviting the candidate—into his home. By now I'd heard Jill prepare the kindling for relationships like this one. I hadn't realized that there was a script until I began, easily, fluidly, to recite it. There were a few logistical items to "pin down"—how much he could spend on catering; how many people he thought would attend; how his people should make out their checks—but we'd get there soon. The candidate, I added, remembering how Jill sometimes seasoned her speech with this nice fib, had already told us how excited he was about the event—this one, yours, in particular.

"I have to tell you, Dave," Blackshear said—quick familiarity, just like Terry's—"I've never had a president. I mean, a *future* president. At my place, is what I'm talking about. I've got friends who do the politics thing, been to stuff like this, shaken the hands. *Hands, hands, hands,*" he said, laughing at an implicit montage of receptions gone by. I could almost see it. I laughed too. "But it never struck me as much of a thing to do myself." Blackshear's tone was basically northeastern: bright and cool, quick and clipped. But then, too, he threw in a few tonal gestures that must've come from a life spent doing business all over the country: ecumenical feints. Sometimes he said *I* like *Ah* and bridged his longer phrases with a rotund, confident *uhhhh* instead of pure silence. And he had those swan-diving, velvety *y*'s.

"But Terry loves him, so I figure what the hell," he said. What's a candidate between father and son? "He likes you too, by the way. Plus, I mean it when I say *future president.* I hope you don't take that as a jinx. In my business we talk about futures a lot. I like to project."

Before long, the date and time were set. All of it was easy. The invitation I sent in an email to donors was a monument to breezy victory.

When the replies came trickling then pouring in, I learned something about names and their proximity to other names. From people I knew, by then, to be more or less loosely acquainted with Beverly—these tended to be black but weren't always—I got emails trying tenderly to figure out the relationship between her and the famous Blackshear. Were they working together now? Had they known each other all along? Others who'd of course heard of Blackshear but only faintly, if at all, of Beverly found poorly shrouded ways to ask for a full dossier. Both angles testified: some of his prestige had started, within hours, to blur onto her. And in a more muted way—via RSVP—I caught some of the runoff, too. People whose names I'd heard Jill say in a reverent way, who only rarely answered our emails and were still skeptical about the Senator and his prospects in the campaign, who sometimes said so publicly in response to questions from the press, now called the office and—as Blackshear had earlier done—asked for me by name.

At night, Beverly would call, sounding casual. Without having happened yet, the event had made us closer friends. She wanted to know about checks, whether so-and-so had sent theirs yet, what the numbers looked like. The event was filling up. More than once she talked with Blackshear—"my man Earn," she'd started to say with a cold smile in her voice—and prevailed upon him to make space for more bodies and, by extension, more cash.

"How's it feel?" she asked me one night, just a few days before the party.

"To be party to your big success?" It was late. Terry and Howland had gone home. I could hear Jill—tirelessly present—tapping softly at her keyboard in the other room.

"That I know feels good," she said. "Thank me later. But I mean in the office. Everybody's happy?" She was only asking in that declarative/interrogative way because she knew the answer and wanted to hear it said out loud. News of the night at Blackshear's had already hit the papers. It was, they said, a sign of the Senator's rising popularity—and a sign, too, of the arrival of a "new class" of political donors, those who hadn't made their mark in a campaign before the candidate's, Beverly being a leading example. Her name had made the *Post*—a glamorous item you couldn't quite savor in public.

"Everybody loves it," I said, pandering to my one-woman audience but also telling the truth. Jill was happy with me, I knew, and her boss was happy with her. "Everybody loves you."

Beverly laughed. "Yeah," she said. Then, suddenly: "You told me once that you wanted to be a writer. Which: fine. We need those." *We.* "But I do think you should go to law school. In terms of learning how to think."

We said little else but stayed on the phone together for a while. From her side, I could hear the muted buzzes, twinned and converging, of the river and the street. I'd seen her apartment—mostly without her in it—but, I now realized, never her office. It was somewhere in the East Thirties, not far at all. Dawdling as my ear sweated onto the receiver, listening as she talked in her way—skimming between tones of voice, sometimes maternal, sometimes sisterly, often teasing in a way I liked—I imagined her at ease. Her often-bunned hair was loose, maybe, scraping her shoulder, her stocking feet up on a nearby chair.

THE BLACKSHEARS' APARTMENT ON FIFTH Avenue was an exercise in angles on Central Park. From every window you could see a grouplet of trees or a curve of benches or a striped swatch of open green field. I walked back and forth in what Earnest called his parlor—horizontally oriented; many paintings of ancient faces; sloping eighteenth-century chairs in startling reds, tightly stuffed—looking out at these segments and creating a mental picture of the whole they implied. I'd walked the park more than anyone I knew, but seeing it like this, from above, was an alienating but not unpleasant shock. It had always struck me as a place to be lost, experienced passage by passage, in a series of unfolding images—not something you could take in in one possessive glance.

During the preliminary VIP reception, I stood in a privileged place at the Senator's left arm, making sure nobody lingered too long taking their picture with him, helping him remember names. He'd remembered me, or pretended to.

"First few months didn't scare you off," he said, and I made a small efficient smile, trying to project good humor while keeping up my subordinate's restraint.

Then he lowered his voice, parodying intimacy: "Now watch me do the cardboard-cutout routine." And, yeah, he had a point. People half-heartedly tried to engage him in deep policy discussions or rounds of pontification about the mood of the country, but in the end they did treat him like a sign, like something whose outward image was intrinsic to its identity. They knew as well as he did that his platform wouldn't change as a result of their chatter. They were there to size him up and, in the process, to be sized up themselves. That watchful, watched dynamic showed up later, in the photographs they took. Taking pictures, thinking about pictures: fatal to the integrity of their poses, but I could tell that it was a more or less natural aspect of their world. The event was just another forum for mutual scrutiny, the candidate as much a pretext for ritual action as a subject in himself.

And, yes, seeming to know this but not to care, he did his routine: a sculpture in vivid paper, chin royally high, his intelligence as evident in his gestures as in his words. My own routine seemed to be working, too. I'd gotten a new suit—untailored but it fit fine. Men with slicked hair and soft hands kept giving me business cards, placidly eager to "stay in touch" with "your office." Some even recognized my voice from the phone.

When the photo line was done, Jill took over custody of the candidate before he spoke. I was in the parlor alone. As I looked out the window, Beverly and Blackshear, together like a team, approached me from behind.

"Here you go," Beverly said, tapping me. I couldn't tell which of us, me or Earnest, was being presented to the other. Blackshear was shorter than he'd seemed in the pictures online, and looked much older. It was hard to believe that the easy voice over the phone had been his. His mouth was a wide pink stripe and his eyes were proud, his hair long and feathered front to back. He made a motion with his finger toward the window, and raised his eyebrows in a friendly way.

"That view—" he said in a tour guide's tone.

"It's perfect," Beverly said, utterly comfortable butting in on his sentence. "And I like how it's off in this . . . room. Away from where he speaks, right? A little private thing." Blackshear seemed to mouth that word, *private*, to himself without emitting any sound. "Maybe it attracts the bold and the nosy, like you," Beverly went on. "But otherwise it's kind of forbidding. Some mystery." She didn't even look over at the window—or, for that matter, at its owner—as she spoke, just at me. "Usually people plop the candidate right in front of the best window in the place. Earnest's got restraint.

"You know," she said, loosed into free association by her happiness at the shape of the night, "all the younger ones here—or, well, *most*: it's a big crowd—are Earnest's. His little employees, right? Charges. He really whips 'em into shape."

I still had an eye on the park. Somehow it seemed closer the

longer I looked, as if it were a patch of long-sought land and
Blackshear's apartment a great ship bobbing steadily toward
the harbor. Earnest—perhaps the captain in this whipped-up
analogy—seemed content (or resigned, given Beverly's expan-
siveness) not to speak, even when he and his employees came
up. I'd met almost all of Blackshear's "younger ones" over the
phone. They'd all called, offering their contributions to the
campaign via credit cards whose numbers they'd dutifully recited to me, all of them indicating his company when asked to
divulge—by necessity of law, I informed them—the name of
their employer. News of the event had traveled fast, and well-
off oglers from all over were present, but Earnest had filled
almost half the party's capacity on his own.

"Total triumph," Beverly said. "Good day at the office."

I started to say something to Blackshear—I hadn't decided
what just yet, but my mouth was already opening—but before
I could get going, she had steered him away, out of the parlor
and into the crowd that had formed around the Senator as he
started readying himself to speak.

AFTER THE SENATOR LEFT AND the donors were gone, another
party started up in the first one's wake. Terry had invited some
friends over for a whirl of food and drinks, to bask in the af-
termath of his dad's triumph. Everybody was our age, early
twenties, all dressed up nicely in sleeveless dresses and creamy
button-ups. Some of us were in the back half of the apartment
(even more hidden from the donors than the window in the
parlor), where the bedrooms were. Others sat at tables and ate.

The wall opposite Terry's bed was bare except for a painting by Renoir. The painting—I thought I recognized it but

couldn't remember where I'd first seen it—was of a woman splayed out on a beach, atop a wrinkled white sheet. Her back is propped against what looks like a mound of rocks, and her head rests on something red but indistinct. I worried over the red thing for a while, wondering whether it was man-made or vegetable, velvet fabric or an overgrown rose.

The woman's eyes are closed, but I don't think she's meant to be asleep. She can't be: her posture is tortured and her face is taut. She must be remembering something, or feeling the rocks as they dig into her skin. Her left side is on the ground, right buttock in the air. One of her hands cradles the back of her head; the opposite arm, closest to us, echoes the curve of her spine and ends in a wrist limply folded, forming something like a crane's head.

Beyond the model on the sheet are shrubs and sand, water and air. The blue from the latter two elements—sea, sky— intrudes on everything. The woman's thigh, the one that's up and free and bathing in the light, is a muddle of green and blue and gray. So close to the water it resembles a shoal. In turn, there are hints of her—russet blushes, changing flesh tones— dabbed over the face of the deep. The sand near the water might be liquid. At the crests of certain waves, tiny islands seem to appear. Sky is sea, sea is shrub, shrub is sand, sand is the body lying naked on the ground. Most of the painters I like create a kind of blur with the brush, a zone of uncertainty between one item and the next, but here—and in some others by Renoir; I recalled one: hundreds of blushing faces at an out-door party—things proceed from one another, are in some way elements of one another. The result is that everything glows and floats. Everything casts a halo. No trick of light was ever so complete.

I thought of Renoir's Catholicism, then of my Jesuit middle school principal (he'd made a point of not liking me; too much of a smart-ass, too little of a jock), and how, in his religion class, he'd taught a poem by Hopkins—"The world is charged with the grandeur of God / It will flame out, like shining from shook foil"—in order to show us what he meant by a sacramental view of life. Not only the wine and the host but trees and sunrises, sea and sand could act as a kind of portal into the action of the Trinity, he said. Once, during a late-summer week before the fall semester began, our class took a camping trip near Lake Placid; we summited a mountain and Father Duncan waved outward, toward a panorama of trees and lesser hills. He turned to us and lifted an eyebrow, quietly but obviously exulting, as if he'd proven something irrefutable about existence.

Terry noticed me looking at the painting, and he seemed, for a moment, as if he might say something about it, but the party chatter whipped up, as if by some simultaneous agreement. Mercifully he turned to talk to someone else. Nobody cared about the painter's chubby subject, her nipple facing skyward, her body one with the world, but me.

Howland was less merciful; when he saw me by the painting he walked over and mirrored my pose. I'd made the mistake, early in our acquaintance, of telling him that I wanted to write. "You should be taking notes instead of checking out nudes," he said, his voice, as always, happy and low. "This party's great material."

Terry fretted around the apartment, making sure no one sat alone. His father must have been almost fifty when he'd been born. Maybe that explained Terry's perfect old-world manners. To those of us standing or sitting in his bedroom—

a talkier scene, through another half-hidden door—he issued reminders of the food and music in the hall.

"Who *is* this guy," Howland said, watching him work.

Soon, not long before midnight, Terry swept through the house, urging us upward several flights, onto the roof. We looked out over the lip. Southward were the lights and jagged roofs at Fifty-ninth Street. Just below us, to the west, were the gently troubled trees and lit walkways of the park.

HOURS EARLIER, I'D STOPPED FOR a moment on the sidewalk below the Blackshears' place. Light from across the park—even, perhaps, from Jersey beyond—had traveled over the trees and collected in an orange wash on the building's many-eyed face. I'd often noticed this sunset effect on the East Side—another of the neighborhood's amenities, evanescent but real—and I found myself remembering a church on Lexington I'd been inside only a few times, where I'd been awed by the windows. How would the light look, just now, through that ecclesiastical glass? The window I recalled most clearly was a setting of Moses and the burning bush. The prophet, outfitted like a flame, kneels on the rocks, his cane falling crookedly to the ground. His right hand hides his eyes. The bush has two natures: flora and fauna. From its branches and leaves—mint, kelly, candy—comes a manlike figure, robed in purple, fire spouting from the halo that circles his head. Fire gives way to smoke, and the smoke is a gorgeous collage. The panes that make it up are various in color: maroon and prune and fuchsia and gray. The smoke floats up beyond the frame, who knows how high. Off to the side, we see a sliver of sky in deepening blues.

The figure in the bush presents a problem, I think. The scripture calls him "the angel of the Lord," and so the most straightforward way to understand him is as a mere emissary, neither human nor divine. But I was taught to read the Old Testament in terms of the New and, therefore, to look for traces of Christ centuries before he bodily appears. Thus the priest Melchizedek, who makes a mysterious, Dionysian appearance in Genesis, prefigures Christ, his feast of bread and wine a communion in advance. My Pentecostal pastor had a card collector's interest in these appearances, and could recite them in a mystical flurry: Adam, David, Jonah in the whale's gut, the Passover lamb, the ram in the bush, the boys in the fire, the second person of the Twenty-third Psalm—each was an early draft of the Savior to come. Maybe the angel, so called, is another. Christ, in this conception, reaches backward, through time, stunning the transcriber of the law he'd later fulfill.

Once, at the height of my belief, I'd tried to explain this—the Bible's hermeneutic density, made pretty by symmetry—to a kid named Jonah Weiss, the first strict materialist I'd ever known. We sat side by side in the church on Lexington, St. Jean Baptiste, looking up at Moses and the bush. I exegeted as he shook his head in mournful crescents. "If it were true," he said, "it wouldn't need so much interpretation." We'd been granted a break from a dress rehearsal for our high school Glee Club's fall concert, a program of Jewish songs. One was Kurt Weill's Weimar-era "Kiddush," jazzy and almost chaotic in its passing use of major sevenths and ninths. Another was a recently written Holocaust remembrance, "Kaddish for the Six Million." Large portions of the Kaddish were simple, spoken chants of the names of haunted places—after much practice, *Ravensbrück* rolled off our tongues.

Both songs had been chosen, at least in part, to showcase Jonah's transitory voice. He was a baritone in the morning, a low tenor at night (stuck, like an angel, between ontologies), and had a round, smooth timbre that made even his whispers seem amplified. He assured me that he brought no religious feeling to the job—little feeling at all: he barely moved the upper regions of his face when he sang—and that he had utterly ignored the many cantors of his youth. *Baruch atah Adonai* was nothing but vowels and notes to him. Sure, he went to shul, but only so that his parents could appease *their* parents. He'd practiced tone and breath control by listening to Enya, he said. When I asked to go with his family to temple sometime, he politely declined.

Our choirmaster, Mr. Somary, walked back to his place behind a black, metallic music stand, our sign to rustle back to attention. Weiss said one last thing: "I try not to condescend when we have these talks, but sometimes, man, you make it hard."

Somary had crooked teeth, furry breath, and a phlegmy Swiss accent. His eventual obituary in the *Times* would note his love of "neglected choral masterpieces, primarily from the Baroque and Classical periods" and his brief stint directing the singers at St. Patrick's—hence, I guessed, his access to one of the city's finest churches as a venue for his high school choir. He was a relic of a crusty disposition whose moorings in time and place I couldn't've named but whose emphasis on discipline—on a kind of priestly focus—was attractive to me, although I could never quite rise to its rigors. He was a Catholic born in Zurich, and at the beginning of the school year he'd distribute a handout, handwritten once and photocopied down the years, full of epigrams on the virtues of precision and hard work. "Pursue ex-

cellence; eschew mediocrity," one went. "Elephants have memories. Humans have pencils," went another. Nothing was surer to
enrage him—and rage he often did—than an unmarked score.
He was also, for two years straight, my music theory teacher;
in the margins of one of my longer papers, on Dvořák's Ninth
Symphony, he wrote this: "Florid. But what, exactly, does any of
this mean?" The Jesuits who'd given me my primary education
had been fairly frank about the doctrines of the church, but at
this nonreligious private high school I never met an adult, save
Somary, so willing to rail, at length, against the creep of secu-
larization, as embodied by our comfort with cultural items like
hip-hop—which he considered "sub-musical"—and abortion,
which, apropos of nothing that I can recall, he decried at every
available opportunity, including, somehow, during lectures about
the evils, almost equal, of parallel fifths. Somary's wife, Ann,
was also on the faculty; she led warm-ups every morning before
rehearsals, gave voice lessons, directed the Girls' Ensemble. An
alto cough is what I remember of her voice. They had three
rarely mentioned older children.

If Johannes Somary was a moral medieval—on this, everybody, including his exasperated fellow teachers, agreed; he had
a liberal enemy in every department—you also, to be fair, had
to acknowledge his more modern approach to music. He spoke
ecstatically of tonality, how it managed to enact the many
moods of God. He used his Boys' Ensemble as a delivery system for perfectly contrapuntal English harmony. At Christmas-
time we stood in the shadows of trees all over Manhattan, at
private clubs and in minimalist corporate lobbies, and, in our
semicircle, sang moody English airs set by Ralph Vaughan Williams. But Somary also taught Schoenbergian seriality, and his
own strangulated compositions—an a cappella Forty-second

Psalm came floatingly to mind as I stood across from Terry's building, my back to the wall of the park—substituted odd formalities of rhythm for anything resembling a home in chords. His appearance was another atonality—uncombed hair, every day a blazer and tie but also Keds and khakis, his belly distended like a child's. The tender aspect of his tyranny was this: he had long, fine fingers and would take your face in his hands if you sang particularly well. "Excellent," he'd whisper hotly as he rubbed your jawbones and ears.

I recalled those brief touches when, much later, after the obituary, the *Times* published another article in which Somary prominently figured. I hadn't, by then, spoken to Jonah Weiss in years, but soon after the piece appeared online he sent me a message on Facebook, asking if I'd seen it.

The article, written by a freelance journalist who had graduated from Horace Mann much before our time, was a long and methodically reported chronicle of pedophilia and sexual abuse at the school, told through sequential portraits of three especially egregious offenders, the last of whom was Johannes Somary. I responded.

I already have, twice.
And, yes, I knew when I saw it.

During his tenure at the school, Somary had molested a series of boys—several were quoted under altered names in the piece—after befriending them in slow, increasingly inappropriate degrees. One babysat and performed other odd jobs chez Somary until the first encounter: fly unzipped, fine liver-spotted fingers down his pants. He took a second boy on trips to Europe, sometimes in groups and at other times alone, where,

invariably, Somary insisted they share a hotel bed. Once, when
the boy expressed discomfort with the arrangement—not with
the rape (serial and senseless as Schoenberg), or the solo trips,
but simply with the sharing of the rooms—Somary showed up
at his house and begged him, in front of his oblivious parents,
to reconsider. Another kid—private lessons; Europe again—
tried suicide twice and succeeded in the end.

Jonah sent me messages in an urgent flurry, telling me how
many times he'd stayed at Somary's house without anything like
this happening. How he was robbed abroad and Somary had
wired him money. They'd gone to dinner all the time, alone, and
talked about singing. He didn't believe a word of the article.

The emotion and illogic of Jonah's messages surprised
me. We had never been best friends at school, but such that
he lingered in my memory, he did so as a symbol of half-
disgusted reason. Surely he couldn't dismiss Sunday magazine
reporting—too many accounts, too similar to have been coor-
dinated or faked—armed only with the graces of his own experience. His disclosures of closeness with Somary were startling,
too. I hadn't noticed the extent of their relationship at the time.
I began, eventually, to wonder—how not to?—whether Jonah
Weiss, with his vibratoless voice, had been a victim while I
knew him. We had both gone on a summer Glee Club trip with
Mr. Somary, between junior and senior years, singing Handel's
*Zadok* in cathedrals in St. Petersburg, Tallinn, and Helsinki.
Had Jonah made nighttime disappearances or acted strangely
by day? Was there something I'd missed? I tried to remember
but couldn't. I answered lamely.

Haven't figured out what to say.
Sorry, man.

# 3

I ONCE HAD A TEACHER WHO INSISTED THAT WHENEVER WATER IS mentioned in a black book—that is, in a book written by a black person, about black people and the fact of their blackness specifically—we are meant to think of the passage of African slaves over the Atlantic. Water, "for us," she would say, is a reminder and a symbol of trauma, wherever it may be found: flowing from a faucet, pooled in a gutter, pouring from the sky, or—as I saw it that summer, from the window of a ferry to a fundraiser on Martha's Vineyard—spread out endlessly, like a rippled blue floor.

The teacher was herself a novelist, and so, presumably, in a position to know. She taught at the City University branch I'd enrolled in—and failed, so far, to graduate from—after I'd come spinning back home, having flunked out in New England. She was very fair-skinned, with long, wet-looking black hair. Now that I think of it, this notion—water as invariable echo of ancestral pain—was what held her entire course on black women writers together; there was always water, and the more it appeared, the better and more animatedly she taught.

She especially loved, and insisted that her students love, a book about a bourgeois black woman, Harlem-bred but forgetful of her roots, coming unraveled on a cruise to the West Indies, in the middle of what was supposed to be a vacation. The woman, a widow, has strange, ominous dreams, portents of the past's unwillingness to die; when awake, she feels a stifling distortion of the trappings of her middle-class status: clothes, hats, a rope of expensive pearls—they tighten and threaten to choke her to death. Eventually, under cover of night, she packs her bags (there are lots of them: the baggage, I'm sorry to say, is a metaphor) and leaves the ship for good when it stops in Grenada. From Grenada she takes another boat, this time a wave-thrown schooner, to Carriacou, for a ceremonial dance in remembrance of the little island's slave history.

That latter voyage, the one to Carriacou, is written as a kind of exorcism. The widow falls into an italicized dream, about an Easter Sunday sermon, and when she awakes her "entire insides" erupt into violent, spasmodic waves of puke. Other women, islanders, hold and soothe her while she travails, muttering—it's unclear to whom—in a calming francophone patois. *"Bon,"* they say, in what I think we're meant to read as a chant. *"Li bon, oui."* After emesis into the water comes another urgent bodily retreat—shit. The scene ends with the woman, a vessel mercifully empty, again hanging between plateaus of consciousness, alone in a deckhouse. She senses others around her—crowded, crying, moaning, suffering. On the way to honor her ancestors, she's been joined by some of them, if only phantasmically, and if only for a while. This is the book's motion—a haunting and a casting out, then, later, a reckoning: all of it in some way occasioned by the sea.

Sometimes I laugh when I think of that teacher and that

book, because although I have been taught, and have sometimes almost accidentally taught myself, so many symbol structures like this one, and have come, in some ways, to love and depend on them—creaky explanatory crutches that they are—I have some trouble taking them totally seriously. This one, for instance, amounts to a kind of racist joke: A nigger walks onto a boat . . .

So as the ferry sped across the water toward the Vineyard, I remembered the Middle Passage thing but couldn't feel it. No metaphor, no bodies, no voices, nothing: just an illegible motion away from the city, and the occasional smell of salt and sound of birds.

I went down to the bottom of the boat, where an older man sat on a high stool behind the counter of a concession stand. He stood when he saw me coming.

"Welcome to Seastreak," he said. "How can I help you?"

I wondered what kind of sandwiches there might be, and he pointed down at the counter. Beneath a thin layer of glass was a short-winded menu. While I looked, the man made conversation.

"Isn't it great to get back on island?" he asked in a high, pinched voice. "It's so fun this time of year."

I'd overheard this phrase, "on island," a few times since the boat had skidded away from Manhattan; it was always half-sung, always intoned with a sense of escapist relief. It sounded like the safe zone in an aquatic game of tag.

"I've never been," I said, "so I guess I'll take your word for it."

"Oh!" he said with a weird force. He opened his blue eyes wide, and I could see their unnatural pitch and depth. They were almost navy. "How long will you be out? The longer the better, especially the first time."

"Just two or three days; not really a visit. Just work."

We went on like this, inanely, about the island, where to go, what to see and eat, until I interrupted us by settling on roast beef. The man reached into a mini-fridge, produced the sandwich, wrapped in plastic, and placed it on a glossy paper plate. Happy not to have had to mention the campaign, I paid and said goodbye. "You're in for a treat," the man said, referring, I thought, to the island, not the sandwich.

You might as well read water biblically, too, while you're at it, I thought as I pulled the thing apart and ate it segregatedly: meat and cheese, mustard and mayonnaise on bread. There's water all over the Bible, most of it oddly important to the stories in which it suddenly shows up. Still, there's no single interpretive rule—none, at least, that I can find—that stretches across the Scriptures. On a boat you think of the Old Testament punishments: Noah's ark, then Jonah hightailing it away from the will of God and into the belly of the whale. Jonah's disobedience gets him tossed overboard and underwater. Gravity does the rest—the renegade prophet can't help but sink like a stone into the monster's waiting mouth. In Genesis the rain's a straightforward death sentence, an agent of God's brutal logic: you had an ark or you didn't, world without end, amen.

Look, next, at the apostle Peter, doubly typological, a better Jonah and a worse Jesus. For him the sea is a test, and his reward for passing, at least at first, is a suspension of normalcy. Peter's bones hollow out and lighten drastically, or the water grows a skin—he walks over waves toward the Master, until, of course, he loses faith and breaks the surface. Jesus saves and scolds, but the story is triumphant—a little comedy with water as a slapstick trapdoor.

Water in the Writ achieves a different, more mysterious

kind of sense at a moment in John's Gospel where Nicodemus the Pharisee sneaks away from the Sanhedrin to talk with Jesus. Nicodemus flatters first, then asks questions, some leading, some earnest, as if in search of an entire improvised theology. In answer, Jesus offers epigrams that sound like jokes, or evasions, or muffled dispatches from the world Nicodemus wants so badly to understand. My favorite part of the exchange is the beginning: Jesus tells Nicodemus, apropos of very little—the scholar hasn't asked about salvation or sight—that in order to see God's kingdom one must be born again. Wanting something clearer, Nicodemus feigns a funny, literalist confusion. "How," he asks, and here I imagine a smirk, "can a man be born when he is old? Can he enter a second time into his mother's womb, and be born?" Comes the famous reply: "Except a man be born of water and of the Spirit, he cannot enter into the kingdom of God." It's like something from a sonata—a restatement by way of deepening, distortion, distention, modulation. The sentence isn't necessarily easier to understand, but it is somehow, by way of image, more precise.

Born of water, I love that. The phrase comes almost prewrapped, calls to mind baptism and the bath, but when I hear it I see something else: a man, alone, at the center of a limitless ocean. He's treading desperately, howling whenever he gathers enough breath, and sometimes the sky flushes purple and it rains. Nothing interrupts the hopelessness of the scene: no great fish, no planes, no bugle blasts, no buoys. The new birth is whatever comes next, a miracle or a death. Salvation, then, wouldn't be a walk across the water but a memory of the depths.

That kind of extremity is hard to come by; almost nobody

faces it—despite my occasional troubles, I couldn't relate. I felt
like what I was: on the way to somebody else's vacation. My
water—the stuff carrying the Seastreak vessel—was just trans-
port, nothing dangerous. I finished the sandwich and tried to
sleep through the hour before the boat reached the island.

Soon there was a staticky announcement, and through the
window at the front of the cabin I saw the long, lamp-studded
pier at Oak Bluffs. We floated closer; a cluster of big chalk-
striped rocks and a whitish sliver of sand came into view. There
was something familiar about the shore, to do, maybe, with its
simplicity—the slick faces of the rocks, a long service house
with its peaked roof, a vanishing series of blues, sea to sky. It
reminded me, just slightly, of the sleepaway camp I went to,
two middle school summers in a row, with kids mostly from the
city and the commuter-rail-accessible precincts of Connecticut, in a tiny, fuzzily bordered town in western New Hampshire. The camp was built on the side of a hill and presented
itself in levels: the older you were, the higher you climbed back
to your bunk at night. Down at the bottom of the hill were
fields, courts, courses, and, most importantly, the lake. This was
an all-boys camp; we shared the lakeside with a girls' camp
whose grounds began beyond the fence of our tennis courts,
and whose name, like ours, sounded vaguely Native American.
The rest is B-roll: color war, Anthony Kiedis's voice, dances
with bad outcomes, "That Don't Impress Me Much" through
speakers. Once, for a skit, the counselors dressed me in a wig
and had me play a neck-snapping woman named Rita Con-
chita. That I recall with weird clarity; I was good in the role.
But, sure, most of what bears remembering is the water. The
lake was called Upper Baker Pond. I went tubing once and

lost my shorts. Tread some water, learn a C-stroke, let the surface glint just so, and suddenly—if too briefly—you feel like a
duskier Kennedy, a B-list Bush rolling dice against the walls at
Kennebunkport. Add money to the list of meanings. Maybe
that's the one that sticks.

Just as the boat reached the pier, it began to rain. Thin, siz-
zling drops troubled the water, but only slightly.

KAREN COX WORKED IN CORPORATE responsibility (that private-
sector soft landing for the political at heart; a near oxymoron,
by my lights, to boot) at a big life insurer in Boston. She'd
worked for Carter in the trenches, and later sat on a minor
commission under Clinton. Now she gave money to the Senator and goaded her friends into doing the same. She was small
and brown-skinned and held her body a bit like a mantis—
head forward, arms rigid, thin legs looking ready to spring.
Her hair was lotioned back into jet-black swirls. Karen and
her husband, a former banker named Benny, had owned their
canary-colored house on Oak Bluffs, near a pond and the boat-
cluttered harbor, for twenty years. The porch and the roof were
fringed with a stripe of white scalloping that looked like lace.

"You work all year to earn your summer on the Vineyard,"
she told me, smiling, after I'd marveled at the place while getting the tour. Marveling was a skill I'd recently picked up. "I'm
glad you like it," she said. "You're always welcome to come."
The Senator was set to arrive the next evening; tonight, Karen
told me, the two of us could talk. Benny was gone; he'd get
there just before the party.

We sat in the dimly lit living room. Karen plopped down

next to me on a pure white couch, one veined leg slung over the other. On the table in front of us was a spreadsheet set horizontally on legal-sized paper.

"I thought we could go through the list," Karen said. "You'll be happy."

She'd promised two hundred thousand, one twenty-five of which was safely in hand, checks stacked neatly in my desk drawer in New York. The rest, I figured, we could collect at the door. "Oh, we already are," I said, but Karen had slipped on a pair of gold-rimmed glasses, picked up her chart, and begun to tick down the rows with a pencil.

"Governor Patrick's coming," she said. "Did I tell you that before? We did an event just like this for his campaign; he's a friend." I hadn't noticed the black pouch at her hip. She pulled out a check for a thousand, signed by Massachusetts's black capitalist turned governor, and shoved it into my hand.

After twenty minutes, I was holding about sixty thousand dollars, twice my salary. "There," she said, looking pleased with herself. "And more to come."

IN THE MORNING, BEFORE THE party, Karen asked if I'd like to see Chilmark. There was a book festival in town, and her friend Skip Gates would be there to give a talk on his new work, on genealogy. I couldn't think of a reason to decline. We got into her faded green car and drove cursively down a hill and across the island. As we went, Karen tossed off thoughts about the Vineyard's black history.

"It's true," she said, "let's face it. Part of it was that they just wouldn't have us anywhere else. So on some level, it's true: chalk Oak Bluffs up to nice Methodists. But what is much more impressive, and much harder to explain"—here she let one soft hand slip from the wheel and patted me gently on the arm—"is that the new ones keep coming. Look at me and Benny. We're not like some of these people, you know, *la-di-da*. At least we weren't born that way. But look at us. We came. It's not just some hereditary thing, passed down. Young people like you," she said, patting me again. "You get a law degree—are you going to law school? You should: you'll make some money and you turn up here in the summers. Nobody's looking backward when they come. It's something to reach for, so we do."

Every few miles, Karen slowed the car to a roll and began to point. Here was Vernon Jordan's house, or Ken Chenault's, or the one people said the new president—knock on wood— might rent whenever he came around. She asked how I'd come to work on the campaign; I understood it as a question about pedigree. "A fluke," I said. I told her about Thadd Whitlock and his parents. "Wow," Karen said, giggling. "Wow!" I was nobody; I could see her relax. "What an opportunity. You're, what, twenty-five, twenty-six?" "Close," I said, teasing her without knowing why. I felt good. "Twenty-two." Her hand lifted from the wheel again; this time she let it rest on my arm. "Wow."

She was quiet for a moment. Then she said, "That's exactly what I mean."

The fair was a procession of white tents, waving like sails over a lake of grass. Under the largest of them sat about a hundred Vineyarders, clapping then settling into silence as the professor approached a wooden lectern. We found two empty folding chairs up front; Karen and the professor traded barely perceptible grins.

"Well," he said, "looks like the whole team came out this morning."

The professor was clothed in cream-colored linen and wore a smile that I recognized from his appearances on dust jackets and TV segments. He shrugged slightly as the crowd laughed at his joke about the similarities among them. The line could only have gone over so well at a gathering like this one, its members (three-fourths black; relatively lighter on the swatch scale) interested less in the particulars of the professor's recent findings re Oprah's genetic makeup than in the looser notion of having simply been with him for an hour or so on a Sunday morning.

I remembered my favorite joke of the younger Bush's. Back in 2000, during the final weeks of that campaign, he stands in white tie at the dais of a Catholic gala in New York. "This is an impressive crowd: the haves and the have-mores," he says, smirking. "Some people call you the elite; I call you my base." The attendees titter over the sound of silverware on plates. Michael Moore later tried, via a series of hysterical jump cuts, to turn this into an admission of nefarious intent—even, it was implied, a hatred for the poor—but the comment has always struck me as basically sweet. He couldn't help what he was. Gates at the fair and Bush at the fundraiser both remind me of church. My mother, when teaching early-morning Bible study before Sunday service, would always start by saying, "Isn't there such a sweet spirit in the room this morning?" The class would hum and nod—they felt it too. "Amen." The Holy Ghost was like money or mobility: a Great Leveler, a ground from which mutual understanding could grow, a precondition for irony.

Soon the speech and a handful of questions and answers were done, and the professor sat at a table to sign books and shake hands—to "touch and agree," the Sunday schooler in me thought. "Let's say hi," Karen said. She grabbed me by the wrist and pulled me to the front of the long line. Nobody seemed to care that she'd skipped ahead. She chatted with the professor about his semester, her kids, how was so-and-so from however many years ago. Then, before Karen could introduce us, the professor looked at me and wrinkled his nose.

"Don't I know you?" he said.

"I . . . I don't see why you would," I said, hoping he'd laugh and let it go.

"Negro," he said, "I know your face!"

Karen came to my rescue. "You will soon if you don't already," she said, patting my back. She was still thinking, I could tell, about my accidental upward motion. "He's on the campaign."

"My man," the professor said, stretching his famous smile. He shook my hand.

I never shared with the professor, or with Karen, that his bricklike anthologies of black lit used to sit on my mother's shelf, lonely among a congregation of apologetics texts and translations of the Bible, or that they had provided my slow, scattershot introduction to slave narratives and the fruits of the New Negroes. I recalled that the great man—Karen was saying, just then, what an underratedly great man he was—had grown up in Nowhere, West Virginia, and had read and written himself into acquaintance with the likes of Baldwin and onto the lawns at Harvard. It didn't matter how it had happened, or whether the path might be traveled by anybody behind him. That it had happened was the principal thing, the outward sign of election. Black advancement was a kind of Calvinism: no such thing as a fluke. The whole island was standing at the shore, friendly as Karen Cox in the morning, waiting for your boat to reach the dock.

Back at the house, a staff of caterers had materialized. They darted around, heating appetizers and setting tables near a tree on the lawn. "He'll speak out back," Karen whispered, as if it were a secret. "We'll do the photo line in here."

I was standing at the front door when the Senator's car rolled up to Karen's house. He burst forward from his seat looking like I'd never seen him look before: his sandy face loose and untutored; his skinny frame swathed in a baggy white polo and a pair of sun-spotted chinos. His walk to the porch was almost a bop. He looked how the professor had looked: at home.

"Hey now!" he said to Karen, projecting an intimacy that was more astral than real. They had "people in common" but had never met. Her face was purple with pride. "Hey now!" she crowed back.

I hoped my face said, "Hey now." I didn't want to speak up and ruin the mood.

But the Senator, in an invincible mood, looked over at me, drawing me into things. He cocked his head and cocked his palm skyward. We two were feeling the same thing, he seemed to be saying, and whatever it was couldn't be—didn't need to be—forced through any process of language. I nodded back.

"You ready?" he said.

I STAYED OVER THAT NIGHT in a cool upper room of Karen's house. She'd outfitted it with thin, luxurious sheets and a mound of towels, more than anyone could use in so short a visit. Above the foot of the guest bed was a small shelf of books, mostly about the island or about the kinds of people who, by whichever means, belonged to it naturally. There was a frayed black-and-brown paperback version of E. Franklin Frazier's *Black Bourgeoisie*. There was a book of Dr. King's speeches and a biography of Andrew Young. There was a surprisingly fat volume on the history of debutante balls. I liked looking at the spines. The room smelled of lavender and salt.

Maybe the slimmest book said *The Wedding*. Partly by instinct—that innate drama of betrothal, so deeply coded— and partly out of boredom, I pulled it down. I felt agonizingly excited, too stirred up to sleep. My heart raced, as it had some-times done at night when I was a child. The slight static of seashells sounded at my ears. I used to read the Bible on anx-ious nights—I liked the sure, strident, spastic rhythms of the Epistles. Those letters seemed so obviously real: only genuine agitation could make a person write like Paul. His wild voice would rock me to sleep. *For we know in part, and we prophesy in part . . .*

Over time I started to resort to novels, on roughly the same grounds. Despite the fakenesses of character and plot, my antic, self-soothing style of reading—each paragraph combed quickly but repeatedly, at a sweeping diagonal angle, hoping to swallow whole each chain of thought—gave me the impression (maybe it was a delusion) that I could glimpse past the narra-tion and see the heart, hear the voice of the novelist herself. The real person at the desk, squirming stylishly to be seen. I thought of fiction as a flexible tarp, easy to pierce and asking to be pierced, thrown over an attempt at correspondence.

So I read instead of slept, and as the dawn began its blush-ing I finished the book. A young woman, in every way ex-emplary of the black mannered class—beautiful, smart, well reared—chooses a white boy, some artist, over a crowd of re-spectable black suitors. It takes place on the Vineyard, among its most hale specimens. The author, a woman named Dorothy

West, whose name had never come up at a school I'd gone to, had dedicated the book to Jackie Onassis: *Though there was never such a mismatched pair in appearance, we were perfect partners.* A nice compression of her book's own themes. Apparently Jackie had edited the book.

Little flashes of fate like that did make me believe, however slightly, in serendipity. The Kennedys, those beneficiaries and victims of fate, Catholics with Anglican looks and pagan luck, tended to come up all the time back then. Their myth, their *thing*, hovered in the air over the campaign. The Senator reminded people of JFK, for one: he was handsome and spoke well and had a pretty family. And then, it felt good to see Camelot in a guy who wasn't white. Maybe there was the hope that *black*, that portentous designation, could finally be subsumed into the mainstream in the way that Kennedy had helped *Irish* to be. That some long passage of travel was almost done. That the candidate's easy manner, his insouciantly held like of hip-hop, and his high-Protestant restraint could help, by symbol more than law, to make a contradiction finally resolve. Help assimilation—the good kind; call it a final stage of integration—along.

But, no, it was mostly the look. That unplaceable intrigue. One day, a big black man swaddled in a silk caftan and, over it, a floor-scraping fur had walked into our office. He was tall, fat, and chic, with speckled hair and a gap between his front teeth. I recognized him from TV, *Project Runway:* André Leon Talley, some paragon of fashion—yet another world I couldn't fathom. How he'd gotten the address nobody knew, but he came in almost yelling. "Hello! Hello, please? Excuse me! I need to hand somebody my twenty-three hundred dollars!" He was excited by the glamorous Senator, you could tell. Jill, recognizing him, raced up from her desk to meet him at the door. He kept on shouting. "And *with* me I have the gorgeous Lee Rad-zi-*will*!" It was true: from his arm hung a frail-looking older woman, tart and puckering about the mouth, wearing a pink tweed Chanel suit with black fringe, with a fur whose hue was a tad lighter than Talley's. I had to be told later that the wobbly woman was Jackie O's little sister.

When I took a walk into Oak Bluffs later in the morning, several of the white people I saw—outnumbered for once— wore hats that said CHAPPY in big white letters. As in Chappa- quiddick, at the far east end of this island. I wondered, walking, what Dorothy West had thought of that ordeal—the president's brother and the car, and the bridge, and the water, and the girl. Maybe it had further troubled her idea of her hidden-away home. I made a note on my phone for later, to see if she'd writ- ten an article at the time. Troubled writer at her desk worrying over troubled water. The girl beating at the windows of the car, gurgling, hoping to break the surface and breathe.

# II

# 4

IT WAS WARM IN NEW YORK THAT SEPTEMBER, BUT AT NIGHT A
slight chill rose, as if from the ground. The candidate spoke
from beneath the high white Parisian arch at Washington
Square Park. Thousands came and trampled the grass. The
air in the park smelled of citrus and mud and, faintly, of weed.
He stood atop a tall, curtained stage with big, curving speakers
on either side. He seemed to be having fun. The crowd at the
rally was made up mostly of students—NYU's real estate hold-
ings, ever proliferating, ringed us all around, like the walls of
an amphitheater—and people only slightly older, early twenties, like me, just embarking on benign careers. The latter you
could identify by their short jackets and collared shirts, or by
the thin straps on their black and beige flats. They stomped and
shouted and cheered, waved signs, and sometimes cried.

The atmosphere was like the one at the announcement
speech I'd watched from home seven months earlier, an aspect
of the campaign's activity that raising money had made me
all but forget. Now, having heard him speak more times than
I could count, I tended to watch his rallies in Iowa and South

Carolina and Pennsylvania and Michigan with the sound muted, often cradling a receiver with Beverly on the other end of the line. The papers reported on all the money we'd raised—just as much as, if not more than, our dynastic opponent: more than anyone had predicted—and the polls had risen, almost in response to all that diligently harvested cash. And now that the press and the voters in the early primary states all thought we could plausibly win, the call-and-response modulated and reversed itself: every time the candidate gave a good speech, money flooded in online, from regular people, probably none of whom had heard of Beverly Whitlock or Earnest Black-shear. Least of all of me.

I'd walked around, through the crowd, taking in its sounds and mentally photographing the faces, before the speech had begun; as the candidate spoke, I stood behind the arch and the stage. I watched the candidate's back flexing as he made his gently practiced gestures, saw how the heel of his left foot left the ground when he stood still. I studied his movements and the corresponding movements in the faces of his listeners. I'd made this a habit after Jill gave me a piece of advice about small fundraising meetings: Don't look at the candidate while he speaks, but at the faces of the attendees. You could track their feelings that way, see how his words moved or failed to move them; afterward you'd know which ones you could ask for a check. This was politics to me now: not the speech but its harvest, not the spectacle of mass democracy on television but the mess behind the stage.

After the candidate finished speaking, a frictionless pop song played; he waved, then jogged down a flight of stairs from the stage. He walked quickly, matching the mood of the music, if not its beat, and I followed him into a black SUV, just north of the park, where his traveling aide, a bald former power forward, sat behind the wheel. I was in the backseat, next to a pizza box on which slick gray spots of grease were quickly spreading. We were headed to a small gathering over cocktails, hosted by the editor of a music magazine. My job that night was to remind him of a few important names.

"If he wanted me to mention the website, he should've told me before I went on," he was saying to the aide. Some reproving call had come from headquarters. "I could've said it toward the end, but it's too late now; it's not like I can just walk back out onstage. You ruin the magic that way." This discussion of logistics—plus the meeting we were driving to, clearly an annoyance—were, I could tell, a disappointment to the candidate after the frenzy of the park. He spoke like a man coming unhappily down from a high.

From his shotgun seat he pointed with his thumb without looking back at me. "Have some of that pizza if you want. You're a young guy. Me, I can't eat that stuff."

The campaign was always finding subtle ways to emphasize his fitness habits. He seemed to jog every morning, and was the kind of thin I'd always hoped to be: his body never got in the way of his clothes. Still, it was funny to think of him as especially watchful of his metabolic movements, some strict dieter. I almost said yes to the slice, but I nervously remembered the task Jill had given me.

"So," I said, more loudly than I'd hoped, "this next meeting is hosted by—"

"Yeah, I've heard of him," he said, tapping his finger against the belly of the glove compartment. The aide had taken the streets downtown instead of trying one of the highways. We'd been stuck at a red light, but as he tapped away the energy he'd absorbed at the rally, we started to roll slowly forward. I could tell that he wasn't planning on hearing the rest of the briefing.

"People like this," he said, "they just want to say they met you."

THE NEXT DAY, A FRIDAY, around noon, Beverly called me at the office. Usually we talked later on, so that her endless ribbons of informed gossip about the campaign and other intrigues in the world of politics could grow long, unimpeded. A couple of weeks ago, I'd learned about a particularly flagrant affair blooming in the ranks of the candidate's informal group of foreign-policy advisers. Before that, about a donor who kept asking about ambassadorships.

"Hey, come downstairs," she said. "We're having lunch. A couple hours. Tell Jill it's me, it's for work."

Ever since Blackshear's party I'd earned some latitude around the office. My faults were just as apparent—congenitally I couldn't speed myself up or make myself better at small-bore administrative tasks—but the definition of "good" in this world, I now saw, was closely implicated with the quality of the relationships you could maintain, the kinds of people you could cultivate. By this standard I was fine, and my many laxities mostly ignored.

Beverly was on the far side of the sidewalk, pacing Park Avenue's small curb foot over foot like a tightrope walker, her phone pressed to her ear. She held her finger up when she saw me, telling me to wait. I leaned against the side of the building and watched her as she talked.

She was wearing a sleeveless dress, dark gray and loose-fitting everywhere but at her hips, whose shape the soft fabric smoothly reiterated. Her free arms shone. Her shoulders were skinny—you could see their bones, round and irregular as skulls—but just above her elbows sat small hillocky deposits of fat. Her heels were neither low nor especially high; they were open at the toes, showing paint so deeply and luxely maroon that it looked textured, velour. Her hair was pressed into big careless curls. She pushed it aside with a flick of her pinkie when she stopped to listen. Her eyebrows descended from the center of her face, and so did the outline of her lips—her features were like the echoing f-holes of a cello. Beyond her, in the median of the avenue, was a buzzing strip of dark red flowers. She looked over at me frankly, as if she were speaking to me through a translating intermediary on the phone. Despite the gaze, she used her body as if she were in the real presence of her interlocutor, whoever it was. She waved her free hand and shrugged wildly, extended her middle finger whenever *fuck* escaped her lips. It was a kind of acting, bespeaking an utter commitment that only her eyes called into question. I knew now why she was so fun to talk to over the phone—and, incidentally, how simple chat could make you respected in politics. Banter was a skill.

"That was Blackshear," she said. "It's funny: he's totally detached and then he's not, right? He always sends people with checks my way, but you never get him on the phone until *boom*." We were walking downtown. One of my lifelong fantasies, often lived out in dreams: I was headed somewhere new under someone else's control. "He says he had fun last time. He could maybe be convinced to do something at his place in Connecticut. I've heard it's nice." I sent an email to that effect to Jill, then put my phone away.

Lunch was with Wilson Taylor, whom Beverly had kept mentioning to me whenever she indulged in speculation about my future career. He was one of those old-school black men who look absolutely white. I'd pulled up his picture in the office once and, hearing the skepticism in their voices, found myself explaining to Jill and Howland the wacky distortions of the one-drop rule, using pictures of long-dead HBCU presidents as prime examples. Wilson was one of those products of twentieth-century New York who seemed to have popped, fully formed, out of one of the small gardens in the plaza near City Hall. He'd run the Parks Department under Koch and helped bring jazz to Lincoln Center. "He's close with Wynton," Beverly said. *Wynton.* Just like that.

He'd beat us to the restaurant; it wasn't far from Rockefeller Center. Outside, tourists fidgeted with their cameras. Near Christie's, a group of women in black suits stood close to one another, holding cigarettes. A line was already forming in front of Radio City. Young guys in boxy suits, striped with what looked like crime-scene chalk, walked dully toward Sixth, where office buildings stretched like sunning bodies. The restaurant was a famous meeting place for media personalities, Beverly said. Wilson, sixty-five or so but with a bodily carriage like an overgrown boy's, was sitting at a table near the center of the floor, wearing a dark flannel suit. He was tall, but slouched in his chair. Hair flew almost horizontally away from his temples. His eyes were watercolor gray. His sarcastic smile never left his face.

As soon as we sat down, he called out to a nearby waiter: "Three Cobbs, three martinis. Beefeater, olives, cold." What a choiceless afternoon! I worried about going back to the office smelling like gin, but I knew, too, that I couldn't refuse. I didn't want to, either. Beverly introduced us once the waiter had left.

"Hammons? Like the artist?" His grin said that he knew the answer was no.

"Hammond," I said. "Like the organ."

But I did like the idea of à distant kinship with the art-world prankster David Hammons. I could faintly remember a photograph of him standing on the sidewalk wearing a bored smirk, selling snowballs lined up in neat white rows.

The Cobb was humongous—a circular coliseum piled high and proud. As we ate, finishing our drinks and ordering a fresh set, Wilson talked about the kind of politics he liked: quick, dirty, unambiguous in intent and in result. Understanding the genteel implications of his skin tone, he seemed to have developed his tough-guy act in drastic contrast, with a comic seriousness not unlike that of the artist with his melting goods for sale, committing intensely to pulling off a huge joke. As he talked, I found myself flattered that Beverly thought that he was someone I could emulate.

"Bev told me you want to be a writer," he said. I fidgeted, embarrassed. Beverly looked at me placidly. She hadn't spoken much during lunch—just looked happily back and forth at us, with an ease in her eyes I'd never seen.

"Which: fine, whatever, good. Or *wanted* to be, I don't know. But, I mean"—he glanced around, gesturing with his eyes and hands at himself, at Beverly, at me, at our formerly statuesque salads, now scattered, at our glasses, again empty, at the famous faces in the restaurant and at the working world outside—"you're smart enough to know that you've really stumbled into something here. Maybe you didn't totally stumble, but . . ."

I looked over at Beverly and laughed.

"Exactly," Wilson said. Then, not as a series of orders but in the mood of an expert navigator pointing out a possible route: "So maybe it goes like: you stick around in politics after the campaign, whatever happens. Here, D.C., we'll see. You study law—it's about how you think. See what this whole . . . *world* . . . has in it that you want. And *then* you can responsibly decide whether you're Paul Laurence Dunbar or not."

He was right in at least one way: I'd somehow groped my way to the middle of the world. The middle of *a* world, at least. Or an unseen perch quite near the center, with an excellent view. In a sense I'd always felt central: the peculiar arrogance of an only child born in New York. But now another previously invisible New York, and, with it, another America, had come striding into view. My new citizenship in it made my head buzz. Detachment was my constant effort; I could sometimes feel it failing; maybe that's why, lately, I found myself—even here, dividing my attention at the table—so strongly drawn to Beverly, herself a study in uninvolved involvement, a participant-watcher so practiced at both poses. At first, my feelings for her had been those of a student toward a teacher. Now they were something else I didn't particularly want to name. And maybe this, the aloof thing, was why she'd insisted I see Wilson, with his thrummingly engaged irony. I couldn't tell. I was getting pretty drunk.

Wilson was on the board of the Studio Museum in Harlem, he was saying, pointing at me as he said it, as if suggesting where the roads of political influence and artistic interest might meet. My tongue felt loose, and I was happy. "The Studio Museum," I said, "is—pardon me—the first place I ever saw a vagina." Nobody flinched, so I kept going. "I was in, like, sixth grade. Maybe seventh. My mom's best friend had this husband named George who'd taken an interest in me. Interest or pity—upstanding black man taking on fatherless black youth. That kind of thing. I was really into art back then, took classes at this place in Harlem called the Children's Art Carnival—"

"Of course," Wilson said. He knew the nonprofit, had given money to it. I could tell this made him like me more. He'd helped make me.

"I painted," I said. "I had this teacher named Lenny, who was always encouraging me. Once he used me as a model for a children's book he was illustrating, about the young Louis Armstrong. He came to my house and made studies.

"Anyway, George. He knew I had this art thing going on. Tall guy with really nice white hair that he must've had cut every week. It was always in a fade. He had this huge face, like a boxer, but skinny arms. He figured he'd take me on this fatherly trip to the Studio Museum. Enrichment. He was really a great guy. I'd always passed the museum on my way to church—saw that red, black, and green American flag a million times before I knew what it was or meant—but had never been inside. We went from room to room, talking about my life and then talking about pictures. Most of what I saw that day I don't remember at all. But at some point we take this turn, and there it goes, huge, on a wall right next to a doorway. This photograph, six feet tall or something, close up like a portrait. A vagina in color. Pierced! At first I thought it was abstract or something, I didn't know what I was seeing. Maybe George didn't either, because we both just stood there squinting.

"My mom had recently slipped a sex-ed book, *It's Perfectly Normal,* under my pillow, though, so after a while the whole thing came into focus for me. I started laughing for some reason, and George, like, physically grabbed me and pulled me not only out of that room but out of the museum and down the street. It was fantastic. He gave me this little speech about shock value and art, right out there on 125th. Then I guess he called my mom to apologize, and that night she gave me a slightly different speech, about the dangers of unnecessary perversity."

By now they were both laughing. "I love that museum," I said.

# 5

IN DECEMBER, LOTS OF THE JUNIOR STAFF GOT TEMPORARILY RE-
assigned, away from fundraising and into the early states where
votes would soon be cast. (The terminology was military:
we called it being "redeployed.") The candidate wouldn't be
in the big cities much for the moment, so there wouldn't be
many events. Howland and I were sent to Manchester, New
Hampshire. One morning at the beginning of the month, we
arranged for a rental car. As we waited for the guy behind the
desk to give us our key—we had to pay extra for insurance because neither of us was twenty-five—I asked Howland how far
back he could trace his family tree, without thinking too much
about why I wanted to know.

Pilgrim John Howland, his great-great-great-great-grand-
father, something distant like that, was a passenger on the *May-
flower* in 1620, he said, and is known, chiefly, for having fallen
overboard and into the heart of a storm. John Howland was
educated and exceedingly pious, and a manservant to John
Carver, who soon became the first governor of Plymouth Colony.
Some say Howland got swept away in the wind while carrying

messages from one end of the vessel to the other. William Brad-
ford, the famous diarist of the voyage (and another eventual
Plymouth governor), called Howland a "lustye young man"
and rendered his rescue as proof of a providential God. There
are several kitschy paintings of the drama—they form a kind of
historical sub-genre, and are these days displayed in an online
gallery by the Pilgrim John Howland Society, of which Howland's mother remains a member. Pilgrim Howland's hands,
foamy with the residue of waves, grasp the rope thrown by his
fellows. His forearms writhe with strain. He survives.

Thereafter a living token of grace, Howland became a
minor celebrity in the New World, admired for his loyalty to
Carver, his kindness to all he met, and, as time went on, his evident knack for buying and selling choice parcels of land. The
latter might be the truest source of his longevity: his name lives
on on innumerable deeds.

Howland—James—told me about his ancestor—"the Pilgrim," he called him—as he turned our rental car, a cherry-
red PT Cruiser, onto the West Side Highway and away from
the city. I sat on the passenger side, holding a set of directions, feeling guilty and sort of childish because I didn't have
a license. Howland didn't care, he said; he liked to drive. His
great-grandfather Howland had been a Presbyterian minister
in Rochester, New York—maybe we'd stop there on the way
back to New York, in a month or so, so that I could see his
family's summer retreat, he said. None of the Howlands of
his generation (or, for that matter, of the one before) went to
church anymore; they'd all settled on post-sixties social justice.
Their family name still adorned a plaque or two in the middle
of town.

The slick gray Hudson whizzed by, Jersey's roofs dissolv-

ing gradually into bluffs and carpets of trees. An occasional
spire of brick or stone poked through the green. Howland had
grown up along the seaboard—between Greenwich, Connecticut, and Naples, Florida—drinking beers and joyriding in carts
on golf courses where he and his friends made pocket change
as caddies. When I saw the long, deep, unanxious breath he
took as the car forgot Manhattan, I believed him about his
love for I-95, and I knew, somehow, that he wouldn't last in the
city very long after the campaign. He was extremely pale, with
clammy, pinkish cheeks and very curly—almost Negroid—
reddish-blond hair. On weekends he stayed at his mother's, in
Greenwich, and during the week with his girlfriend in Tribeca.
He'd met Meron, whose parents were East African doctors, at
Johns Hopkins, sophomore year; she shared an apartment with
a guy who, several years earlier, had almost won on *Top Chef*.
Sometimes Howland brought leftover experiments to the office
in Tupperware containers. There was something very Presbyterian about him—something in his constant and seemingly
uninterruptible decent (but never exuberant) mood; in the
plainness of his dress and of his speech; in the way he made his
best and smartest jokes about people who took themselves very
seriously, or seemed to—and he was all the more mainstream
for his indifference, verging on happy ignorance, regarding the
church, which was, for him, less a repository of transcendent
belief than an article of the past.

When I was younger I'd lived under the misapprehension
that when people described themselves as Christian in answer
to questions about their religion, they were signaling some
fervor—some absolute metaphysics—like the one into which
I had been born. I'd learned slowly, from people like Howland
(by now, at least in this respect, I recognized him as an instance

of a recognizable type), that they often meant only that on holidays their parents had dragged them to a church instead of a mosque or a temple. They hadn't shaped their lives—organized their guilts or sorrows or hopes—around any particular creed. On most Sundays they watched TV and ate cereal. "You're, like, *into* church, huh?" Howland said when I asked whether he, or any of his Howland cousins, had ever, even as children, been as religious as their great-grandfather (and, before him, the Pilgrim) had undoubtedly been.

"In a certain way, yeah," I said.

We had so far, just by dint of being young and unexperienced, enjoyed the kind of distant camaraderie that I have since learned is common among male coworkers—circular conversations, brief commiserations, mostly jokes. Something loosened in the car. I have never been quite proud of my ability, when prodded—or, more truthfully, simply allowed—to monologue at length. I think of the quality as essentially feminine, despite the fact that the men I've loved most have been talkers: preachers, writers under interview, certain uncles, my father. I found myself narrating to Howland the basics of my passage through stages of belief and unbelief. The faith had begun, I told him, to loosen its hold on me while I was away at college. "I guess that's typical," I said. Less supervision, less—as in: no—nearby compulsion to go to church. Some of the kids from my residential hall—I remembered a Nick and a Clark—were Catholic, and once, on the Easter of my freshman year, I'd gone with them to Mass. Everything felt *light*. These guys seldom attended otherwise and were clearly going just in order to tell their parents that they'd gone. Even the priest—probably drunk on the high attendance—cracked jokes. "Now we'll just take these little pieces of Jesus," he'd said with regard to the host. Not—

I hastened to add; I felt a pang of protectiveness—not that there wasn't any levity in Pentecostalism. Most of my dead pastor's sermons, for example, had had a tripartite structure, and the register that corresponded with the first third—before the hoop, the holler, the speaking of otherworldly tongues—was mostly, if not all, jokes. That early part of the sermon had the texture of cultural criticism or some kinds of stand-up comedy— a constant stream of references, all pointing back to a languid, strolling exposition of the text via current events. The art was in a kind of tonal travel: a message that started with a comic riff on popular TV might end with the bleakest eschatology (I had believed in the Rapture, and expected, even sometimes hoped, that it would come before I died) and, on the way, indulge in lyrical, almost euphoric passages on such topics as sodomy, hellfire, the—inevitable, soon-arriving—wages of sin, etc. I'd never thought of any of it as necessarily severe until, when I was away from home, the twin forces of rurality and the ease of others sent me wondering what use—toward what happiness—was my faith. But even then, perhaps by habit, I was too intense: I started reading Richard Dawkins and some of the lesser polemics of Christopher Hitchens, then, finding their tone annoying, settled into a weakly felt position of undogmatic theism. I came stumbling back to church after the baby was born and I was home, stunned, from school.

"So," I said, "I just don't know. Yeah, I'm *into* it, I always have been, but I also just don't know. I'm jealous of people who do know or just don't care." Howland was quiet for a while. "I take it you just don't care," I said.

"I don't." He gestured toward my iPod—he wanted me to DJ. I put Crosby, Stills & Nash's first album on and he gave me shit about it but never asked me to change away. Soon he returned to our talk. "So, having a kid . . . what were you, twenty? That had to be . . ." Terrifying, I told him. Nobody had expected it from me. "I mean," he said, "it's not at all the same, I know this, but at Hopkins I was *sure*, for like a *month*, that I'd gotten this girl pregnant." The young woman had been his girlfriend and was, in his telling, "awful"—"which," he conceded, "says more about me than it does about her"— and soon after he'd ended the relationship, she came knocking at his dorm room door, saying she'd missed her period; she was sure he'd knocked her up. Obviously, the story ended on a note of relief—she wasn't, he hadn't—and reminded me of the many others I'd been told. Since the baby had come, I'd heard all the variations: quick scares, close calls, quiet abortions. I was an icon of a life they might've had. Everybody seemed to want to say, *It could've been me, too.* I never knew how to respond, so I shared with Howland the details of the actual article: dozens of dinner trays left crusting over in my junior-year dorm room; the persistent smell of vomit. I'd chain-smoked and kept secrets, read books, lost most of my friends on campus. After a while, I'd stopped showing up at class.

"Damn," Howland said.

Before long we had to navigate between major highways, and so I picked up our dissolving talk by reciting the directions out loud. Even in dictation, my inexperience showed. "Next exit's in five-point-three miles," I said. "Coulda sworn it was five-point-four," Howland replied. There were firs at the sides of the highway, and many black, looping ropes of bird-flecked wire overhead. At a rest stop we pulled over and got Wendy's and barely talked. Back on the road, when the route turned straight and promised to stay that way until New England, we got to talking about fathers. Howland didn't know his. The guy had left early on, and his mother soon changed James's last name to match hers and her famous family's. "This part of your story," I said—I didn't feel close enough to him to joke about his coiling hair—"sounds very recognizably black." He smiled and shrugged. "I don't really know anything," he said, sounding befuddled and cheerful in equal measures. "My mom doesn't say anything." I told him, in turn, about how my dad had died when I was ten. When he was alive he was a church musician. We moved to Chicago when I was a kid so he could play at a Catholic church.

"That'll do it," Howland said, not meaning anything, just before we fell silent again.


THE CAMPAIGN HEADQUARTERS IN MANCHESTER occupied the top floor of a long, L-shaped, brick-skinned office complex. The only other tenant, just downstairs, was a dentist who seemed to have no patients. In front of the building was a wide parking lot, and beyond the lot a narrow road and a snatch of woods. We'd stopped for burgers and a pitcher of bad beer before arriving at the office; it was black outside when we finally showed up; we were slightly drunk. Despite the hour, the office was full. Staffers—our age, more or less; exhausted-looking as a group—sat in rows at long tables under the bright fluorescent lights, looking at laptops and huge stacks of paper. They must have been accustomed to strangers wandering in at odd hours. Nobody seemed to notice—or, much less, be worried—that we'd appeared. We stood unspeaking, looking around with hopeful expressions on our faces, holding the duffels we'd stuffed plump for the month, until a tall, chubby, round-faced guy wearing a washed-out Red Sox cap walked over to welcome us. His hands

were wrapped around the stem of a wooden baseball bat. The
tip rested on his collarbone. "You're the finance guys?" he
asked. "Welcome to field," he said when we'd answered yes.

*Field.* The word described an aspect of political activity in
which our campaign prided itself especially—and especially
loudly. While our opponents spent their money on impressive
but ultimately ephemeral displays of administrative compe-
tence such as lawn signs and television commercials clogging
cable channels in the early states, we, the story went, had invested in the tougher, more lastingly effective work of what
was quasi-mystically called "organizing," which consisted, as
Rob, the guy with the cap and the bat, had begun to tell us,
in recruiting, meeting by church basement meeting, an army
of volunteers—college kids, small-time party hacks, retirees—
who, on foot, went door to door and, from the office, made
hundreds of phone calls, each evangelizing on the candidate's
behalf and keeping strict records of the support or resistance
or, most often, indecision they'd found. Since early in the year,
when the Senator's support in the state had been basically nil,
they'd done what they could to persuade voters to his cause
and to turn the already-convinced into new volunteers. There
was a numerical scale to chart each potential conversion. A 5,
barring some miracle, was a definite no; a 4 was all but gone;
a 3 was most perplexingly opaque: totally undecided; a 2 liked
the Senator and only, one surmised, needed a nudge into his
arms; a 1 you could consider squared away. This data was what
we saw the organizers feeding their computers—every evening
brought the drudgery of input. After input came time to carve
neighborhoods into walkable routes to divvy up among the next
day's canvassers—this was called "cutting turf." One result of

so much administrative duty, after such full days of recruitment and contact with voters, was a basically insane disregard for the limits of human capacity for work. The organizers typically showed up at HQ around six-thirty or seven o'clock and worked—"as you can see," Rob said with a smile and a flourish of his bat—long into the night, often well past nine or ten.

Soon I learned that this kind of martial discipline was essential not only to success as an organizer but also—more crucially, I've come to think—to the maintenance of a persona that matched the subtler valences of that word, *field*. The organizers lived in cheap apartments near the office, in various states of perfect, monkish austerity. Nobody had furniture they'd call their own. Everybody wore takes on the same colorless outfit every day. Some had roommates (they were yoked equally with other organizers, of course); some lived solo; but domestic details were all but meaningless—life as understood in Manchester occurred here, under the office's ugly lights, or, otherwise, somewhere outdoors, among clipboards, sheets of talking points, and clusters of fellow zealots. I hadn't imagined the hint of disdain in Rob's voice when he'd said *finance*. Like the suits in Chicago, we fundraisers—settled, as we were, mainly in major cities—trussed up our devotion in business attire, semiterrestrial office hours, and a focus on numbers instead of individual hearts: so many high-church smells and bells, aimed not so secretly at assimilation into the wider culture toward whose transformation the effort was aimed. The campaign had already seemed wild and unprecedented to me—in addition to the more than mild intoxication of seeing our work discussed every night on cable news, there were the ruptured relationships, urgent hookups, and occasional personal meltdowns that were, or at least seemed to be, symptoms of monomania and protracted stress. But here, away from the city (Manchester was technically a city, but . . .), you could feel an even deeper and purer current of intensity. If the candidate was Christ, the fieldies were, together, John the Baptist, eating their locusts and honey, twigs caught in their dreadlocking hair.

Manchester's—and Sioux City's, and Greenville's, and Carson City's, and Ann Arbor's—relative isolation from the cosmopolitan outposts (and attitudes) from which the campaign carried out its more cynical functions conferred upon its inhabitants, weary as they looked, a kind of glow. Rob grew almost emotional as he explained how his office did its work.

JAMES AND I WOULD LIVE, we learned from Rob, with an especially dedicated volunteer named Derrick, who had offered up his trailer as a site for what was called "supporter housing." (So much of this hyperofficial, nationally drastic work depended on the kindness of strangers.) As we drove from the office to the "mobile community" where Derrick lived, it started to snow. Flakes filled the cones of light that shot out of the front of the Cruiser, and were otherwise invisible. Tall evergreens and lines of electric cables overhung the two-lane road.

"Where the fuck is this," Howland said approvingly.

Derrick answered the door by extending both of his skinny, hair-swamped arms and grabbing our bags before we could object. Then he smiled and let his yellow teeth gleam. "Take a load off," he said. "I'm Derrick." A clear plastic tube cut an equator across his face, and two prongs stuck upward, into his nostrils. "Emphysema," he said when he saw me looking, but the air in the trailer was tart with smoke. I looked past him and saw a lit cigarette hanging off the edge of a narrow computer desk. He saw me notice that, too, and he shrugged. "I could do a bit better," he said. He wore thin-rimmed glasses over big, bulbous features and open pores. He looked happy to see us. We stood there, returning his gaze, until he waved his hand inward in a mock-courtly gesture and said, sort of grandly, "Welcome home."

The door of the trailer opened directly into Derrick's living room. There was the desk on which the cigarette sat, alongside a blocky, cream-colored computer monitor and several neon-green-and-yellow dinosaur figurines. A tyrannosaurus with sharp, triangular teeth stared at James. On the screen was the home page of the website RealClearPolitics: stripes in red and white with a bland black font. "All I do is check the polls," Derrick said. Across from the desk and next to the door was a television, on. Two rose-colored, scratchy-looking couches, one longer than the other, slouched on perpendicular walls. Taped onto the walls at irregular intervals were figures—people and animals, mostly; a building here or there; one wild abstraction in blues and greens—drawn in crayon. At the end of the room was a cube of a kitchen, cordoned off by a chest-high bar and several stools. In a corner stood the oxygen tank that provided Derrick's air. It made a loud, gasping, efficient noise.

"Where should I start," Derrick said after he put our bags down next to his tank.

"Thanks so m—"

"Oh, pleasure's mine," he said. "You guys are doing, like, *God's work*. Least I can do. I mean, New York, that must be great. Anyway, like I said, I'm Derrick. James and David—those are easy. Been helping out at headquarters for a few months now, mostly data entry, doors every once in a while. Most fun I've ever had."

He stood for a moment in the middle of the room, his mouth screwed into a bud, looking up at the ceiling.

"What else? I'm, uh, very recently divorced. Which is why I'm *here*." With that *here* came another comic flourish. "For now. Temporary solution. Kids are with their mother at the moment, but they'll be here sometimes too. So, you know. I hope that's okay."

The kids' names were Grace and Turner, a girl and a boy; the dinosaur belonged to Turner, and the drawings were the work of Grace, who, Derrick said with some pride, was also a budding writer. Maybe I could read some of her stuff: she'd be thrilled. There was a bedroom—Grace's—where one of us could sleep. The other could take the longer couch, which unfolded into a bed.

"What else, what else? I'm trying to think . . ."

Howland put Derrick at ease by sitting down, thoughtfully, on the couch. Soon Derrick sat, too, and so did I. Derrick's nervous bubbliness subsided; he asked us what it meant to raise money for a campaign—what it *really* meant: whether, as it seemed to him from the outside, it all happened online, via that famous (and growing infamous) flurry of emails and text messages, or were there also some telephone calls involved; he was flabbergasted, and, I could tell, sort of put off, to learn the high-toned truth—and Howland asked him, in turn, why he had given himself so completely, sans compensation, to the candidate. There was something very subtly aggressive about the question, I thought, though I doubted Derrick—having known Howland for only twenty minutes or so—would have noticed it. Howland had his reasons for having joined the campaign, including, no doubt, a measure of real respect for the Senator. But his nature was essentially (if also lightheartedly; lightheartedness was the way he expressed his dissent) hostile to evangelism. He couldn't understand how you might get carried away.

"Well," Derrick said, "Of course I saw the guy and just *loved* him right off. And then . . ." He was quiet for a while. "And then, I also honestly just needed something to keep me busy. This thing is kinda saving my life." His mouth trembled a bit as he spoke.

I CAN'T RECALL THE SPECIFICS of the negotiation, but I ended up sleeping in Grace's bed that first night while Howland took the couch. I found it hard, at first, to fall asleep. The bed had sheets the color of Pepto-Bismol and a flimsy canopy of purple faux satin, decorated with vivid drawings of Disney princesses. The drapes were white from within, and when I burrowed into Grace's overstuffed pink pillow, I saw the princesses as pale inversions of themselves. On the bedside table were signs of Grace's seriousness: a squat lamp (also purple; also princess-themed); several precisely sharpened, pastel-hued pencils; a pack of markers; and a book printed on hole-punched construction paper, held together by strings of yellow yarn. I started to open it but then felt guilty for the impulse and stopped. The cover, white, was wordless: just a neatly executed drawing, in marker and colored pencil, of a fair-haired girl with wavy tresses, wearing a sky-blue dress and holding her hands wide open at her sides.

Grace's lines seemed precociously confident, her even application of filled-in color perhaps the product of hard-earned control. Her lonely figure floated unmoored atop the grainy, unmarked surface of the paper. A surge of pity and slight awe—that precise emotional admixture that runs so easily from guilty adult to unwitting child—passed through me. The kid's parents were splitting up. Suddenly she stood in for my daughter, wholly blameless but already burdened by my mistakes, and by this substitutive logic (by now I was slipping away . . .) I was Derrick, hosting a pair of strangers, one conspicuously tenser than the other, in the spare spaces of my temporary trailer. I smoked one final, possibly explosive cigarette as the tank that was my air made noises strangely similar to breath.

# 6

WITHIN A WEEK OR SO OF ARRIVING IN MANCHESTER, I'D DRIFTED into a routine that bore no resemblance to the one I'd kept in Manhattan. The office was busy as early as six in the morning and never fully quieted until after nine at night. I could never tell if the glut of hours was really necessary. With the added intensity, and the relative youth of the staff, came a different approach to group activity. With Jill and Ashley and Hannah in New York, we'd sometimes share a dinner, or pile into a cab to an event across the park, but otherwise maintained more or less cordoned-off private lives. The organizers, by contrast, spent most of their time outside the office together, at meticulously planned office-wide meals or, most often, at darkly lit house parties, accoutred with junk food and local beer in a heap of cans or a keg; they reminded me of the parties I'd thrown with my roommates in our junky freshman triple when I was away at college. And, sure, there was something undergraduate about the atmosphere. Nobody among us foot soldiers was older than twenty-four or twenty-five. And the relationship between time and incident was compressed—made sometimes unbearably urgent—in a way that resembled campus, too. We'd come to New Hampshire just a month before the primary, and so every moment of the day, and of those nights spent messily dancing and drinking with an edge of desperation, seemed charged with potential—and, at a lower but still perceptible pitch, with portent. People fell into and out of operatic sexual affairs, often in betrayal of some rumored boyfriend or girlfriend back home. Petty disputes over turf turned into screaming matches in the open vault of the office. Rashes bloomed. One guy, behind on recruitment targets, descended into a state of unshowered neurosis and had to be sent quietly home to the outer suburbs of Portland, Oregon. Underage and dizzy with world-historical significance, our interns would occasionally get into trouble with the police for drunken public obnoxiousness or, worse, driving under the influence. They were immediately and summarily fired, then purged from all of the campaign's records. (The only comparably unforgivable offense, as in fundraising, was talking to the press without permission.) All of it seemed stoked by the overhang of that early January deadline: the mental image of lines of voters hugging the bland sides of churches and Elks lodges and public schools, exerting their captainship over our candidate's fate. That and the snow, which came in pricking colorless sheets and never stopped.

At one of those group dinners out—maybe the first I went to; it's difficult now to remember—I met Regina. We sat next to each other by no special intention and found ourselves sharing a basket of brittle tortilla chips. She was from Marin County, born to a Ghanaian father, all but absentee, and a quiet black American mom. Before the campaign, she'd taught at a public school in the Bronx, and we talked, that first time, about the city. Her apartment had been on 125th Street, just off Lenox—right around the corner, I told her, from the church where I'd grown up. In order, I guessed, to make me feel closer to home, she drew a crude map of the intersection on the paper tablecloth, indicating by arrow the location of the big Starbucks franchised, famously, by Magic Johnson and, across the street, the skinny building where she'd lived, between a furniture showroom and a tableau of small-time restaurants.

She was tall and substantial, with dark, enthusiastic eyes, a negligible forehead, and a low hairline that sprouted handfuls of thick, near-black hair. A birthmark floated between her verdant eyebrows. Her face was plump and heart-shaped, interrupted in its edgelessness only by a sharp and subtly rippled chin, and the size of her calves pulled smooth the lower quadrant of her jeans. Soon our legs were gently touching under the table. Around the table, other organizers kept looking at us and whispering, dragging grins across their faces.

We flirted for a few days, dense days that felt like weeks, and soon found ourselves in bed. I wish I could remember the first time we kissed: in the fumbling dark of her apartment near the office or in the overlit bar where we'd started out that night, pushed together by another stilted group outing. Regina had a big green Chevy truck, glazed matte by layers of scum and spoiled frost, and as she drove us from the bar to her apartment, we held hands over the cup-holders between our seats. There was something ridiculous about the gesture; I felt its silliness in the moment just as acutely as I do now, recalling it; we had no basis—none, at least, in experience with each other—for such assured and quiet intimacy. But we drove on, down a wide highway whose emptiness was kind of

scary, fondling each other's fingers like lovers of long tenure.
Regina steered the truck with her left hand at twelve o'clock.
The road was quiet and so were we, until it struck Regina—
I had no reason to notice—that we'd gone too long without
turning.

"We missed the exit," she said, smiling like she'd delivered
good news.

AT HER APARTMENT, WITH THE lights off and our clothes in piles
on either side of the bed, we made strange confessions. Figuring
that the month would prove too long for serious omissions—
and also, I think, as a bid for a feeling of acceptance; as almost
a test—I told Regina about my daughter. "I'm a father" are the
words I used, which now seems to me funny but also somewhat
sad. I affected, throughout a longish rendition of the story, a
blasé peace with my life as it had unfolded from my junior year
at college onward, culminating in the facts of dematriculation,
"co-parenting," tenuous employment—I told her about Thadd
and, in the vaguest terms, about Beverly—and now, somehow,
this. She nodded gravely, tracking the movements of my face
with her eyes, often making noises of understanding and great
feeling, as though she understood herself to be the recipient
of some grave trust. In a way, although nothing I told her was
secret, she was.

Her confession was that she'd like someday to be mayor
of San Francisco. Her father had largely ignored her, she said,
while she was growing up. The hardness of his life before his
arrival in America and brief marriage to Regina's mother mud-
died the meaning of his negligence somewhat. Was he a trau-
matized person, due more forbearance than he might otherwise

deserve, given what ravages his psyche must have undergone—
and still be undergoing? Or, Regina wondered aloud, was he
just an asshole with an impeccable excuse? Her therapist tended
toward the former interpretation and her mother toward the
latter. Regina floated between poles, her feelings on the matter depending upon the day. Not that it had much bearing on
her behavior: she adored her fat, squat, bespectacled father
with his dark face, livid with lines; she thought him funny and
smart; and whenever he resurfaced, she welcomed him back
into the innermost corners of her life—offering details about
boyfriends, existential anxieties, hopes such as her hope to be
mayor of the city of San Francisco—as if he'd never shown
himself lacking in love. Eventually, inevitably, he'd find a way
to disappoint, usually by simply ceasing to answer her calls and
texts, and in a few months—or, a few times, years—the cycle
would repeat. Each time, Regina ended up convalescent in the
arms of her mother, who, she now realized, was rightly bitter
about the dynamics of the arrangement: she'd never gotten
so much forgiveness from her child, nor ever—not close—so
much open devotion.

Regina talked more about her father, and I about my
child—how scared I still was, how hard it had been to tell my
mother—until, soon, we became comfortable and started to
kiss. She had thin, dry, protrusive lips, which she often pursed
in the manner of the Buddha in certain sculptures. Each of my
lips was as large as both of hers, and so she suctioned one at a
time, drawing cool, inscrutable patterns with her tongue. Her
hands were long-fingered and strong; one cradled my neck,
and the other made sweeping forays between my thighs. Mine
rested on the skin at her hip, which was hot to the touch. The
night was cold, and swirls of gelid air sometimes slipped under

the sheets—we pulled them closer to our bodies and ourselves to each other.

Regina's apartment was on the dark bottom floor of a shabby-looking dun-brick building and had the dank, earthy, briny smell of softly rotting clothes, old wood, and dirty snow salt as it caked into corners. There were three rooms: the bedroom where we lay squirming; a haphazard living room with a low corduroy couch and a large Old Glory hanging framed on the wall; a junky bathroom whose sink and bathtub drains were clogged by long corkscrews of Regina's hair. On the lip of the sink several exhausted toothbrushes lay like corpses alongside the newer one that was presumably in use. There, too, were strewn a series of dull razors, used and discarded in the mornings in a hurry to reach the office.

I have always felt happy in spaces like these, those whose states of stubborn but basically benign dishevelment disclose something fundamentally earnest, well-intentioned, serenely industrious, and refreshingly self-accepting about the characters of the people who live in them. These mess minders are people who drive sport vehicles up and down the interstate looking for important things—causes, crusades—to sacrifice their lives to. They've changed apartments innumerable times in the years before you meet them, and so their belongings take on an incidental relationship to their ever-changing environs. The stuff sits there like a set of figures pasted onto a background, paper on cardboard or CGI over the details of real life. These people constitute a kind of priesthood.

"It's really fucking gross," Regina had said, lively with pride, when she'd walked me in and paraded me through her rooms. Now she sat on top of me and licked the open palm of her hand, and applied the spit to herself and to me. Soon we were moving in rough tandem, and her hands were grasping at my neck and the sides of my head.

I WOKE UP TO THE sound of Regina stumbling around the room and pulling clothes on. I watched her through a small opening in the blanket we'd slept under. Instead of the jeans, T-shirt, and fleece she usually wore to the office, she was slipping on a sleeveless kelly-green dress. She struggled with it for a while, her arms groping helplessly forward and her head lost, like a turtle's, within the body of the dress. When, finally, she had the thing on, she stepped into a pair of cream-colored canvas flats that were pointed at the toes. Then she looked over and saw me watching, and started to laugh. Her face was purple with the effort of dressing. She slapped her palm over both of her eyes, pantomiming exasperation.

"I'm *so* sorry," she said. "I guess I forgot? There's this . . . church thing." She stopped talking for a moment and looked at me helplessly. "I'm getting baptized," she said.

Goffstown, New Hampshire, was the largest town in her "turf" as an organizer, and her most reliable volunteer there was a Presbyterian pastor named Bill Buechler. When she'd first arrived in the state as a new hire, Buechler had acted as her host, and she'd quickly fallen into the habit of accompanying him to his church on Sunday mornings. Now—although she'd be gone in a month, off to organize another town in another state—she was joining the congregation and going under the water. The pastor would be her new godfather. She wanted to think of the decision as sincerely felt, but worried that there was something opportunistic about it, too. Maybe, subconsciously, she'd converted in order to win a few "faith-based" votes.

"Pastor Bill talks about a God I can sort of understand," she said after I'd asked more about Buechler. "He talks about action: politics, looking out for the poor, fighting for justice. All the hippie, Jesus-people sort of stuff that I remember from some of the nuns that used to teach me when I was a kid. Maybe there's some self-flattery going on; my job makes me basically a saint to him. He says I've 'given my life' for something 'bigger than myself'"—she rolled her eyes while pronouncing both phrases—"and that this makes me like a miniature Christ. And he tells me not to worry that I can't totally buy into the idea of some invisible Person watching over me while I—excuse me—shave my pubes or sit on my ass at the office, or whatever. Or, for that matter, into the idea of a virgin birth or a resurrection from the dead. He says God's the stuff I already care about, the people I already love. Which, to me, makes sense.

"And then he's also just truly sweet—just *good*—in a way that makes me think that he's got something that I want to have. So I trust him more than I tend to trust these kinds of people. He uses very little jargon, which is comforting."

She asked if I'd like to come; I said sure. As we crossed into Goffstown it started to snow, first in a scattershot way that suggested it might stop just as quickly as it had started, but then in solid gray-white waves that made it hard for Regina to see as she drove. We slowed to a roll and got to the church late. The building was low and square and made of large bleached stones, with a white wooden spire at the top. It didn't much matter that we were late—the pews were half empty, presumably, Regina whispered, because of the snow. We slid into a pew a few rows back from the pulpit, just off the center aisle.

Regina gave a short, embarrassed wave toward the pulpit, and a man who must have been Bill Buechler smiled broadly and returned it. Buechler wore round glasses with thin, gold arms and had a yellowish mustache that rushed over his upper lip. He was tall and sat in a plain brown chair, facing the congregation, with his back perfectly straight and his thin legs extended and crossed at the ankles. He might have been watching TV or lazing at a coffee shop, but, instead, in his pose of total comfort, he sat watching the people in the pews as we were led by the choir—ten or fifteen graying older ladies with leprous voices—in the singing of several hymns.

Finally, the songs done but their sound still hanging in the air, Buechler stepped up to the pulpit and called Regina to the front. Two of the stooped choir members stood waiting for her; one held a metal bowl, full of water, and the other a wooden cup. As Regina stood, head bowed, listening to Buechler's short preamble and waiting for the ladies to wet her head, I felt my cheeks growing hot. Tears snuck into the corners of my eyes before I could stop them from coming.

# 7

THAT NIGHT—AND, REALLY, FOR THE REST OF THE TIME I KNEW her—I told Regina lots of stories. She told hers too. We sat there, back on her bed, in various stages of undress, trading confessions. She had a way—I noticed this as she was telling me how she'd decided, for good, to give up singing—of wrinkling her small upper lip in the manner of a furrowed brow. She'd make that gesture, turn her face into a gentle wave, and look off somewhere just over my shoulder as she spoke.

Her baptism, I told her, had reminded me of a time when I was away at college and, back home, a miracle had happened. One Sunday night, the phone in my dorm room had rung, and my mother told me excitedly that Brother Charles had died and been coaxed back to life that morning at church. Brother Charles was a short man with a shriveled face and stubby fingers who always smiled and cooed nice greetings but never spoke. The only indications of his age were his eyebrows, which groped outward in sparse gray tufts. If I saw him today, I'd know to call his condition Down syndrome. Back then, we all just smiled at him while we made conversation with his sister, Sister Janice, who brought him to church and looked after him.

That morning, during the music—he was known to love faster numbers, and this was one of those—Brother Charles started to grab first at his face and then at his chest. Then he let out one long groan, unmetered by syntax or meaning, slumped in his chair, his eyes rolling wildly about his head, and slipped from his pew to the floor. (By this point in her telling, my mother had already started to cry. Now, telling all of it to Regina, including the bit about my mother's tears, I tried to set my face neutrally, betraying neither belief nor disbelief.)

At our church there were women we called "nurses" who wore thick white sneakers, thick white stockings, and shockingly well-starched white dresses as uniforms, and were nonetheless not at all actual nurses. The function of the "Nurses' Board" was, alternately, to fetch water for the pastor; to cover up ladies' bare or stockinged legs when they lay on the floor, slain in the Spirit; and to catch people who fell out before they hit the floor. Pentecostalism is a contact sport; these women were somewhat like training staff, ball boys, and referees. Sister Janice was the head of the Nurses' Board, and the rare nurse who was also by profession a nurse. Immediately she slipped down at Brother Charles's side and started pumping at his chest and listening for breath. She cried out that the breath was gone and so was his pulse.

This is what the church was like: the choir stayed where it was; the organist stayed in his seat at the Hammond; almost everybody kept to their pews, except for the pastor's adjutant and a few others who ran to call for the paramedics. The rest of us—I wasn't there, but this is, without a doubt, what I would've done too—simply started to pray, holler, shout, run, fall out, cry, imprecate the Devil, and beg God to change His unchanging mind. The place went up in a holy roar. The player at the Hammond swerved away from the up-tempo number and into the wandering minor-key dirge that always accompanied deep worship—the sound reserved for moments of highest emotion, like on Pentecost, when kids and recent converts dressed in white would approach the altar and have hands laid on their heads and prayers prayed over them, tarrying there in hopes that they might, by service's end, receive the Holy Ghost and begin to speak in tongues.

Now tongues were spoken with an urgent fluency—glottal gasps, rolled *r*'s, sobbing vowel sounds tuned to the organ—over Brother Charles's body. Sister Janice made the few congregants who'd left their seats give him space, fending them off with her arm between pumps, but a loose circle did form around the brother and sister; the din of prayer came at them from every angle.

"This is the kind of people we were," I said to Regina, still showing—or, at least, *trying* to show—no feeling either way.

The pastor came down from the pulpit—my poor, dead pastor, around whom many similar circles were later formed, to no avail—and walked through the throng, and placed a hand on Brother Charles's slick hairless head. He muttered inaudible words as Sister Janice kept administering CPR: two sciences, spiritual and physical, at work at once. The organ struck a glancing chord—loud, attacking, Gothic, almost lewd in its dissonance. The sound of prayer—the name of Jesus moshed among many mouths—went up in another unbearable wave. Audible, too, my mother said, was an extramusical sound, like metal chains grinding. A feeling of wind shuddered through my mom's body. The purple upholstery on the pews went blurry. Moan, moan, moan, moan. The Blood of Jesus. So many syllables put indecipherably together. So much sweat. My mother couldn't tell me how long the praying went on. But just as the ambulances were arriving—from the sanctuary you could hear the whoops, and, through the stained windows, see a burnished wash of the sirens—the congregation fell quiet, and the organ stopped its thrum.

Sister Janice and the pastor were shouting. Brother Charles was alive. His head swiveled wildly and his hands grabbed at the air. His eyes fluttered; he was breathing. The next wave of prayer was all hallelujahs. My mother had offered her own hallelujahs as she cried, relaying the good news over the phone; now I relayed even those to Regina as we lounged in her bed. She didn't ask what I made of the story and, grateful, I didn't say. I'd only mentioned Brother Charles, I said, because his resurrection and Regina's baptism had given me new ways to think about the history of God's interaction with people. I'd worried so much about salvation—heaven or hell, in or out— that I'd crowded out promises of earthly healing or prosperity. Who cared, when death was coming either way. And I'd never once considered that God could be implicated in politics other than those of his own kingdom. Current affairs and divine healing had both been worldliness to me. I was "living to live again," as the old folks said.

"Huh," Regina said. "My mom took me to church maybe once a month. She believed, I think, but she wasn't hung up. Dad didn't care about that stuff at all. So I never once worried about hell. I guess I thought that this stuff had mostly to do with *here*. But—not, like"—she fanned her hands, waving toward the immense weirdness of the story I'd told her—"nothing with miracles. Nobody near me thought a lot about miracles." She stopped and considered for a moment, her lips gone italic again. "Yeah, no, not at *all* about miracles."

"One time," I said, "that guy David Blaine—do you know David Blaine?"

"Uh-huh," she said. "The Criss Angel guy."

"Much better than Criss Angel."

"Ah," she said, starting to smile. "Serious preferences among magicians."

"I just know Blaine's the best," I said. "One time—this is before anybody knew about him, before he'd been on TV yet in any real way—he came walking down the block of my church. This was before the thing with Brother Charles. There was a really small camera crew with him, and all the guys around my age—fourteen, fifteen—were hanging out on the sidewalk in our suits, after service. He said hey to us, told us—I guess this was a joke—that we looked like we were in town for a yearly accountants' convention. Then he told us his name—his name was David Blaine—and said he was an *illusionist*—'magician' being far too vulgar a word—and he was filming a special for TV. He wanted to know if he could show us a few tricks. We said okay, sure.

"First he did something involving my friend Corey. You know, pick a card. Corey looks at the card and puts it back into the deck. So far, so normal, so corny. Baby's birthday party stuff. We were all sort of getting ready to clown David Blaine. Then Blaine gives Corey this short but weirdly deep stare. Like, soulful. And he gives Corey the deck back and tells him to throw the whole thing in the air. Chuck the deck. We all started giggling—what if the dude was crazy, that kind of laugh—but Corey did it. Made a mess, cards all over the sidewalk, everywhere. David Blaine starts pacing, like he's looking for Corey's card with this weird stressed-out energy. He fishes one out of the gutter. 'This your card?' Corey says no. He pulls one out of the patch of dirt near a tree. 'This one?' No. The last one he grabs comes from the church's front step. He looks at it like it's his last hope, like the TV special and his whole career in illusionism hangs on this moment. 'This one?' he asks, sort of pleading. 'Is this your card?' Corey looked almost genuinely sad. 'Nope.' David Blaine looked like he wanted to cry. By now the rest of us are standing around Corey in a huddle, laughing even more.

"But then, like it was an afterthought, Blaine said, 'Oh, just one last thing. I think I forgot something. Could you—Corey, right?' I always thought that toss-off of his name was an incredible touch. 'Corey, could you check your inside suit pocket?' We all got quiet *fast*. Corey reached into his pocket and, feeling the card there, he started yelling before he could get it all the way out. When he brought it out, of course that was his card. Everybody screamed. It was mayhem."

Regina was laughing hard. "Black people love magic," she said.

"Yes, they do," I said. "And while his crew was picking up the cards, David Blaine showed us one more thing. He turned his back to us, asked us to catch him in case he fell, and before we knew it, both of his feet were off the ground."

"I saw that one on TV!" Regina said. "Levitation!"

"He levitated for us," I said. "Right in front of the church, like a minor demon. We just started running around, up and down the block, with our hands on our heads. When we stopped and got ourselves together, David Blaine and his whole crew—and all the cards on the ground—were already gone."

After that first night and day, I spent more evenings at Regina's than with Howland at Derrick's. The move wasn't really a move—I had my bed or the couch in the trailer whenever I wanted it, usually when either Regina or I was working too late for the other to stand—and it required no logistics. I wore the same outfit on most days, a gray knit hoodie and my stiff, dark jeans. I didn't need to move my duffel—I bought a new toothbrush and a washcloth and the maneuver was done. We saw each other in the dark of the morning and the dark of the night, mostly. Because we were halfheartedly hiding our quick coupling from Regina's fieldmates, we talked in little snatches during the day, in a hallway almost nobody walked down. Otherwise I'd sit at my desk in the unwalled office and look over at hers—from where I sat I could see only the back of her head: the two big braids she often wore, arcing playfully from the middle of her forehead to the nape of her neck. It was as easy to fall in love as it was to be pulled into the excitement of that office, and that time—extremity, in both cases, wrought a kind of unshakable belief.

At night we spoke for hours, then fucked intricately. In the mornings we showered together without speaking, and Regina drove us to the office after we'd scraped a fresh layer of frost off her windshield. We'd end up in our seats before the sun was fully up.

———

AS A KID, I LIKED to read the Song of Songs. It felt illicit to see sex and love so openly discussed in the Bible. The book isn't just some blank description of Eros: it contains an argument, if only through the context of its inclusion in the canon, even if it doesn't spell it all the way out. It goes something like this: Sex is, yes, an evolutionary necessity, an animal instinct, something to enjoy and exult in and herald with song in its own right and for its own purposes. But it is also, much more pressingly, a metaphor—but somehow a *real* metaphor, utterly different from the kind we encounter in books—for the ever-intensifying love between the human and the divine, the created and the Creator, the all-engulfing lover and the meekly attracted beloved. To practice it as an art would be to grow closer, as one does by prayer and fasting, to God.

I'd liked that idea. It twinned my pinings after girls and spiritual depth, and assured me, too, that both could be satisfied, perhaps even at the same time. But when I started having sex, I could feel that old connection fraying. I went to a tiny liberal arts college in Vermont, among slope-shouldered green mountains. Away from home, I seldom went to church, although, for reasons I never stopped to consider, I held on, at first, to my hope to preserve my virginity until I got married. But mostly I was a kind of pagan, looking at long intervals out my dorm room window at the ridge of mountains, sculpted into softly textured shapes like resting bodies, that loomed outside. Most of the kids at the school were from New England— "just outside Boston" took on a chiming resonance in those years—which, in the early two thousands, hip-hop seemed only glancingly to have touched. Everybody wore Patagonia and carried around bulky Nalgene water bottles and listened

to sanded-down acoustic music by "singer-songwriters": flagrantly lesser heirs of Joni Mitchell and James Taylor, whose
work I was coming to know by way of a constantly applied
osmotic force. Lots of people seemed to have gone to boarding
school and had learned to binge drink responsibly, according to
a byzantine set of rules—stuff about spacing over time and the
correct liturgical order in which to imbibe various spirits—that
I could never grasp. More than once I ended up in the campus
health center with vomit on my clothes.

I didn't listen to much of the classical music I'd sung at
high school, but one composer I did pick up, in a matchy-
matchy and almost corny pairing with my pastoral surround-
ings, was Aaron Copland. I'd known his stuff before but not so
well. Now—maybe hoping to experience some spray of Ap-
palachian water against my face, that Copland *thing*, the sound
of assertion and refreshment, of American belonging—I dug
into the CDs of his that I could find uploaded onto the college's shared file system. But soon I settled on a series of pieces
called *Four Piano Blues*. None of them had a trace of that fresh
optimism. Instead the "Blues" were chilly and standoffish, with
chords colored in cool pastel yellows and greens, and fluctuating melodies that flirted with, then frustrated, my desire for
a romp. When I learned that Copland was a New Yorker, I
began to understand. For me, the *Piano Blues*, which I played
over and over in my room, conveyed the image of a person,
black or white, slouching elegantly near the curb on a city corner. A cosmopolitan, simultaneously American and a person
of the world. The person who would like this kind of music—
the person I started to realize I wanted to be—was a street
citizen, moving chordwise up or down the sidewalk, appreciative and aware equally of the Renaissances uptown and across

the water, of "Bessie, bop, or Bach," as Langston Hughes once wrote.

Maybe it was the music—my Copland-inspired image of an enlightened sophisticate—that made me briefly stop believing in God. Well, even as I say it, I'm not sure that that was ever really true. Certainly I stopped *wanting* to believe. It may also have had something to do with—at long last—my acquisition of a girlfriend in the spring of my sophomore year, not long after I turned nineteen. I surprised myself by how quickly, without even the short struggle of a decision, I shed my (theretofore entirely untested) commitment to virginity. After a few squirming failures—condom mishaps and misplaced boners—I was freshly made, initiated into a world that had been everywhere around me but whose contours I couldn't, until now, perceive. Yes, I was flesh-rendingly guilty, vibrated with guilt, had soundless dreams whose only substance was a dark image of reflecting water and silhouetted trees. But I never once considered changing course. I'd achieved sex and love, and they'd thrown me into antagonism with God. She was from Harlem—weirdly, almost all of the black people on campus were from New York—and had round, smooth, ballooning cheeks that folded and came almost to peaks when she smiled. She danced in the hip-hop troupe on campus. Her style was wild and emotional; onstage she tossed her short, slender body wantonly, into a whir of elbows and precisely placed knees. She was incredibly good, as far as my untrained eyes could tell. Her style was a small clue to her character: all we did besides have sex was argue. In our short intervals of peace, she'd play Sims on her computer or trawl *American Idol* message boards, and gleefully tell stories of fights she'd been in back home. She'd had sex before, had been pregnant before, and told me things

I couldn't decide whether to believe—she was always trying
to shock me—about more than one ex-boyfriend now in jail.
She showed me what were supposed to be letters they'd written, without displaying a hint of sentimentality or regret. We
broke up over the summer and then got back together, again
in spring, and almost immediately after that, she was pregnant.
She stopped going to class and I did too. At mealtimes, I went
to the cafeteria and came back to my dorm room—a new one
by now, no mountain view—with two plates on my tray, saw
almost nobody. By time the baby was born, we were both back
home in New York for good and we'd broken up again.

I couldn't think of any of this as following a pattern of en-
croaching closeness with God. There had to be some other way
to understand it—not totally animal, but shot through with a
roughness I hadn't let into my prior neatly allegorical vision.
If I could come to understand this spectacularly strange first
attempt, and subject it to the logic that seemed clear to me in
Copland's *Blues* (one was marked, simply, "Freely Poetic"; those
two words yanked at so many of my yearnings, made my heart
hurt), perhaps I could revise it over time, make it lovely.

I have been waiting all my life—was waiting long before I
met Regina, I've come to realize, and am still waiting now, long
after—for the emergence of a criticism of sex. Something that,
say, porn won't satisfy. The data set on porn and its various effects is by now large enough, I think it's fair to say, to conclude
that it has basically zero beneficial—or, more to the point I
have always fumbled to make, pedagogical or interpretive—
effects on the development of sexual performance or creativity
or integrity over time. Porn (minus plot) is a kind of parody of
untrained sexual desire, manufactured with the subterranean

purpose, it often seems to me, of exaggerating (not for clarity but for clicks) the cruelest and least savory aspects of those desires. Beyond climax it serves no good purpose. I've heard arguments to the contrary—guys who say it taught them how to please their future partners—but I just can't believe them.

What I've wanted, instead, is something that would culminate in a discovery, and reliably carry forward, into the present, the insights won by prior generations. It seems absurd that each of us has to invent sex on his own, like some coital Prometheus, alone outdoors.

I don't mean arts-section reviews. That only puts us back at porn.

One night, with all of this very much on my mind, I cradled Regina's head to my chest and, hoping to sound offhanded, I gave my spiel about sex and criticism—about wanting a manual of aesthetics and manners that could ensure some kind of growing cohesion.

When I finished the complaint, Regina seemed moved—almost sad for me, I thought. "No!" she said. "That's exactly what's good about sex. It's like . . ."

She hesitated for a moment, tilting her head just a tick.

"It's like something vague coming into focus," she said. "You start out with someone, and it's not like you can bring the moves or, like, *techniques* you've already learned into this new situation. Not all of them, at least. You've got experience—unless you're a virgin, of course—but you've also got something like innocence. Naïveté. At least when it comes to this new person. And so you figure them out, encounter by encounter. You experiment, and—if they're good—they'll help you to know what's right, what works. And at the same time they're trying too. So the only real skill that's portable from one person to the next is maybe openness. The kind that allows you to guide and be guided at the same time. Do you know what I mean? This is a good thing! It wouldn't be so good if you could do it under the influence of some, like, literature. It wouldn't be so *different*."

Call it unresolved, this problem. Regina's free, poetic attitude helped me relax. One nearly artistic effect of our pairing was that it dredged up memories. An alternate history of my own life. Talking with Howland in the car, I'd thought of all the men whose monologuing I'd loved, but now—under the influence of so many conversations with Regina—I remembered how conversation among women had helped create my own talk. My mother would catch a ride from church with one of her friends, and they'd somehow end up talking for hours in the car, idling in front of our building instead of going upstairs. I'd sit in the backseat, half asleep but always, on some level, listening. They'd glide easily from gossip to the trading of serious sorrows, then further interpret or elaborate upon or outright criticize the sermon that had been given that morning or afternoon. My mother's best friends were three pretty ladies who towered over her, each of them six feet tall or somewhere close. They sang in harmony spontaneously, along to records or improvising their own renderings of Protestant hymns, and went to far-flung diners just because they liked the service; often we'd end up somewhere in Yonkers on late Sunday afternoons. They treated me like a fifth friend.

Maybe that's why it didn't strike me as strange that the boundaries of formality between me and Beverly kept dissolving. She called me often, three or four times a week, while I was in New England. Just as I stole away to see Regina, I sometimes snuck off into an empty office within the complex to lie on the floor and talk with Beverly. A lot of the time it had nothing to do with work. She'd spin her wheels about her son, Thadd—he was fine, thanks, acting like a shit but essentially fine—or about the stream of annoyances that flowed through her office.

Once I asked her the same question I'd started to ask everybody—the one that yields Pilgrim ancestors and lost immigrant fathers, and keeps others talking as I follow the paths of their eventual arrivals. Where were her people from?

She was born and raised in a St. Louis suburb by quiet hymn lovers—lifelong AME congregants both—who were quiet about their churchgoing, quiet about their work, quiet unto total abstinence about their only daughter's virtues. Praise was scarce but Beverly knew, more or less, where she stood. Her mother, like mine, was a teacher, and her father a structural engineer.

That was more than enough pedigree for Beverly. Talking about herself made her antsy, almost mad. Instead she quickly diverted, asked me what it had been like growing up in both Chicago and New York. I didn't know what to tell her, having come from nowhere, and not wanting to sensationalize or to bore. Wanting to reciprocate, though, I told her everything I could remember about college and the baby, about Vermont in the muddy, desperate spring. I looked at the gray grain of the uneven office carpet, sometimes letting my head rest on the floor, as I rifled through its rhythms. I never told her about Regina.

Sometimes she was in the mood to talk about the rest of her life: how she'd become close with the candidate, what she thought of him. Those short conversations became a collage in my head, one that I pasted together with conjectures of my own.

The candidate, I knew, had moved to Chicago not long after his graduation from Harvard Law School. He was looking, it has always seemed to me, for something to cling to—just as Beverly would later cling to him, and I to her. This was no great insight: fundamental to any close reading of his biography (there are already, understandably, several) is an acute sense of self-conscious placelessness and, therefore, of confusion. Peripatetic childhood left him dizzy. For him, identity had been a kind of curation or collation—he picked up aspects as he went, freestyle.

He came down from the steeples of the law school having probably proved something of great importance to himself— foremost that his self-possession is a kind of continent, his own hometown, as much a place to be "from" as anywhere else—and plopped down hungry for politics in Chicago. He organized tenants and met and married his wife and started attending the church whose articulation of the Gospel would end up so radically overrich for his blood. Membership at Trinity seemed, at the time, pretty aspirational-middle-class, though; it was a sort of sign of arrival. He took up residence as a lecturer in the law, ran for state legislature and won, then for Congress and lost.

By this time, he was a father, and when the babies were asleep with his wife, he'd go on long nighttime walks around the city, hewing close to the lake and looking up at the lights. In Springfield—the symbolism of that place was never lost on him—he practiced a brand of ostentatious collaboration: he smoked cigars and went to poker nights and sparred mildly with Republicans who duly deemed him not so bad and let him put his name on a bipartisan bill or two every session. He had his eyes on higher ground from the start; nobody didn't know that. His cloakroom buddies called him Mr. President and hummed "Hail to the Chief" when he entered rooms. When a Senate seat opened up, everybody looked his way.

But he did still have his wounds. That failed congressional campaign had given him the slightest flinch. His problem had been twofold, probably. His bearing needed a tweak, and his conception of politics—this kind of politics; neighborhood hyperfocus; rec-center democracy—was plain bad. He labored under the misimpression that people—voters—wanted to hear him talk. As it turned out, he wouldn't be wrong about that for long. But nobody in Cook County cared to diagram his speeches.

His opponent was a former Black Panther given to entertaining and almost jokey irruptions of black nationalism on the floor of the House. He said wild shit in Washington and stroked his base back home. He played the inside-outside like a harp. He knew what he was doing; eloquence didn't figure in. And here came this pontificating light-skinned kid offering inspiration and going on about "good government" and "special interests" and scolding about the war. Nobody gave a shit—their man handed out turkeys on holidays and knew people's names, like a noble mobster or some street-smart Robin Hood. For him Springfield—hell, pick a capital—meant a mud fight, an evolutionary struggle among fledgling germs, not a virtuous orator in a big hat.

At a summer fundraising event for the doomed bid, attended by the variegated upper-middle-class group that had flocked to the candidate and adopted him as a potential savior almost immediately upon his arrival in Chicago—former Harold Washington staffers; former Weather Underground homemade-bomb manufacturers; faded Alinskyites; an array

of professors and lawyers and middling money managers—
he'd become acquainted again with an old friend from law
school.

*Friend* was a stretch. He and Beverly had both worked on
the *Law Review* and attended meetings of the Black Student
Union, held signs in the same crowds at feeble campus protests.
She'd cut a weird figure at school; hadn't had as easy a time as
he'd had at surfing the many social structures and pretending
to belong. Caught between Black Power and black profession-
alism, she'd worn headwraps and tweed jackets and jeans and
sandals on her walks across the quad, looking with every outfit
like a box-checking survey of attitudes about the powers of the
world in which she now moved. She spoke a lot, in class and at
meetings and everywhere else, kept up a nearly constant, heavily informed, densely eloquent chatter that kept her "known"
among her peers but also, almost forcefully, staved off real intimacy. Back then, that was the whispered rap about Beverly:
Everybody liked her, but who was her friend?

At the congressional event, she cornered him just after
his short speech and formal, minimally tense period of question and answer, when he was supposed to be breezing around
the room, thanking people and promising he'd do better the
next time around. By now his mistakes were nothing new to
him, but she pressed him afresh with their gravity—and, more
creatively, connected them implicitly with the small but still
visible freckles of fault in his personal character. He was an
egghead, impressive but ineffectual; he cared more about daz-
zling people than about winning their support. He'd proven
that he could get along, but not that he could get over. She
saw a great performer in him—a president!—but he'd go nowhere until he dropped the outer Kennedy act—the handsome

winsomeness, the good-boy flair—and got in better touch with Kennedy's deeper realities: his familiarity with party bosses, and with worse actors than that; all those voting corpses in— where else?—Illinois. He knew, he knew, but he couldn't shake her off. The party ground to a halt and watched her hector him. Annoyance turned—in the audience and in the candidate himself—into a kind of respect, just at her endurance. Before long, the candidate took her number, promised to call for more advice, and finally, wearing a real but tired smile, earned his freedom from the exchange.

They'd been allies of a kind ever since; on the Senate campaign that became his big national break and paved ground for the presidential, she'd helped lead his finance committee and served informally as a liaison to the old law school crowd. She called the classmates she'd known but not known, picked up their old skin-deep banter just long enough to evangelize them to the candidate's cause. Sometimes she wrote long, intricately reasoned emails about him, like a latter-day Saint Paul. She'd started her long climb in finance and, tapping into deep synergies between the worlds, found it fairly easy to make a commensurate mark in politics by trawling for checks. This produced an ouroboros: her proximity to the rich made politicos open their doors; her growing renown—still little real closeness—in D.C. gave her an extra bit of mystique among the marketeers in New York.

Beverly became the great constant in my life. She'd call to ask about New Hampshire or to catch me up quickly about New York. Each time, though, she'd give me a few names, along with their credit card information and addresses. "Some gifts from Blackshear," she said. The new donors, always credited to her, always worked for Terry's dad's firm. I emailed Terry about it once—he was still working in New York. Why didn't his father just give *him* the names? "No idea," he wrote back. "Dad likes Beverly and Beverly likes you. So you get to do the honors." By *honors* he meant data entry. I saved the money stuff for the very end of each day, just before I left the office.

# 8

SOMETIMES AFTER WORK, THE THREE OF US—ME, HOWLAND, Regina—would drive down a short hill from the office to the bar and restaurant where Howland and I had stopped on our first day in town. The place had bleeding burgers, pallid beer, and crispy, tough-skinned fries, salted generously, that we loved. They always had the Celtics on. We'd go and eat and drink and watch Howland get red, then split up. Howland would carry a hello from me to Derrick—who didn't care, Howland assured me, that I was only sporadically at the trailer.

One night, the night before my twenty-third birthday— never before had the day snuck up on me like this—we sat in our customary booth across from the door, from which Regina and I could see the TV in the back of the place and How-land could see the big one up front. The Celtics were playing the Detroit Pistons. Detroit, back then, still got a measure of respect because they'd won the championship only four years earlier, and they still a couple of my favorite personae from that year: Chauncey Billups and Rasheed Wallace. I liked Billups because, as a kid, I'd read about him when he was in college,

in my favorite basketball magazine, *SLAM*. Rasheed I liked because he was an asshole and seemed to have more courage
than I did. So I was more or less even on the Pistons.

Howland liked to watch basketball but didn't care very
much about it, or keep track of most of the players' names.
Regina was a die-hard Lakers fan and therefore couldn't watch
the Celtics without *motherfuck*ing them all game long, which I
liked because she otherwise never cursed. Like most New Yorkers, I held the Celtics—all things Boston—at arm's length, but
I couldn't hate them too much this year. They were a kind of
experiment. Two superstars, Ray Allen and Kevin Garnett,
had made their way onto the team to join Paul Pierce, the
star Boston had already had. Now, the sports talkers said, they
were a "super team," hastily arranged—like the thing between
me and Regina, like even the best-organized state primary
campaign—but still perhaps unfairly sodden with expecta-
tion. If they couldn't win with all this talent, the talkers said,
they were a failure. My favorite sportswriter at the time was
an openly partisan Boston fan who pitched a fit in his column
every time they had a bad loss. Since the Knicks were bad and
better ignored that season, the Celtics were what I thought
about when I wasn't thinking about Regina, or the candidate,
or the sublime but inscrutable workings of a constitutional re-
public.

My favorite Celtic to watch was Pierce. He was a strange
player—for me, at least, in my youth, the first instance of a type.
He was a big wing—six-seven or six-eight—with a big trunk for
a body. Wide shoulders gave way to an equally wide midsection
and thick legs. Big in every dimension though he was, he didn't
look, at first glance, particularly athletic or strong. His arms

were smooth and unmuscled, and, especially early in most seasons, the barrel of his torso sometimes seemed to be toting a substantial gut. He looked like he could've played back in the seventies or eighties, when even the best players never worked out over the summer and, during the season, rode charter buses and smoked cigarettes. Now, at the beginning of the new century, all the guys looked like Adonises freed from blocks of stone—so much so that I often worried that there'd be a steroids scandal in basketball like the one in baseball, some shock that would trouble my belief in the game. Neither of my parents had been big sports fans—I'd found basketball on my own, like a solitary seeker, and guarded my love of it like a treasure.

Pierce was comforting, then: the real untainted article. He looked like an overgrown uncle and played like a boulder. He would dribble slowly in front of his defender, then take a surprisingly quick first step into the paint. The defender would try to scuffle over to throw his body between Pierce and the bucket, but Pierce would tap him with the side of his butt, the way you close the fridge when your hands are full, and the guy would go flying or crumple to the floor. Plays like those often ended with a big dunk—Pierce could get his bearlike frame magically high above the ground. He celebrated by punching the air and squishing his face into a grimace, directed at one of the cameras or the opposing bench. He had a bad beard—scrubby patches on the cheeks—that wouldn't connect with his rainless cloud of a mustache. Some players seemed to get a haircut before each game; Pierce's hairline was a scribble. His mouth was small but his eyes were big. He was too bizarre to dislike, no matter where he played.

It was close to Christmas, two weeks from the primary,

and the restaurant was almost empty. As the game started up, the waiter who came over was a black kid—the only nonwhite person I'd ever seen working at the place. I'd noticed him before; he sometimes peeked out of the doors to the kitchen. I didn't know he waited tables. As usual, he wore a small wool cap of dark purple or blue, with forest-green trim, which sat cocked atop his head in the manner of a kufi or a navy officer's hat. Under the cap and always escaping it was a mop of loose, playful curls, which often settled—to the young man's annoyance, you could tell—on the bridge of his nose and in front of his small, dark eyes. He was complected like a fading manila folder, and had a wrestler's short, brawny bearing. He wore a long white chef's coat flecked with brownish smears that looked like old blood.

My body was warming up, and basketball was on, and I was with my friends—I felt good, so I started a conversation with the young man after he'd taken our orders. It might be useful, I thought, to try to become a "regular." "Hey, it's good to see you again," I said, feeling for some reason a need to establish that I'd seen him before. "You know, I always thought you were a cook."

He smiled and looked almost shy—a bit of color crept into his face. "You're right," he said. "Yeah, I cook back there most days, but on slow nights I'll take a few tables too. Owners try to keep the payroll down in the middle of the week, especially this close to Christmas. We don't really fill back up till after New Year's."

His teeth were slightly spaced out, each making room for itself, and he had a high voice that lilted, only slightly, in a way I recognized. Each of his vowels started out sharp and clear, but then shaded into a near rasp just before it hooked onto the next sound. The "Christ" in "Christmas" was a short, efficient mesa over whose edge the "mas" fell gently. Over the kid's shoulder I could see Billups hit a dead-on three-pointer from the top of the arc. I let out a little scream—my lifelong habit of brief, sports-induced excitement.

The cook turned around and made an appreciative noise too. "I like Billups," he said.

"Are you—I'm sorry—but are you Haitian?" I asked. Maybe I'd been further emboldened by learning that he liked basketball.

"Haitian!" Howland said, enjoying how specific things were already becoming. Regina, next to me, was still rejoicing over the three. Billups was from Colorado—for her this made him, by adoption, a citizen of Greater California, and therefore a fitting proxy in her coastal battle against the Celtics.

The cook grinned his gapped teeth back into view. "How'd you know?"

Figuring he'd understand what I meant, I said, "I'm from New York. I know a lot of kids from Brooklyn." Just as he started to laugh, someone yelled, "Hey, Prince! I need you!"

The bar up front was three-sided—the fourth surface of the square was the wood-paneled wall on which the huge TV hung. On both sides of the screen were tableaux of fake taxidermied animals: deer, elk, big cats, flayed fish. Around the bar, here and there, were guys in washed-out jeans, big boots, and heavy jackets. It was the bartender, a tall, slim kid with brilliantly active acne ravaging his face, its colors a Doppler map of pus and scabs, who had yelled out. He was holding up an empty bottle for the cook—"Prince"—to see. "Be right back," Prince told us.

Prince seemed popular with the patrons. Soon the bartender was pouring shots—all the guys got one, and so did Prince—and they all cried out "Priiiiiiiiiiiiiiiince!" Prince blushed and took his shot and hurried back into the kitchen, carrying the pad on which he'd written our orders and the empty bottle.

The first quarter of the game was slightly awkward. Billups was hitting shots, and so was Ray Allen, who'd just come back from an injury, but both teams' timing was otherwise off. The rest of the players seemed tired. We watched Billups hit another shot, and, after a few listless passes around the Celtics' perimeter, Allen replied with a three. Prince came back through the kitchen door and left it swinging in his wake. He brought a fresh bottle to the bar, and again his presence occasioned a wave of happy shouts and recitations of his name. On a tray he toted our watery-looking beers. There were four of them instead of three, and when he came over, he clinked glasses with us, scooched Howland over on his side of the booth, and started to drink and watch the game with us as if we'd all come together. "I like Allen," he said, in the same tone he'd used about Billups. "That guy *works*." He took a sip with an approving look in his eyes.

Prince looked across the table at me. "So," he said, "Brooklyn?"

"I'm from Manhattan," I said, "but yeah, a lot of my friends are from Brooklyn."

"Lotta Haitians," he said. "My dad is, my mom isn't. She's white, from up here. But when my dad came to the States, he went to Brooklyn—'Bwookleen'—first." When Prince did his dad's voice, he made his eyes big and his fingers taut with stress. "You know Nostrand Avenue? Never been there myself, but he lived around there. Nostrand, close to Flatbush. It's all Haitians down there, huh?"

I nodded. "Lotta Haitians, yeah. I could tell you were because of the kids I knew—kids of immigrants but, you know, more or less American themselves, educated next to white kids like I was. A lot of them had voices like yours. Just a hint. Softened versions of their parents'."

"My dad's always mad I can't speak Creole," he said, "although as far as I can tell that's his fault. He'll be happy to know"—and you could tell, just then, that Prince was, too—"that I'm recognizable as a Haitian anyway."

His hair fell steadily out of the hat. As he spoke he kept batting it away from his eyes and trying to tuck it back into his hat. "So it's like Little Haiti, huh?"

"Little Haiti but also Little Jamaica and Little Trinidad and Little Saint Vincent and Little Barbados. Down where your dad lived, Haiti's probably most prominent. There's a street named for Toussaint-Louverture and another for Jean-Jacques Dessalines. Big deal. Sometimes I'll go hang out in Brooklyn and be the only black *American* in sight." I'd talked a lot with Howland about how almost nobody he'd grown up with had been black of any kind. Now he listened with a look of neutral curiosity, happy, I knew, to eavesdrop on a kind of inner life—blackness within blackness, subtle gradients of color and colonial origin.

Regina took her eyes off the game. "Back home, I was one of the only black second-generation kids I knew. Everybody was American. All the black kids, that is—there were more Mexican kids than maybe anybody else. Most of the black kids' parents—like *all* of them, to a weird degree—were from Louisiana."

"Southern," Prince said, looking like he was drawing a map in his head.

"Louisiana specifically," Regina said. "To a startling degree Louisiana."

Prince looked over at me. "My grandmother's from Georgia," I said. "Grandfather's from Sierra Leone, but I didn't know him. No connection to any of that except for a nice great-aunt. My dad's parents I don't know anything about. Uptown in Manhattan almost everybody's like me: Georgia, Carolinas. But Flatbush? Crown Heights? All islands."

Prince looked satisfied. "Everybody around here was white," he said.

"So," Howland said after a moment. *"Prince?"*

Prince shrugged. "Not really, but it works. I told the guys my dad's Haitian, and somebody—I can't remember who; maybe it was Brian, over there, in the glasses—anyway, somebody had heard of Port au Prince. Then, *boom.* Nickname. I didn't try to stop it. Name's Max—Maximilien—but, yeah, Prince is fine. Now my friends call me that too. I don't *not* like it." He'd just graduated from the University of New Hampshire, he told us. These days—basically uninterested in a career; he liked to ski—he was taking his time and figuring out what to do. "My dad wants me to be a lawyer, now that it's basically impossible, as far as he can tell, for me to be a doctor."

I was happy to be talking with Prince but getting annoyed by the game, whose score I didn't care about. Pierce was having a bad game, sort of floating around. He missed a wing jumper just as the quarter ended and Prince got up to grab our burgers and fries. When he came back he also had new beers we hadn't asked for. I hurried up with the quickly warming bottom third of my first. Prince sat next to Howland again. The second quarter started; Allen hit another three. "Dammit," I said, not really begrudging Allen but feeling bad for Pierce, who, I thought, was unfairly eclipsed by his two new, better-regarded teammates.

"You don't like Allen?" Prince said. "I *love* Allen."

I explained: Allen was fine, but I was pulling for Pierce.

"So you want the Celtics to win, but only if Pierce is the reason?"

"Sorta," I said. "I don't really care about the Celtics. Just Pierce. They can win or lose or whatever. Technically I'm supposed to hate them."

"I don't know, man," Prince said. "I'm not sure Pierce cares about Pierce as much as you do. I mean, look at him—he's clearly not as interested in the gym as the rest of these guys. I think he probably plays basketball because he happens to be good at it, you know? I'm not picking up a lot of passion. At least not for getting ready."

"That's what I like about him," I said, starting the new beer. I wondered whether it would be free. "He's not perfect. Maybe he's not as athletic, maybe he likes to go home and listen to music after practice instead of spending the rest of the day working out. But he's still awesome; he does cool stuff. He sort of works within those limitations—his body type, his love for R&B or whatever, I'm making this up—to produce what's good about him on the court. That's art." Right then, Pierce unfurled one of his exceedingly slow stutter steps, moving just deceptively enough to shake off a defender. (The guy guarding him was Rip Hamilton, whose game I didn't mind. He was a good midrange shooter who ran incessant, elegant routes when he didn't have the ball and, because he'd broken his nose one too many times, always wore a plastic mask sculpted especially for his face.) Pierce shot and made—finally—a seventeen-footer. "See," I said. "That's what I mean. He'd never have developed that little fake first step if he'd been a faster guy. His body breeds innovation. It's a good thing."

"Fuck Pierce," Regina said.

Prince shook his head disapprovingly. "No way. If his 'limitation,' as you say, is laziness—which, okay, I get it; it's mine too—he should be working to overcome it *off* the court, *away* from me. I don't wanna watch that. Bring something, like, *refined* onto the court, and then work from there. You say innovation but what you're really talking about is a band-aid." He took a big gulp. "I've seen you guys a bunch of times before," he said. "I like that you really watch basketball. Those guys"—here he gestured toward the bar—"those guys really only care about baseball—Sox, Sox, Sox—and football: Pats. They just put basketball on when there's nothing else to watch. It's my favorite, though," he said. "Because it's so easy to see how much *work* they put in. On their jumpers, on their hops, on their bodies, whatever. I feel like one of my old math teachers when I see them, you know what I mean? Like, show your work!" He made himself laugh really hard with the math thing. His cheeks grew roses. "It's like a showcase for self-control," he said. "If my dad—he's an engineer; all he cares about is being right, getting stuff down—if he could hear you say all that stuff about Pierce, justifying his sloppiness by turning it into a quirk, he'd slap you to death and then die himself. He couldn't even sit here and listen to you say it; he'd have to leave. I mean, look at Allen. That's what I'm talking about."

Allen was just then hitting another jumper.

"He came into the NBA pretty good at shooting. Remember him on the Bucks?"

I nodded. I was amused and egged on by the conversation, partly because what Prince had said about my view of Pierce—sloppiness as quirk, weakness as false strength—sounded to me like the kind of indictment I often lobbed at myself.

"He was already good," Prince said. "And now he's so obviously better. Now he's like the best shooter in history. And it's not like he's happy with that. Every single time he steps into a gym—have you heard this?—he has to make—*make*, not *take*—a thousand jumpers. And then he's getting better at other stuff, too. Not so stiff dribbling, jumps higher every year. On the Celtics, he's learning all this stuff about moving without the ball. The other day I saw him dunk like he was Kobe or something. I'm not Mr. Excellence in my own life, don't get me wrong—but that's the whole thing: I want these guys to be something I'm not. Pierce depresses me."

Pierce inspired me, I explained: he showed me a way through life as *myself*, showed how limits—lifelong limits, irreversible except by something like a miracle—could point beyond themselves. Allen hit another shot before the half ended.

Prince lifted an eyebrow as if to say, See? Then he jumped up to get our table a round of shots from the bar. "On me," he said. "Nobody really cares, especially now." He got the shots—sweet Irish whiskey—but not before having a separate round with the guys at the bar. Another wave of howls sounded at his presence. He came back with the shot glasses looking tipsy. "You guys work on one of those campaigns, right?" We told him which one. "Figured," he said. "The whole town's full of new young people, it's cool." We saluted each other at the center of the table before we took the shots.

"Speaking of Kobe," Regina said. "The reason Prince is right"—she gave me an apologetic glance—"is clear to see in

Kobe. He has a million character flaws, right? Hardheaded, arrogant, demanding, rash, sort of strange socially? All that's true. As a Laker fan I can admit all of that. But he seems— I don't know him and I can't claim to really *know*, but I feel like I basically do—he seems to have figured out how to turn all of those things around and put them in service of his strengths: insane ambition and weird willfulness. He thinks he's the best— bad—but decides to express this by actually becoming the best. He's bringing all his . . . *weirdness* together and making it work out for him. That's part of what we like about him, right?"

I thought his hard-work act was just that, a bit of an act, even if—you couldn't deny—it was grounded in something true and bore real fruit on the floor. Something about it seemed strained, showy, bootstrapping, I said, where, instead, Pierce— I couldn't let the thing with him go—showed you how you could accept yourself instead of undergoing some monstrous transformation and still, somehow, make something, or be something, worthwhile. I remembered then, too, without making it part of my argument, that Pierce had been stabbed almost a decade earlier, at some nightclub, after a fight whose rationale I'd never been able to figure out from the news reports. You couldn't blame him for being stabbed, of course, but this was something that shouldn't have happened to someone like him. He shouldn't have been out so late, so unprotected, so open, with a body—frail thing—as provably valuable as his. His great flaw was consistent behavior, vulnerable integrity.

Prince shook his head. "Take your boss. Have you seen the pictures of him as a kid? Bit pudgy—looks like I used to. He talks all the time about how he was lazy in school too. How he's this skinny workaholic who went to Harvard or wherever. He's a model of hard work. He did fucking *coke*, and now he's . . .

this. My dad sort of hated him at first. He liked the other ones better because they seemed harder and more prepared. But when I told him how much this guy has *changed* throughout his life, like walked him through how much effort this guy has put into himself—that's what won him over."

"You changed him over?" Regina said. A note of pragmatism had slipped into her face—pragmatism, in her case, being almost interchangeable with inspiration.

"Yup," Prince said. "That story did it. Character. That dude's like Ray Allen. That's how he can appeal to guys like my dad."

"That's really smart," Regina said, excited. Then, more casually: "You know, if you wanted, you could be a volunteer. Like, whenever you're not here and you've got some time. Intern, whatever. I bet your dad would be impressed."

Prince seemed to be thinking about it when he got up to make his check-in with the crowd at the bar. Now I saw this routine—the sheepish smile as he approached; the happy surprise he feigned when the men started shouting his name—as part of his job, a component of the experience the older men expected when they came and paid and drank and watched sports. To the extent that it was a professional obligation, he fulfilled it well—he never once seemed to be annoyed, whereas I got irritated and vicariously embarrassed just watching it happen. When he was back, Regina started in again.

"So," she asked. "Are there more Haitians out there like your dad?"

Prince nodded. "A few in Manchester, some more over in Nashua. They're all married to white ladies, and sort of mysteriously in touch with each other. It's like a society."

"And you think this Ray Allen thing would work on some of them too?"

The Celtics lost after Pierce missed an open shot late in the game. All the beers ended up free.


THAT NIGHT, DRUNK, I DROVE the rental car back to Derrick's trailer under Howland's supervision. On our way up to New England from the city I'd told him that I'd never learned to drive. Every so often, he let me drive the Cruiser up and down empty highways at night and gave me pointers. Now I sped down the two-lane road toward Derrick's, buzzed enough finally to feel no fear, the Cruiser's headlights glossing with a ghostly white—like the sudden flash at a crime scene—the profligate branches of dead sumac at the sides of the road. What was hardest for me, always, was steadying my foot and finding a balance. I crawled or sped, with little between. Howland did his best to tutor me, but every time I tried to adjust, I only made the car lurch.

As we came closer to Derrick's, a dark squad car came over the slight swell of the horizon behind us. Howland elbowed my arm so hard that the car swerved gently left. By some scared impulse I righted the car and at the same time elbowed him back. I saw, I said. He asked, "You know where we are?" I shrugged. "Close." "Fuck," Howland said. "Fuck. Shit, I'm sorry. You can do this." He looked not so much scared—that I would've understood—as gravely serious. I'd never seen him even close to serious before then. He put his hand on my shoulder and took a deep breath.

"Listen," he said. My hands were sweating. The police car came closer. None of its lights were on. "I know—well, no, that's not true: I don't know. I have heard, I have read, I've tried to be *aware* that this whole thing—a situation like this one—is scarier—not, like, personally, I don't know, but maybe *historically*—scarier for you than it might be for me. I don't— I mean—I get that. Okay?" I nodded okay, but by the end of his speech I was laughing hard; tears made the road ahead of me swim. Howland saw me laughing and he laughed too. "Okay, yeah, sorry," he said. "Have you ever been arrested?" I'd had cuffs on once but never been "brought in." "Pulled over?" I reminded him that I wasn't a driver, and that I didn't have any kind of license or permit on me now.

"Jesus," he said. "Okay. Take a deep, cleansing breath in case you have to take a blow test. That works; I've had a miracle or two. But, forget that, you're not gonna get pulled over anyway. In maybe a half mile, you're gonna take a left. One smooth left. Hand over hand, and you can ease up on the gas. Smooth turn." I drove more steadily than ever for the half mile, noticing nothing but the double yellow line ahead and the car behind. The left came and I took it—smooth. The squad car kept rolling. Howland howled.

# 9

THE WHOLE OFFICE, SLEEP-DEPRIVED AND DRESSED EVEN MORE horribly than usual, watched 2008 roll in at a huge Chinese restaurant close to the bar. (New England Chinese: the sweet and sour's saucier, crab rangoon easier to find.) Regina bought a pitcher of something called a Scorpion Bowl—a pink-orange substance that stank of vodka and rum—and we passed it back and forth until the countdown came. At midnight, she gently held the back of my head as we kissed. We woke up in the New Year past noon, with the smell of the bowl wafting out of our pores.

Two days later, the first votes of the campaign were cast. The fluorescents in the office lit the room undramatically as we watched on several small TVs as the totals in Iowa were counted. I think we were all secretly happy to be second in line, not first. The amazing pressure that we all felt must have been doubled out there among the haystacks and cows. It was strange, watching him win. None of us could afford to express surprise, really—part of the bargain of our work was to seem, always, to believe. Still, there was something surreal about watching someone I'd known—even in such a small way—

stand to give a speech like the one I watched him give. Strange thing: I remember looking at him and feeling like there was a haze in the room; I couldn't tell whether it was in the office or in the hall in which he spoke. He'd never been skinnier, or taller, or more proud. He looked like a monument to himself. (Somewhere along the line I'd realized that all of my private language about his physical bearing was statuary: he could talk, and move, and make his mark felt in time, but his deepest significance to me was as something solid, sure, impossible not to reckon with in space, yet ultimately frozen—something with a plaque affixed, asking to be dutifully studied.)

He started his speech with an artfully stuttered anaphora.

"They said . . . they said. . . . they *said* this day would never come.

"They said our sights were set too high.

"They said this country was too divided, too disillusioned . . ."

He was talking about his race but also not, dog-whistling at a high and perilous pitch, making gently buzzing sounds for those with ears to hear. I especially liked the "they" thing. They who? Well, white people for one, I guessed. The "media" too, always them. But also those older black people in your life—in my experience, these people were often your barber—who hadn't allowed themselves to imagine that he'd win. *"They."* Everybody needed a hater to make success a tad sweeter. Everybody, even this guy, needed a "they."

"You have done what the state of New Hampshire can do in five days," he said at one point, and I could feel the ecstatic atmosphere around me tense up.

ON THE DAY OF THE New Hampshire primary, I was assigned to
sit in the campaign's "war room," a small, cleared-out meeting
room on the ground floor of the Radisson hotel. There, Rob,
the field director, and the other higher-ups would sit at a bank
of phones, fielding calls from the organizers on their turf. This
would give them a picture in real time of how close they were
getting to their vote totals, and hopefully they'd be able to quickly
help with any irregularities that might pop up at polling places.

Upstairs, in the ballroom at the Radisson, the candidate
would give his speech. We all expected to win. The victory in
Iowa had made its mark—*was* a mark in the national ground,
had already become a kind of sculpture—and when the candidate touched ground in New Hampshire for his final visit, his
lead, according to the polls, was ten points. The biggest and
most important newspaper in the state had endorsed him. It
was time, they said in their editorial, echoing the campaign's
ceaselessly consistent message, to move on from an older era, to
look for new leadership to solve a new century's problems. At
the debate at Saint Anselm College, the candidate seemed to
win, although some of the pundits on cable news said that he
was beginning, at this moment of prosperity, to act a bit conde-
scending. While talking to a group of women about the rigors
of the campaign, our main rival, not known for her emotional
attunement, had spontaneously started to attractively and relat-
ably cry. A day of news about the crying had ensued. Nobody'd
seen a bad poll for us yet. We'd notch another win, maybe even
start forcing our opponents to quit, and begin wrapping up the
primary.

My job in the war room was to keep several internet tabs
open on my campaign-issued laptop. Despite the campaign's
ever-hardening disdain for the "bed wetters" in the media, ev-

erybody acknowledged that the news organizations did a good job of reporting vote totals promptly after the precinct officials had finished their counting. Once the polls closed and the results came rolling in, I'd write the results down and pass them along, so that the bosses could keep score.

For hours I sat there with nothing particular to do, eavesdropping on Rob and the rest of the team on the phones and slipping whatever information I could over email to Regina. She was running around Goffstown, getting her voters to the polls and managing a fleet of vans for senior citizens. She was also making personal calls to the informal statewide network of Haitians that she'd built with Prince's help. Her tone over email was optimistic but unsure.

When the polls started to close, the numbers came in fast. The big gray precinct map on Politico's website—they were the fastest—filled up with bright colors. Something, we could tell early on, was going wrong. We'd expected to lose in big, vote-rich, machine-dominated Manchester, but not by so much. And in the places we knew we'd win—wealthy, progressive "wine-track" hamlets, college towns—the margins were far too close.

My desk became, awkwardly, a site of focus. Rob looked over my shoulder constantly, and when I called out a new total, I felt as if the result were somehow my fault—as if my vocalizing the disappointment had called it magically into being. That kept happening, my voice turning numbers and colors on a screen into concrete realities. Like the judge who now pronounced you husband and wife or the priest who announced that this—this bread—was now a body, my words had an insane heft. I can't say that I didn't like it. When we'd gotten into the room, the winter light had blared coldly at us, our shadows hard and definite against the wall. Now the curtains were closed, the atmosphere stifling, the only light coming yellowly from one standing lamp in a corner, and bluely from the several laptops still open. My stomach felt loose and my leg kept twitching. When I saw that we'd lost too many counties to have a chance, it was my job—unbelievably to me, evidence of a kind of chintziness in the process that you couldn't glimpse on TV—to tell the leaders in the room that we'd lost the primary.

I looked up at the TV hanging from a corner of the room, opposite the lamp. Soon the candidate was on the screen, at a podium just upstairs from where I sat. Suddenly I noticed that I was sweating, my hands wet. I left my body behind again when the candidate began to speak. It was funny: barring a brief acknowledgment of the loss, the speech he gave sounded like a victory address. Technically, it was much better than the one he'd given in Iowa, perhaps because it was undergirded by a kind of defiance instead of the evident self-satisfaction that Beverly was always complaining about. Belief, among the truly successful and maniacally aspirant, was odd in that way: it worked best when it swam against the current of reality, not with it. I admired the candidate in a way I hadn't before, but also, for the same reason—because despite his veneer of rationality he could access a surreal mysticism that I recognized from my childhood, and had never managed, in the end, to like—I started to regard him with a wary fear, too.

The campaign manager, a tall blond man with huge eyes, pocked skin, and an intense focus on mathematics, watched the speech with us in the war room, then turned around to face us calmly.

"We're gonna drag her out to the desert," he said. The next stop in the primary was in Nevada. "And we're gonna put a bullet in her head."

The room soon emptied out, the laptops shut and the mounds of paper stuffed away. As I walked into the hallway I almost knocked into a body not much taller than mine. I looked up: the candidate. Somehow angrier and more optimistic in the face, all at once, than I'd ever seen him. The look he gave me wasn't stern, or familiar, or upset, or even weary. He knew I worked for him, I could tell from the loosely held authority he regarded me with. He was almost staring, had come to a complete stop, and was looking not into my eyes but—I thought—at a point in the dead center of my forehead. As if he could glimpse past my brain and see the wall behind my head. His hand crashed onto my shoulder. Not a pat but a kind of blow, almost heavy.

"You hear that?" he asked, pointing blearily upward, meaning the speech.

I said that I had, of course I had.

"Good, right?" Needing or wanting to hear it, if not specifically from me.

"Better than good," I said, queasily sincere.

"Uh-huh," he said. "And I meant it."

III

# 10

BLACK AND WHITE. AN ALMOST-HAPPY FAMILY SITS DOWN TO dinner, all dressed up. The table is cluttered with china: a teapot with matching cups, their pattern, from this vantage, unintelligible; a dish for sugar; a pitcher for cold white milk; five empty plates, each cradled by a pair of open hands. I've never seen an apparatus like the one that holds three slices of toast, makes them stand upright like file folders in a rack. The steel loop that is its handle gleams lithely under the flash. At center is a vase, crystal or glass, overflowing with white blooms. A chair, patterned in panels like stained glass, is the closest thing to the lens. The tablecloth is spotless and smooth.

The daughters—I assume that they are daughters, that this is indeed a family—share features: long, dark, bushy-wavy hair and light eyes; flat faces with slight noses; sharp brows and blushing lines for lips. They both wear loose dresses, blue to the part of my eye that looks at shade and imagines color. The dresses button up the front, to the neck, and fold over into big white collars edged with lace. The girl closest to us looks younger, and regards the camera teasingly. A little black clip draws the curtain of her hair.

Seated between the girls, completing the composition's left flank, is an older woman who may or may not be wearing a hair net. She too sports a loose white collar; between its flaps, fronting her broad, flat breasts, is a bow of thin, glossy black ribbon. In the family I am building she is Grandma. Her mouth barely exists, and is beset by deep, soft lines. Her hair waves backward into a bun. The main point of interest—but this is true for everyone, isn't it?—is her eyes. They run in opposite directions, as if repulsed one by the other. The left is glassy, somewhat lighter in color than the right, likely dead. The right is fixed momentarily, of course, but looks possibly fluid, like a marble or a just-cleaned ball bearing. A tremulous second chin cups her face. She may or may not be strictly sane.

If Grandma is looking at anyone, it is at the woman who might be her daughter, and who—just by appearance—is almost certainly the mother of the girls. She is a handsome, somewhat severe-looking woman, with a muscular, natural slope for a forehead and a chiseled-out ramp for a nose. She returns Grandma's glance—the curt, beautiful waves of their hair are the same—and her mouth is tugged into an ironic, possibly disapproving smile. Her neck is fine and clear; she holds her right hand like a Catholic school pupil, practicing for the pencil. To the extent that I *like* anyone among them, it is this woman, a daughter and a mother.

But the father, just right of center, compositional mirror of his (probably) eldest daughter, seated easily next to his wife, is the reason I picked up the photo and began to rummage through the thousands of others. The only person I knew in Los Angeles—the only person, that is, that I'd known before the campaign—was a kid from high school named Brandon, who now worked as a film editor's assistant. After I landed at LAX, caught a cab, and threw my bags into a dismal hotel room not far from the house at which, the next day, the Senator would perform his closed-door routine, Brandon showed up at the hotel in his car, talking in his soft, serious way about a flea market he visited every week, and would I like to go. His older brother, now dead, had been a painter, and Brandon was a hopeful filmmaker and installation artist; the two had often gone together to the market in order to visit the booth of a certain man—a Pakistani named Joe who wore simple, slightly dingy white linen shirts, matching slacks, and soft sandals— whose specialty was found photographs. He bought them indiscriminately, by the hundreds, at estate sales and the clearings of long-abandoned storage units, then sold them to image-hungry artists like Brandon and his brother, Jamal, at a dime apiece. Now Brandon stood beside me, murmuring about the kinds of shots that each photo might inspire. "That's fucking *perfect*," he said, without further elaboration, when I showed him the family at dinner.

It was August: the slow, hot days before the party nominating conventions. I had slid into a valley of fatigue with the campaign. Or, I should say, with the campaign as it was apparent to the outer world. After the loss in New Hampshire, it had taken on a cloying, predictable rhythm: a boost of thin energy, primed by good press, for the winner of the most recent primary or caucus, followed closely by a stirred-up, largely meaningless miniature controversy—some verbal slipup, some

long-forgotten vote—in the days before the next contest. Someone won and the cycle started afresh. Just arrived in L.A., I
thought of the customary description of the city—as, more
than anything, a cluster of loosely related suburbs—and considered that the primary season had taken on a similar shape.
The longer things drew on, each contest its own enclave, the
less I could follow its story.

My interest had veered in another direction. The campaign kept moving forward, along a horizontal timeline, while
my thoughts were oriented downward—down, down, down,
into the core of things. Maybe this was because the primaries,
with their sense of finality and scent of popular authority, had
kicked money totals off the newspaper headlines. All the organizers and signs and rabid rallies and nicely produced commercials that had become the visual hallmarks of the campaign
still coursed with the money I'd learned to collect, but—at least
out in public, where the people could see—the logical tie between the two had frayed. Voting, you couldn't deny, was more
telegenic than campaign finance. You could pick up a hint of
malaise on our fundraising calls with Chicago—we wouldn't
be getting quite so much time with the candidate anymore, we
were told. We'd have to make our days thicker with activity,
pack the events with more bodies, make the dense days count.
Those days of total access—car rides from one event to the
next, hours on the phone rolodexing through rich targets—
were over. Now he had too much security for that. Sometimes
in the office, late at night, Jill would grumble about how her
work paid the salaries of all those organizers who had become
like folk icons for the rest of the country. The wages of our success was invisibility.

Secretly I sided with the organizers: leaving New Hampshire—leaving Regina, for one thing: she'd gone to Florida after January and been hopscotching from state to state since then—had given me a hangover. In New England I'd been close, or felt close, to figuring out something else: the history and fulfill-ment of a feeling. You couldn't quite pick that up on the news. I was interested less in the campaign's plot than in how I was supposed to interpret it. Less in its details than in its coded total meaning.

Beverly was the only one I voiced these troubles to. "You remind me of my father," she said once in response. By the way she said it, I could tell it wasn't a compliment. "He loved to talk about the *country*—tried to *master* it, that was his term, tried to tame it for his own ends. He never got—*you* still don't get—that it's not, like, some abstraction. Understanding gets you nowhere."

But, despite herself, she sometimes let her own impatience slip.

"You know," she said once, not long before I left for Cali-fornia, "everybody talks about how he'll change race in Amer-ica. Erase it or whatever. By this they mean he'll change *white* people, which, if it happened, would be amazing enough. But nobody mentions the better thing, Dave. How he could abso-lutely, all at once, with one big stroke, end *black* politics forever. A 'special interest group' is a group in which nobody's really interested. That shit's over. All these stupid debates I listened to as a kid, going nowhere. Assimilation against separatism. Markets or collectives. Malcolm, Martin. Du Bois, Booker T. All these fucking *men*, first of all, and their precious ideologies. When the real thing is: How about you get some power and then use it?"

The sole hint of something new, a quick glimmer of politics

as art, or something like it, had come in the middle of the otherwise anticlimactic spring, when the candidate found himself
in racial and religious trouble. I was never able, really, to arrive
at a stable opinion of the nature or, at bottom, the sincerity of
his oft-mentioned Christian faith. He seemed, even in his own
well-honed telling, to have joined his church—a mostly black,
rhetorically radical congregation in Chicago, solidly bougie
despite the edginess of its politics—in order to root himself
socially within a recognizably black community, and not, necessarily, in response to some deep and irrepressible metaphysi-
cal urge. (No shame there: What, anyway, is religion, especially
in those first beautiful days of belief, but the acknowledgment
of an agreement among people; or God but the ground upon
which such agreement is built?) For this he'd chosen the right
church: its focus, in citywide good works and during Sunday
sermons, went to civil rights instead of sacraments; its semi-
famous pastor, a liberation theologian of the old school, reserved hellfire for systems, not sinners.

Having been reared under the strictures of Holiness, and
with the nihilist's eschatology that dismissed politics as firmly
"of the world," and therefore just another inevitable casualty
of the soon-coming Rapture, I'd been only dimly aware—via
King, I guess; maybe Jesse Jackson too—of churches like these,
with pastors like shadow congresspeople, and mission state-
ments like party platforms.

Someone had found and released to the press a video
of the pastor—bespectacled and very light-skinned, almost
fat—at the crest of an imprecation. "God damn America," he
recommended, and for the next week or so it seemed that the
sermon, which was no less or more shocking than the offending

snippet in its full context, would ruin the Senator's chances of winning the nomination. This, after so many petty sub-events, was the real article, a kind of cataclysm. Even now I remember the Senator's trouble with a bit of a thrill. In response he gave a speech, and the speech—about black and white, give and take, reasonable grievances on both sides of the racial aisle; a high-minded way to denounce and separate himself from the pastor who had, after all, so recently prayed over him before the announcement of his candidacy, but also, obliquely, to explain the man to the rest of his followers—succeeded miraculously. It never settled the question (stupid anyway) of why he'd continued, for twenty years or more, to sit under Reverend Reynolds's teaching. Nor did the sheen of discursiveness in its treatment of such scarcely related topics as a benignly prejudiced 1960s grandmother and the history of urban housing segregation serve, really, to achieve a new or useful synthesis. It failed—although, to be fair, it never quite tried—to outline the trends in black and/or charismatic religion that would, over time, result in Reynolds.

We already knew the answers—everything was perfectly transparent. The facts, apparent to all but the stupidest and most racist reactionaries, were these: the candidate wasn't all that pious, at least not in the traditional sense; he had stayed at the church to appear—and also, sort of movingly, to *feel*—more naturally and culturally black. The dissemination of the tape had, as a political happening, folded in on itself, was less about its content than about what, if anything, the candidate could do to blunt its superficially negative effect. The tape had—by day two, maybe, of the controversy—become little more than a sport. Or at least that's how it seemed on cable TV. Less so in our little midtown office, where Jill spent the week red in the face and in the eyes, taking half hours at a time to hold her head in her hands.

The great and saving effect of the speech was that it exhibited—presented a *chance* to exhibit, and in this way was on balance a kind of blessing—the candidate's ability to escape, purely verbally, this trap of his pastor's manufacture. He seemed reasonable, and warm, and smart, and in possession of a greater depth than a future reader will be likely to locate in the text. In other words, he passed a test.


IN ANY CASE: THE FATHER. Brandon had asked Joe the flea marketeer to pass me one of the small plastic baskets in which his buyers—of which, I could feel it, I was already one—held their photos as they shopped. "Get after it," Brandon had said as he went off on his own and quickly disappeared into the crowd. The father is, skinwise, easily the darkest item on offer. And his irises, I swear, almost blend in with the whites. The effect is weird; somewhat Gothic; almost scary. His straight, thin nose points like an arrow to a contented grin. He wears a three-piece suit, vest double-breasted, dark, wool, with a subtle, pleasing stripe. I thought—I couldn't help it—about the skin, and the skin started me thinking about time.

Nowhere on the photograph (which, by the way, is one of the few things from that year that I still own; I have it propped up on my desk, right now, as I write) is a year or even a time period indicated. The back is white, blank, a bit grainy to the touch. I have no talent—no focus—for detective work; all my eye tells me is that this is the output of an amateur photographer: the object best in focus is the toast. But from the nice clothes, the relative formality, and the general air—surely imagined, in part, by me—of ruined wealth and gently spoiling fun, I came to believe that this family lives, is frozen, in the 1920s. Maybe this is only because the father genuinely resembles Scott Fitzgerald. Yes, possibly the twenties. And unless Joe's is a coast-to-coast operation (I didn't ask), it's fair to assume that these are Californians and, therefore, for their time and ostensible race, sort of exotic. The father's been there longer, hence the tan. He's a writer for the movies, and the money from some recent hit helped him finally to send for his family.

The other writer he resembles—less than Fitzgerald, but it's there all the long-faced same—is Jean Toomer, who, in flight from his drop or two of black blood, and therefore from his pesky association with the Harlem Renaissance, beat it west, to Taos, where he lived among crackpot Gurdjieffians and artists and houses held together by red mud. Out there he wrote and failed to finish an incomprehensible play. Too much bad religion ruined his art, so fragile and strange to begin with. He drew followers, was always handsome and darkly charismatic, taught them Gurdjieff, or Dianetics, or Quakerism, or his own aphoristic home brew, and then dropped them or strung them along. Awful to his wife, dramatic, hypochondriac, a self-righteous alcoholic, an ultimately pitiful figure until his obscure death. The false allure of the West—Manifest Destiny as final, decadent wheeze—is part of my idea of the twenties, and it played softly as I stood for the first time in Los Angeles—for the first time, for that matter, in California at all. I hadn't told my officemates about the blank space in my travel; nor, now, did I

tell Brandon. I felt ashamed, provincial, low-rent. I wondered
what would happen when I finally saw, no, touched, the Pacific:
whether the country would somehow begin to cohere. I wondered, too, along Toomer lines, whether the father fled west,
away from family, if only for a while, as the holder of a secret.
Whether undergirding his Hollywood "color" was something
more basic and less contingent. He might be the subject of
one of those "passing" novels of, again, the twenties. It might
explain how alien he looks in the company of his family. His
features are evident in the faces of the girls, but his differences
from the rest of the group—dark skin, bright eyes—make him
appear imported from some other arrangement. I dropped the
photo into the basket and went flipping through the mess of
others.

I couldn't help, looking at all the landscapes and faces,
many of them ancient by American standards, feeling that
some law of intimacy had been broken or breached. Other
items for sale at the market had, of course, first belonged to
others. There was almost nothing *new*, in the usual sense, in
sight. There were old campaign buttons, buttons of other and
various kinds, sun-faded dashikis, rows of beads, records (78,
45, 33 rpm), DVDs, CDs, cassette tapes official and homemade,
mirrors, desks, wardrobes, chests of drawers, bed frames, magazines with warped covers, baseball cards, old comic books,
memento mori (brass skulls and little triptychs), toy trains,
crude ceramics, aged houseplants (dust on the leaves), beaded
curtains, outdated textbooks, pearl earrings, signet rings (somebody else's initials), those early Nokia flip phones, T-shirts and
baseball caps, crumbling paperbacks, family Bibles, chipped
china, journals bursting with confessions, wall posters, county

maps, rickety globes, laminated images of saints and long-lost kids. Some of the dresses were new, as far as I could tell. But nothing felt as private—or, therefore, as invasive to peruse—as the snapshots. I imagined, for instance, the descendants of this family, and how I now planned to purchase an irretrievable hint of their history. I had, somewhere on a bottom shelf of my mother's, so many favorite pictures: me in a technicolor shirt and green jean shorts; my father at the piano, singing, with me, also singing, on his lap; my mother and I, asleep, spooning, in a bedroom with one brick wall. What would it mean—what, surely, *will* it mean; the reality of it is almost certain—for these to belong to someone else, to whom I and my parents are nothing but fodder for art? Nothing, I guessed. Besides, this kind of problem was almost extinct: Who had—or, more precisely, who *made*—physical photos anymore? Some hobbyist minority. The Joes of the future will find their wares . . . well, where? Forgotten phones? Auctioned-off email passwords? Twenty-three, sure, but I filled my basket feeling briefly like a relic of the past.

The next picture that moved me was nicely simple. A black woman, light-skinned, stands smiling at the center, a shadow drawing a line under her taut, round cheek. She wears a smart suit—the long skirt and structured top are a set—and lets her hand drop gracefully at mid-thigh. Ring on right hand; left less clear. Her hair's tightly pressed and rests in a short, circular bob. A part reaches brutally back toward the crown of her skull. Behind her is a simple frame house, and at her hip, looking serious, is a little blond girl. The woman is not looking at the girl, but her face and body signal a loving acknowledgment of her presence. Instead she looks directly at us, smiling subtly, her eyebrows betraying a squint. The sun is in her eyes. Behind

her is a window and, just below, a hole in the ground next to
the house. The little white girl squints too, and her brows cast
shadows on her cheeks. She wears a perfectly pressed gingham
dress, the checks running diagonal. The edges of the photo
are not even; they're frilled artfully, in a way I'd never seen,
meant to resemble a proper frame. Near the bottom, in the
white margin between these edges and the action of the photo,
is written, in a neat, childish hand, the name Becky. I wondered whose name that was, the woman's or the girl's. And also
about parentage: Ole Becky's just fair enough to be Lil Becky's
momma—white pappy perhaps acting as photographer—but
she could also be some kind of nanny, especially beloved. I
kept operating on stereotypes; my vast, half-conscious bank
of American imagery—from ads, TV, documentaries, period
pieces—guided my reading of the time. Something about the
bright bluish quality of the light made me think that the Beckys
lived in the forties.

The prize for most wrinkled picture: a picture of four guys
on a lawn, each down on one knee. Two hold cigars; each
wears sharp slacks and a wide-brimmed hat. The background
is blurry, but I saw many dark-leaved trees, interrupted at intervals by tall white posts that seemed to be made of wood. I
imagined that they sprouted lines for the wash. Of the kids—
I'd place them in their late teens or early twenties—only one,
the second from the right, wears a jacket. All but the one at
far left (he looks like a young, bad-minded Belafonte) wear a
tie. This must be a party in somebody's backyard or on the
hastily trimmed lawn of a public park. These are graduates or
boys about to leave home for the war. (Which war?) The kid in
the jacket, second from right, is also, more generally, the best
dressed. His tie's got a good stripe—but even that's a bit be-

yond the point. His clothes just sort of *hang*. His elbow's resting on the knee that's not on the ground, and his hand, near his dark, funny face, is open in a questioning gesture. This might be the oldest photo yet. I flicked it into the basket, feeling proud about the find.

The first clearly time-stamped photo I found was of two couples: young ladies out front, their men behind, touching arms, shoulders, hips, whatever they can find and grab. "MAR·58" it says along the right margin. So: none of the great acts have been signed—Civil Rights, Voting Rights, etc.—but *Brown v. Board*'s been decided, and the West Coast must feel like a respite. Nobody looks worried. The man on the right's wearing a navy captain's broad white hat. Maybe he survived Korea. Again I felt the voyeur's pang of guilt: I wondered how much the captain's grandchildren would pay for a picture like this one, of their family hero in so total a mood of repose. He holds his lover—his wife, presumably: they both wear shiny little rings—by both of her arms. She looks satisfied. *Satisfied*, strangely, is the word. She smiles widely, and her eyes are untroubled. Guilt, again, when I looked at the other woman in the frame. She has big, smooth thighs and sculpted calves. I caught my eyes lingering there, below her waist, and then remembered reprovingly that the woman—if still alive at all—must be seventy-five years old.

There was also this, undated: a tableau of eight, all dressed unspottedly well, eight perfect variations of spinal straightness. The photo so faded it's brown. One woman gazes off to the left, well past the lens, looking proud and possibly prophetic: she sees something. One fat man's face is so black that it shines. The bust of a hero, rendered in unmixed tar.

And also this: on the back a note:

*Sat. Dec. 12, 1998*
*Here is Jazz Great*
*George Benson.*

I flipped it over, and there, indeed, was jazz great George
Benson, looking as he must have looked in the late fall of
'98. Thin-bridged nose with nostrils like wings. Thin, almost
drawn-on mustache and a sliver of a smile. Thumb pointing at
a person whose face is left out of the capture, and whose plump
white hand has almost settled on his arm.

# 11

I WAS STAYING IN A HOTEL IN A DEPRESSING SECTION OF LOS ANGE-les. I'd chosen the place—I had a room in a dark corner of an upper floor—because the hotel was close to the home of the record producer who would host the candidate tomorrow for one of the most important high-dollar fundraisers of the campaign so far, and because it was less expensive, by quite a lot, it seemed to me then, than the other places I'd seen through the system on which we booked our travel and our lodging. Somebody's spreadsheet said $2.3 million in pledges. The L.A. office had asked Jill to let me come help work the event because—nobody said this at first, but it *was* because—the producer was black, and so were many of his guests. Jill said fine.

I'd found this cheap place close to the house, figuring, *How bad could it be?,* even though both Jill and Ryan Blue, the fi-nance director in Southern California, had insisted that I stay at the Beverly Hilton, regardless of the price. (The people in New Hampshire had said nice things about me upon reluctantly re-turning me to my home among contribution checks, and this afforded me, I noticed, a measure of new respect.) But I didn't know yet how changeable Los Angeles can be from mile to mile, especially toward the center of the city, or, even worse, just how incommodious certain of its hotel rooms are. Plus, I couldn't drive, and I was determined to walk around.

The floor was uncarpeted concrete, polished smooth and almost slippery to the touch of the bottoms of my socks, which I'd decided, just about immediately, not to take off. The walls were made of the same carceral substance and were entirely unadorned, except for the several spots where they were inexplicably wet. A little television carried four or five local channels, and the bed was short, narrow, and hard. I was afraid to find out what lay under the thin sheets, so, after I'd said good-bye to Brandon and found a dinner of pork tacos and several beers from a matte steel truck with a sweet-faced lady working at its counter, I stretched out atop the bedding mostly clothed, wearing black basketball shorts and a black tee with my socks pulled up almost to my knees. I tried to fall asleep but couldn't. It was maybe eleven o'clock.

My heavy stomach was a factor in my sleeplessness, and so was the frankly scary lack of comfort in what I'd already begun to think of as my cell. Another was the noise from the party downstairs. *Hotel* is slightly generous for the kind of place this really was. It was the kind of place you read about in eventually bloody novels where surfboarding and the drug trade meet. The four floors were connected by a set of chintzy outdoor stairs, and formed a half hexagon around a fetid pool. Each California-mint door faced inward, toward the green water and the gray plaza that surrounded it. Now a group of thirty or forty kids—they looked college age through my window—were down there, playing wordless synth-and-bass-heavy music, joking loudly, and folding their bodies into cannonballs as they hopped into the pool. There were lights running along the sides of the pool, submerged but still bright. A fuchsia glow reached my window, and so did the fattest leaf of a tall palm, pressed flat against the glass like the hand of someone desperate for help. It takes too long to learn how to spend other people's money. I lay there fantasizing about the Hilton I'd never seen.

A book I once read, a compendium of quasi-mystical approaches to acting, presented as a series of journal entries by an actor about his guru-director—something like Plato on Socrates but for the development of several on- and offstage techniques—contains a piece of advice that I sometimes think of at night. The apprentice performer, says the guru, should lie awake every night in the quiet dark, calling to memory as precisely as possible every moment of her day. The feeling of her feet on the bedroom floor as she crawled out of bed and the warm plops of shower water hitting her back. The quality and temperature of the air on her face whenever she stepped outside; the look of each stranger briefly encountered. The subtly audible tone of every room. The point of the evening exercise—which, if executed perfectly, I thought, would presumably take all night, and then some, to complete: your whole life would be an act of memory—is to enhance the actor's imaginative powers, under the theory that imagination in acting (and possibly everywhere else, too) is, in the end, just a refinement and an extension of the remembered past. The unreal, the idea goes, is accessible only via the real. She who recalls and can summon, on command, the feeling of AC in the office can project herself, in performance, into the Arctic. Little memories anchored in the senses, and in the subtle emotional movements influenced by the senses, accrue and yield a performance.

Back at school, I'd read the book because I'd been cast in a role whose content I couldn't understand. The third act of *The Cherry Orchard* is a party scene and, at the same time, the sad height of the drama of the lady and her doomed estate. A Jewish band plays lively music and a young woman shows off her talent for ventriloquy as the guests dance and pass drinks; meanwhile, an auction for the deed to the estate is going on elsewhere, and all of it ends with the news that the place has been lost to a rival. And so the party itself, full of people who are oblivious to the tragedy unfolding, feels gruesomely funny, a final joke on the unlucky family. At some point, an anonymous railroad official—this was me—steps onto a staircase, grabs the attention of the rest of the party, and recites a few lines of a poem. The poem was written by a lesser Tolstoy—the novelist's cousin—and the lines that became mine were about a party thrown in the home of a very wealthy man, a party, in other words, not unlike the one the stationmaster interrupts with his recital. For the role, a two-line affair (the one that wasn't the poem came maybe a minute earlier and was adjunct to the aforementioned party-trick display: "Ah! Look! A lady ventriloquist!"), I was outfitted in tight brown trousers and a tight vest, both custom-made for me by the theater department's head costume designer, an older woman named Krystal who wore glasses with green, cat-eyed plastic frames and her hair in a bleached-blond buzz cut, without much attention to—or accommodation for—the loose, ovoid shapes of my stomach and my ass. I took the unflattering tailoring personally and retaliated by leaving my clothes, night after night, crumpled in a pile on the floor, instead of hanging them up on the rack that held the rest of the cast's costumes.

I wasn't much good at acting, hence the sorry part. And it didn't make me feel any better not to be able to puzzle through the few lines I did have. Every time I tried to deliver them during rehearsals, the director—who wore sweatpants exclusively and was also my often-exasperated acting teacher—said that I hadn't recited them with enough tonal variance or physical enthusiasm. I resisted the note; I wanted acting to be something more than a grade school presentation, even if that was all that was called for by the role I'd been asked to play. Surely there was something beyond volume, beyond gestures. If I couldn't be a star, I could turn these lines into an act of compression, a little art-house interlude toward the end of a bigger, more commercial enterprise. I wanted, mostly, to impress the theater kids with whom I'd been having trouble becoming friends.

So I turned to the book: What kind of person was this stationmaster, and what had he done to be invited to such a high-toned gathering? How could I arrange the information offered to me by my own experience—locomotive sounds, occasional marginality at parties, the intermittent feeling of petty, largely useless power—in a way that would make me his facsimile? I never figured it out. In the end, I said the lines like a lost kid, husky in a snug and unloved uniform, and made no impression, as far as I could tell, on the audience.

The Stanislavskian exercise had failed me on a practical level. But, over the years, I'd held on to it as a sleep aid, which had, anyway, been its greatest use to me even in the weeks before the play. In replaying the day in my head, I'd barely make it out the door in the morning before losing the thread and very quickly blacking out. Memory wore me down.

And so, now, writhing around alone on the hard mattress, I started trying to remember this day, which had started in New York and would end in L.A. I'd . . . I'd woken up to a call from Beverly. She was back in New York after a "quick trip" to Brussels, she'd said. She knew some expats there who wanted to know how to be involved in the campaign from abroad. Now she wanted to host another dinner with Earnest Blackshear, and she was hoping that I could help her make it happen. I asked myself, *What were your sensations at the time?* I'd still been under my stiff green sheets, and a stripe of soft purple light stretched electric across the wall. A corner of it touched my face and made my eyes squint. I lay on my back: rare for me. My right leg hung off the side of the bed and my foot scraped the floor—jagged, much cooler than the quickly warming air. The sheets scraped pleasantly at my skin. I sat up in bed to talk to Beverly, and let her know that I had a plane to catch, so I couldn't talk for long.

"Don't need long," she said. "He's in the city at the end of August, right? Right after the convention?"

He was. The time had been only recently procured, and I had no clue how Beverly knew.

"All we need is an hour," Beverly said. "And not that fake hour where you rush him in and out and really it amounts to thirty-five minutes of actual presence. The real thing. We'd want twenty minutes for a VIP reception: maybe ten or fifteen of us, shaking hands and getting to talk. We can get forty-six hundred a head there, easy."

"Okay—"

"I know, I know: You don't know. You'd need to bring it to Jill to find out. But just let me talk for a second. Is that all right?"

"All right," I said.

"All right. Then, after the VIP, he'd spend forty minutes with something like two hundred more people—you know the Blackshears have the space. Those'd all be twenty-three hundred. He'd maybe talk for fifteen minutes—stump speech or whatever. Then the rest of the time he'd be taking questions. Everybody's happy. And if my math's right, we're talking about just over half a million."

She paused for emphasis.

"So that's the number you should bring up with Jill when you pitch this to her. Half million plus." Beverly had never before had any trouble making her own requests known to Jill or, for that matter, as far as I'd seen, to anybody else. So I felt somewhat flattered—then, almost immediately, ashamed to be flattered—that she seemed to think she still needed me to make her plans come to pass. "I'll bring it up, too, of course," she said, sounding just slightly less casual than she usually did. "But hearing this from *you* might help a bit. My people—*our* people—plus Blackshear's people—black, white; probably know each other a bit, by sight, but haven't had the chance yet to work together on something like this, right?" Then, more slowly, clearly smiling although I couldn't see her face: "To *feel* as though they're working together on something as *significant* as this. Do you know what I mean?"

I thought I did, but the longer I worked on this campaign, the more I became aware of how much was hidden from me. How much I totally did not know.

"David," she said, now sounding almost affectionate. "I hope it has occurred to you that we are going to win."

"Yeah," I said, "of course—"

"No, no, not in, like, some peppy-campaign-optimist way. Not because it is the correct or the helpful thing to say, the party line or whatever. This thing is over. Right? The tectonics have finished their travel, Dave. The votes are just a way for everybody else to kind of catch up. Okay?"

I said okay.

"I mean, I know that your office has to keep on raising money in order to keep pleasing your bosses, or whoever. Make the news stories sing. And I understand how that might make it hard to take a step back and really see what's going on—but it's really, really important, David, to cultivate that skill. To know when one thing is over and another thing has already started. Nobody's waiting around for you to figure this out."

I was struggling to keep up with her—I was still sleepy; the sheets were still, I remembered, gathered around my legs, my bare feet sticking through—but I liked it, and was almost immediately ashamed to be liking it. I wanted her to tell me more, to show me her motives. "The half million will be nice," she said. "Totally worth the hour. But we both know that kind of money's coming in online every few hours, with literally no need for him to show up anywhere. The point is that *this* money, from *these* people, will be . . . I don't know, Dave. Symbolic."

What she'd said about the internet was true. Over the summer, on our weekly conference calls, a crux had been reached: sometime just after the Fourth the numbers raised online had started to surpass, first spottily, and then for good, what we "high-dollar" fundraisers could take credit for. What had begun as merely a symbol—how heartening and democratic it was that so many "regular people" could claim ownership of the candidate through their contributions of twenty-five and fifty dollars at a time—had become the most imposing material reality of the campaign. Our larger checks, rustled up in the traditional way, had played their part in making the candidate viable as a real contender for the nomination, and for the presidency, but now they seemed almost superfluous. Not one to struggle against a process so natural, Beverly wanted to see the cycle completed—big money would now become what little money had formerly been: fully symbolic, less a practical necessity than a form of speech.

What else did I remember?

I swung my body around, placed both my feet on the cool floor.

ABOUT AN HOUR LATER, THE chime of my BlackBerry woke me up. On the phone there was a message from Alexis:

> Hey Songbird:
> we're going out tonight
> with Sarah. Me,
> my sister + Ryan.
> You're coming. Send me
> address to yr hotel!

Alexis was an assistant in fundraising like I was, except stationed here in L.A., where she'd been born and grown up. She talked a lot—fast and loud, connecting her thoughts, which ranged everywhere, impressively, by grafting them onto the many people whose names crowded her conversation. It wasn't name-dropping, not exactly. It was something much friendlier than that. Her ideas came riding in on personalities. She knew so many people, some, sure, very famous, some anonymously powerful, some nobodies who were nonetheless cool. She talked about them in a way that halfway convinced you that you knew them too. Both her parents were black New Orleanians with reddish skin and wavy hair that always shone. They smelled like lotion and powder and told a lot of jokes, and were nice in a way that brought the word *benefactor* to mind. Alexis's hair was the same as theirs, liquid and soft and big and bright—I'd seen it unpressed once, at a breakfast, but she almost always ironed it straight. She was always looking at her BlackBerry and taking calls, which made me wonder how a person with the same job as mine could be so much busier. But there was an art to correspondence, one that was related to the particulars of our work but also stood above and apart from it, and I knew that Alexis had already mastered it, and that I never would. There wasn't anything to begrudge. I found her glamorous and sort of funny and I liked her a lot, but for some reason I couldn't name I felt afraid to be her friend. As things stood, she made fun of me a lot—she'd caught me singing under my breath once, hence Songbird—and sent me bullying texts like this one.

"Ok," I texted back and typed the address.

"What the fuck neighborhood is that," she wrote.

"You'll see," I said. "A mistake."

An hour later, Alexis pulled up in her gleaming black car. The air in it smelled like weed—she soon offered me some, and I accepted—and a diffuse pinkish light came from somewhere I couldn't see. A song—bright major R&B chords clothed in synth, an auto-tuned voice—played loudly. Alexis's spotless windows gently rattled. "Everybody else's meeting us there," she said quietly. We sat there for a while, listening to the music and passing a blunt back and forth. "What the fuck," she said suddenly, looking up at my hotel with an expression of gathering alarm and disgust. "Hammond, what the FUCK did you do?"

She had a low raspy voice that was surprisingly flexible and resonant. She also loved to curse; when she said "FUCK" it sounded like a whisper through a megaphone.

"I was trying to save money," I said. "Like I said: a mistake."

She gave me a look of total and slightly irritated incomprehension. "Whose money?" she said, almost laughing. "You work on the same campaign I do, correct? And you know how much money they have, correct?" I did, and I did; she had a point. Alexis shook her head and pressed the gas. We suffered through traffic that was especially thick, given the time; but, then, this was a Friday night, prime party time, so perhaps the proliferation of cars—black sedans like Alexis's dominated, but there were also big hulking SUVs and little brightly colored sports cars, striped on the sides and open on the top, their drivers and passengers wearing dark shades—shouldn't have surprised me as much as it did. Soon we were on the highway and Alexis was free to drive as she preferred to—far too fast, and in a series of tight swerves that averaged out to a line but was terrifying in its momentary particulars. I grasped at the handle above the window on my side and felt my hands start to sweat. At the same time I was tired. I'd spent the day walking among Joe's photographs under the sun, and had had about an hour of sleep, if that. And so I swam between fear and fatigue in Alexis's front seat, sometimes grasping the handle, sometimes keeping my eyes from rolling backward, into my head, and my head from listing backward into the cushion behind me, and into sleep. Alexis was telling me by what provenance we were about to party.

"Sarah threw a party at this club a couple weeks ago for Justin Timberlake—I told you he came to our Oprah event, right? We ended up dancing and he got weird. Weird, but also very sweet—but, anyway, of course they ended up loving Sarah, so they told her to come by and bring friends and they'd have a table and some bottles for her." I'd never been able to tell exactly what Sarah did for a living. She was a chubby white woman who always dressed in black and always wore a wary, almost mocking smile. Based on the things Alexis had told me about her, she was, apparently, some sort of events planner and arts activist and social strategist to the stars. I knew, or thought I'd heard, that she owned a few bars around town. Justin Timberlake often came up when she did, so perhaps there was some special connection there—I was learning that it only really takes one or two of those to get things going.

Some people are mysteries better left unprobed. Many times I had asked Alexis to describe Sarah's occupation in just a word or so and had been met with silence or the answer to some entirely separate question. Sequence didn't matter to Alexis in the way it did to me. "Wake the fuck up," she said now, when she noticed my fluttering lids. From some compartment she produced another joint and took both hands off the wheel in order to light it. "Here," she said, shoving it toward me. "Fix your attitude."

When we pulled up, Sarah was standing on a swatch of

indigo carpet just in front of the door of the club, chatting
with a huge man wearing a clear plastic earpiece. With her
were Ryan Blue, Alexis's boss, and Geneva, her sister. A second
bouncer, the one Sarah wasn't talking to, held a plush violet
rope just unhooked from its brass stanchion, giving Alexis and
me a grim but inviting look. Before I could track or truly understand the exchange—these things were new to me—Alexis had
handed her keys to a valet, and her car was gone. I wondered,
briefly, what was the protocol for handling a car so clearly redo-
lent of drugs. We walked past the bouncers, through the gap
between stanchions, and past a glass wall covered in leaves—
real or fake, I couldn't tell—through the door and into the
club.

Ryan was tall and Waspily handsome, always tan in a suit
with his hair gelled and swooping off to the side, always looking
like he'd just returned from a weekend on a vacation island and
was now "excited" to get back to work. His boyfriend, John—
shorter and ruddier but equally smiling and attractive—also
worked on the campaign. About a decade later Ryan would
turn out to be the United States ambassador to a small central
European country and, somehow, in the course of that work,
a minor reality-television celebrity. All the evidence of such
a trajectory was already on display. He managed, like many
proto-politicians, to be pretty funny without saying much that
you'd remember later on; he allowed only the slightest cattiness
about our donors to sweep past his bright, horsey teeth, and
even that only when having drinks and very purposely "team
building," to use his parlance; as part of his method of recruiting new funders he'd developed a stump speech not unlike the
candidate's, in substance, tone, and rhythm; and nobody ever
had anything bad to say about him. He'd worked as a producer

on several animated movies and made his way into politics one
acquaintance at a time. Although he was her boss, Alexis was
also something like his best friend. When we sat down at the
table that was waiting for us, against a wall and cupped by a
soft couch, he said, "Wow! *Sar*ah! Seriously?! *Wow.*"

"I know," Sarah, smiling, said.

*"Wow."*

The club had a high vaulted ceiling topped by a wide window with the black night beyond it. From the middle of the first
floor, where we sat on a slightly raised pedestal, behind ropes,
you could faintly see the stars. Although this middle chamber
was open, the club had many floors; along each of the walls
were seven balconies, sticking out like stuffed shelves. The light
was a low, impassive blue. We'd arrived at the table, and the
table had been bare, but soon a little squadron of waitresses,
in black leotards and high, chunky boots, brought materials
to us: bottles—tequila, vodka, rum, gin—and carafes of juice
and a stacked tower of squat glasses of thick plastic. From the
tops of the bottles chintzy sparklers stuck up, throwing off weak
heat and briefly illuminating the section where we sat. The
light drew attention; people looked over, obviously wondering
whether we were people worth noticing. A photographer—the
kind who sets up a website and tries to sell your image back to
you at the end of the night, as sometimes happens after a ride
on a roller coaster or a short tourist cruise—trailed the girls,
snapping pictures and wearing a bored expression on his face.
He caught each of us in notionally candid, actually stilted and
surveilled, poses, before he started urging us together, first into
pairs, then into a smiling, half-hugging group of five. Soon we
were alone again.

Alexis's sister, Geneva, younger, with a bouncier personality and a higher, clearer voice, began to tell a story—about her job, I thought—but I was at the farthest point in our semicircle from where she sat, and I couldn't understand what she was saying. I nodded along and pretended to laugh when her face—big eyes, dolphinish teeth, and high cheeks; a truncated forehead met at its shoreline by a spray of black hair—hinted at its cooperation in a joke. I poured myself a cranberry vodka.

I could see the door from where we sat. The stream of partyers entering the space had thickened, and the big dance floor was starting to be crowded. Soon, sensing that the party had entered a new and more urgent phase, someone—the DJ, I presumed, but there might be some higher authority in matters like these—increased the volume of the music. Now we all gave up on stories. A few more drinks were poured and drunk, and we headed toward the floor. Alexis grabbed my hand and pulled me to her. She started winding softly against my crotch. "Wake up, Songbird," she said. I barely made her words out amid the noise.

HIGHER UP, ON THE FOURTH floor, looking up at the windowed ceiling, my back to the banister of the balcony, I stood cradling a fresh drink, alone. I'd wandered away from Alexis and the rest of the group after that one A.M. rush into the club and onto the dance floor had hit its plateau and, an hour or so later, begun a gentle decrescendo. I'd gone to the bathroom, where a man in waitstaff black had quietly demanded to be tipped after passing me a mint and a nice napkin, then gone looking for the

stairs. The open plan of the club made it so that each floor had
the same music, unlike the vertical, warehouse-like clubs in,
say, D.C., where each floor is its own ecosystem, a distinct location in genre and time. In places like those, the musical variety
leads people to cluster, at least loosely, by age—uncleish guys
in vests and Kangols and pleated pants make their overtures
over R&B, while, somewhere lower or higher, kids twitch their
genitals along to newer stuff.

Here, though, under the sign of musical sameness, the differences among the floors were more subtle. As a general matter, the crowd lower to the ground was younger—the idea, I
guessed, being that the rhythm of the one-night stand (meet,
dance, kiss, dance, kiss, abscond) was better served by ready access to the doors—and, sure, the egregiously old (forties?) had
clustered toward the top. But the difference was barely perceptible, really noticeable only if—as I had—you'd walked up and
down several times. More readily apparent was the increase,
as you ascended, in behavior that seemed to me to indicate
an interesting seediness and, you couldn't miss it, criminality.
Guys walked around taking unsurreptitious pulls on blunts of
impressive size, and in the meantime made sales of same and
stronger. Pills in plastic baggies changed hands between songs,
and the club, I saw now, was a kind of churn—up for drugs,
down for the promise of sex—a wheel for the stations of want.

I had always assumed that there must be some fairly reliable, reasonably visible source of drugs in a big club like this
one, and here, finally, it was—visible to me, too. I felt gratified
to have it made plain, and gratified too when I was approached
by a man with one big, glassy eye and the other eye squinting
almost shut and he offered me a spotless white pill, naked in

the pit of his surprisingly slender hand. I was gratified again as I toured the floors afresh, feeling its effect. I walked into a bathroom and poured cold water into my open hands. I sipped some and smeared the rest across my face, which felt staticky. This time I left before the attendant—whether he was the same one I'd met before I couldn't tell—was able to help me and thereby claim a tip. The cash I'd used to buy the pill had been the last in my pocket. I dried my hands against my jeans.

On what I figured was the sixth floor I had my back to the balcony again, now dancing softly against a woman I'd just met, who, without my asking, had bought me a drink. I felt, dancing and drinking, the attenuated consolation that comes from being drunk and sweetly high at the same time—the sense of a real but remote acquaintance with joy. My face flamed beneath the skin. As we moved we talked about—I think I remember—our pasts. She'd had a full ride to USC, she said— "my grades were *that* good"—but she'd squandered the time somehow or other, on older guys off campus and drinks at the dorm, and now she worked an office job she didn't like. With grave seriousness, as if I'd never disclosed it before, I told her about my daughter. "Wow," she said. She seemed impressed. She grabbed my hand in a way that made the gesture seem like the product of a sudden impulse, and she pulled me through the thinning forest—but still it was a forest—of dancing bodies. Everyone was darkly lit, but a thin, bright red crescent of light outlined each of the shadows. Loose strands of hair looked electric. I said "Excuse me" maybe twenty times as we walked.

Gratified again as, after a few flights down again, I realized that she was leading me back to the man with the mismatched eyes and paying for another pill just as she'd paid for the drink.

I tossed it into my mouth and was washing it down with a cup of unknown provenance as I noticed the beginnings of a fight.

To my right there were two men talking with increasing intensity into each other's ears. Their faces were close, almost touching, and the rest of their bodies were already engaged in an exploratory first skirmish: chests pushed together; hands slapping each other, writhing for position in a slow game of pitty-pat; one thumb sometimes pressed into the crook of the other man's elbow, trying to nudge him just slightly off-balance, the better to ready him, just in case, for the delivery of the first blow. The muttered words were all curses; I couldn't pick out a narrative or a cause. Both guys wore dark jackets with bright button-ups beneath and fitted caps on their heads. Someone was going to swing—if you'd ever seen a fight, this was obvious almost immediately—and soon someone did. Which one it was I couldn't say. Things were happening quickly and the two men looked, to me, like twins. Punches turned into upright wrestling, and then they were right next to me—I couldn't move—spinning together in grasping pirouettes, taking turns with their backs against the banister.

One of them pushed too hard—but I didn't know him or his intentions: for all I knew, he'd pushed just hard enough—and the other man bent suddenly over the edge of the balcony, torso first, then, unstoppably, the rest of him. He went flying toward the dancers below. I heard a few people scream, then a sick thud on the floor, then a few shattering glasses, then the music come, after a few seconds, to a stop.

I stood there, still, my systems of comprehension barely alive, trying for the second time that night to relax.

There was screaming below, I could hear. From so far above

I couldn't make out any faces, least of all those of my friends. The guy who'd administered the last blow had disappeared. I felt a panic try to rise in my chest, but it was just as distant as my prior joy. By some half-remembered reflex, I sent all the focus in my body—sent my whole physical intelligence—into the palm of my left hand. I felt the tiny muscles there pulse, tingle, tighten, and release. I subtly flexed them and let them go, five instinctual times, like breaths.

This accomplished, I shifted my attention to the right hand and did the exercise again. I'd learned it years earlier, during high school, not long after the school shooting in Columbine, Colorado. A few of my classmates had been recruited to work as volunteers—guinea pigs, really—at a new nonprofit called End Teen Cruelty, or ETC, as if the mission were some item of lesser importance on a list; it had been recently created by a psychologist who lived and worked, bizarrely, like some foreign eminence or the ambassador to the U.N., at the Waldorf-Astoria. Dr. Debora Phillips—Dr. Deb, as she liked to be called—was a somewhat famous behaviorist known for her book *How to Fall Out of Love,* published in 1978 and the product (and, as it turned out, further spur) of a practice that had thrilled and consoled the lovestruck of New York in that time. The book must have sold well—that, or Phillips was the heir to a fortune she never mentioned. Probably both, I thought. Now she wanted to apply her talents to the problem of bullying in schools, on the assumption that an outpouring of kindness-via-therapy across the country would stop future massacres like the one in Colorado from happening. She was a kind of psycho-utopianist.

Her plan was to train us—a corps of kids of maybe fifteen, from private schools around the city—in her methods, which

were many, then have us teach them to a test batch of middle
school kids from New Jersey. She'd perfect the curriculum and
have it implemented, school by school, across America.

She taught us exercises. Two kids at a time would play
the roles of bully and bullied; the aggressor would shout some
threat or epithet or insult and before the victim would spread,
Dr. Deb said, two options: walk away responsibly after issuing a
self-righteous retort ("I'm sorry, but this is way too childish for
me") or, on an even hokier note, self-deprecate the bully into
submission, trying, if possible, to improve upon the joke he'd
meant as a weapon ("Yep, my skin sure *is* diseased! Ever heard
of *leprosy?*"). These self-defensive measures were a weakness in
Phillips's method. They hadn't come from any particular experience in her clinical practice, I don't think, and if she'd ever
been truly bullied, it had been too long ago for her to clearly
remember, or, certainly, for her to know how the ritual happened now, at the contented—therefore especially cruel—turn
of a new millennium. For no interesting reason that I can remember, very many of the kids in the cohort were black, and
soon we turned these role-playing sessions into vicious rounds
of the dozens. What Dr. Deb took for realism—"commendable
commitment"—was actually a game stealthily embedded
within the one she'd created. We cracked on each other's teeth
and breath and midsections and home situations, pretending
to be bullies but also *being* bullies and groping for laughs from
the crowd, while she, smiling, would say things like "Wow" and
wonder aloud at how much experience we all had in this sort of
verbal violence—invective on the one side and artful deflection
on the other. She was sure, she said, that we were exceptional
and that, together, we were nearing a kind of breakthrough.

I often wondered whether the joke—an even larger one—was on us, and Dr. Deb had enlisted us as subjects in a secret study—fodder, perhaps, for a new hit book—under the guise of trying to save the world. I wondered who we were to her, what idea we were supposed to represent. And I wondered what she imagined herself to have learned from us, what kinds of notes she took when the sessions were over.

Another aspect of our study was more straightforwardly psychological—and, therefore, because of Dr. Deb's much greater confidence in this area, more fun to take part in. These were scenarios during which we'd again pair off, but this time to act as friends and consolers of the bullied or otherwise disturbed. Dr. Deb called these lessons in empathy and started them by saying, "Let's empathize!," laying bare her belief that empathy was a process instead of a feeling or a quality of the heart. One person—the bullied, the patient—would pour forth his troubles: sick or unloving parents, scarce friends, demons at work in the school cafeteria. Then, once the problems had all been articulated, Deb said, the Empathizer should do nothing in the way of offering advice or rote solace—no assuring her friend that hard times would pass and everything turn out fine. No. Just say back to the person what the person had said to you, not in exactly the same words, of course—that'd be mocking—but in your own, making a kind of paraphrase of woe. The effect—like that of certain long book reviews, which seem only to recapitulate a book's plot and redescribe its characters but end up achieving a subtle exegesis, impossible to isolate within just one or two of its sentences—was somehow clarifying. The Empathizer, by that repetition ("Always start with 'Well, it sounds like . . .'"), trained her mind to think in rhythm with another's; the patient had his struggles foregrounded and framed in a new light: someone had listened and could understand; and, in their simple communicability, the troubles seemed somewhat less impossible to overcome.

We did this for hours and days, two at a time. One speaker, one listener turned regurgitator. It sometimes ended in tears. We'd leave the Waldorf and walk down Lex wrung out. Sometimes after sessions, before we left, Dr. Deb would invite us to lie down wherever there was room in her photo-bedecked hotel apartment—on a couch, on the floor, in one of her several beds—as she helped us relax. To "refresh your senses," she said. (We considered, so many times, the possibility that we were the charter members of a small but growing cult.) "Send all the energy into one of your hands," she'd say. "Feel it there. Good. Good! Now hold on to that energy—that power!—for five beats. One. Two. Three. Four. Five." A huge, heartfelt pause between each number. On just like this into each extremity; down into nail beds and the spaces between toes; into the mystery behind the ribs. You either fell asleep or completed the exercise, and in either case emerged feeling like a vial of light.

You could faintly discern a point of view on the human person—how it reacts under stress or persecution—from these spokes of the work. (She always called it that: "The Work.") There was a time for self-armoring, a time for talk, and a time to regard your body kindly, limb by limb, and get it ready to start the cycle again.

I stood there doing the exercise, trying and failing to achieve the illumination I was remembering from the Waldorf. Spurred oddly, as if waking from a dream, I said my sorries to the girl who'd bought me the drink and the second pill, and shuttled downstairs to find Alexis, who was still sitting where we'd started, and was wearing the remainder of a laugh on her face. "Songy," she said, "I thought we'd lost you. And when I saw that guy—did you see that shit?! He might be . . . everybody else is over there trying to see . . . when I saw him falling, for a second I thought it could be you." She said, "You look like shit. Were you having fun?"

# 12

I HAD NO TROUBLE SLEEPING AFTER ALEXIS DROVE ME BACK TO THE sad hotel. I was shocked and stoned quiet, but Alexis was as cheerful as ever. Apparently, she told me, somebody fell from one of the balconies at that club once or twice a year, and so our witnessing the fight and the fall—I'd told her how close I'd been to the guy, and to his ill-fated wrestling match—counted as a kind of souvenir. "See you tomorrow," she said when I got out of the car. I climbed back into my bed at five or so, slept resentfully, and woke just after noon, in time to shower, put on my shirt and suit, and walk over—the sole benefit of my bad choice—to the house where the party would happen.

Ron Clarence, the producer who was hosting the event, and who was one of the campaign's biggest fundraisers, had a kind of late-rhythm-and-blues-era biography, which my mother had made me look up when I told her I'd be going to his house. He was born in South Carolina, last of eleven, and educated in a one-room school with dirt for a floor. He moved north, to Jersey, first to go to college, but then, increasingly, to hang out in the lobbies of and, soon, the recording studios at radio stations, in order, he figured, to find a way into the industry and help move the rest of his family away from the South. He'd sung in a few groups back home, toured around his home state in a very small way, and felt—correctly, as it happened—that he might have some insight into what made a good song and how the minds of artists worked. Before long he was the late-night soul DJ at a lesser, but still well-known, station and had started to manage small-time blues and R&B acts, some of whom, under his guidance, promptly got famous and made him rich. After the normal pattern of such successes, he moved to Los Angeles at thirty-five and never once considered moving back East. Now he was a sort of godfather figure in the movie and music businesses and in the rich precincts of black L.A. His daughter, Melissa, was, of course, one of Alexis's best friends. The Clarences had been Alexis's way in.

I walked about a mile, past quiet strip malls and the back sides of minor chain restaurants, through a color scheme of rich goldenrods on awnings and cool greens on cars and little bikes, until, passing into sudden suburbs, I found the gate of the tree-rich community where Clarence lived. After I asked a guard to let me pass, it was Clarence's voice that I heard staticking affirmatively through an intercom, and when I'd walked up to the huge door of his house—a mansion among mansions—it was he who opened before I could knock. His hair was shorn close to his head and mostly white, and he wore an even whiter goatee, which framed his slanting teeth.

I smiled and shook his hand, and he sort of grunted in recognition, I thought, when he saw that my teeth were unfixed like his. "New York, huh," he said. He stepped aside and drew the door open wider so that I could walk through. His place was enormous, but somewhat less gaudy than I'd expected it to be.

The walls were bone-colored, and a field of a foyer, tiled in shiny squares of white, stretched out toward a pair of downward steps that marked the beginning of a grand sunken living room, a big dimple in the face of the house's ground floor. There was a piano—white—and a feathery rug—black—and several long gray couches with bright pillows. On either side of the threshold of the living room was a set of spiraling stairs, where, toward the outer side of every fourth or fifth step, big green ferns stood in their planters. Off to the side of the staircase on the left I could see a kitchen, where a squadron of caterers had started to cook. "VIPs—my forty-six-hundreds, plus some buddies I'm trying to recruit—are gonna be in here," Clarence said without stopping for preliminary conversation. "He'll talk by the piano." Past the piano was a series of windows through which I could see a wide lawn. There were about a hundred and fifty round tables out there, enough for what would amount to an outdoor midday ball. Each table had nine seats: eight for donors—"Twenty-three hundred apiece," Clarence said, "not a slacker in the building"— and the last left open for the candidate, as if for Elijah at a seder. He'd promised to stop at each table, make every donor feel special in the presence of the future president. "Alexis's in here," he said, establishing a hierarchy that, by now, I already felt in my bones and didn't mind. "You'll be out there with the twenty-threes. There's a list—"

Before he could finish with the logistics, Alexis came wincing down the steps, toward us, with Melissa at her side. Melissa's face was pewter, her features forgettably fine, her eyes honeyish, her hair tawny and huge. Her mother—white, a former publicist—had died several years earlier; the lady's face peeked out from a triptych of family photos in the foyer. Alexis and Melissa both wore big-eyed sunglasses and moved gingerly. I knew what ailed Alexis; I was hurting from a hangover too, but, intimidated by Clarence's reputation, I was trying harder—trying *at all*—to hide it. Melissa must have also been out late last night.

"Hey, Ron," Alexis said, her voice gravel. *Ron.* Alexis's comfort with everybody, no matter their station, made me almost laugh out loud. "The Songbird flies again, I see," she said to me without moving her head in my direction. "David, Melissa. Melissa, David."

Clarence was famous as a motherfucker. He'd curse you out in a second if he thought you were sort of dumb; curse you out, too, if he was feeling bored and you happened to be around; and he'd hurt you in worse ways if he loved you and you disappointed or otherwise betrayed him. That's what people said, and how—I could see even now, having known him for just a few minutes—he liked to be seen. But as he watched the girls walk down the stairs and hold their heads, he looked sort of tender. He answered Alexis with a nod and a smile and, as she approached, grabbed his daughter around the shoulders. He shook her a bit and laughed when she groaned.

"Your sorry asses fucked around all night—*knowing* you had something to do," he said, glowing, "and *now* look at you."

"Ron," Alexis said.

"No," he said. "True shit, Alexis. You're gonna be breathing vodka all over my millionaires and my president. Real nice."

Obviously he couldn't have been happier. This was something like the envy—and the admiration—of youth. What kind of twentyish kid would Alexis be if this early turn around the center of the civic-social world didn't accompany—didn't outright urge—all kinds of commensurately intense private experiences? *This is healthy,* he was saying. *Have your fun.*

"New York over here is all professional," he said, gesturing toward me. "Grabbed my hand like I had a job to give him. You could learn something." Alexis smirked. Melissa skittered off to the bathroom.

This was light mockery and a false compliment, I knew. He was calling me a square, a fool. My attempt at concealment was a mistake. This was supposed to be fun. It was a job, but in many ways it wasn't. I felt embarrassed—but also, really, when I thought about it, just fine. I also felt like I might vomit later on, but to say it now would be lame.

FOR THE REST OF THE early afternoon, we worked alongside Clarence's domestic staff to set up place cards and affix fragile bouquets, and put up lengths of rope and stanchions where we thought the VIPs should stand in line before their pictures. By the time the party began I was tired, but my stomach had settled.

I was out back when the candidate arrived, but, looking around the side of the house, I could see his car as it pulled up. He got out stiffly. He gave Clarence the faintest wave, not feigning any special intimacy, and kept walking to the door. Through the back window of the house, I saw him give his quick, intimate-seeming address to the larger donors. I could see him from behind, in silhouette, delivering gestures whose naturalism I'd now watched him hone for months; I had a passable impression that I sometimes used to make Howland and Regina laugh—a stiff, open hand jutting outward, a drawling stutter, a dependence (like Beverly's on *right*) on the word *look* to stud the pauses between his well-worn phrases. I stood outside on the grass, watching the twenty-three hundreds settle in.

Sitting alone for now, dressed in black with big rings on the fingers of his right hand and a white collar at his throat, was a preacher I'd watched on television as a kid. He led the Church of God in Christ, a national Pentecostal assembly not unlike—but much larger and more famous than—the one in which I grew up. I'd always liked him because he was a good singer; the hooping final sections of his sermons were always wonderfully tuned, and he had a bandleader's rapport with the organist, who sat on the far stage-left side of his huge pulpit. He was a baritone, and reveled in the lower end of his register, which was rare for a preacher. He'd looked old for my entire life, and here, in front of me in the flesh, he looked even older, and sort of papery in the skin. His skin was dotted with moles, and seemed to sprout new ones as he sat there in the sun. He was breathing hard for a reason I couldn't discern.

I was surprised to see him—and surprised, too, to realize that I was also kind of excited. He talked often about how he'd started out as a political preacher, counseling solidarity on Sundays and attending civil rights rallies when they bloomed in L.A. But the rub of those anecdotes, always, was that though he was proud of what he'd helped accomplish in the sixties—he'd known King in a marginal way; hooked arms with Heschel—he was glad now to keep his sanctuary set aside for the Holy Spirit and nobody else. Politics was a distraction from the work of holiness. Seek first the kingdom, and all the rest—even temporal change, without the peskiness of protest—would be added unto you. I usually held back from starting conversations with donors I hadn't yet met, but before I could stop myself, I was walking over and tapping his shoulder gently. Lacking much to say at the outset, I told him how often I'd seen him on TV and how much I liked to hear him talk. But then I asked—this was why I'd gone over—why exactly he'd come here. I knew what he thought about politics—I recited to him almost verbatim his thoughts on the matter—and couldn't figure out, *respectfully*, why he'd spend his money on a few moments with a politician. I found myself riddled with something like suspense for his answer.

His voice had been feeble when we were trading those early pleasantries, but I could tell I'd interested him—helped him seemingly shed a few years—with my question. He started to talk about how he could discern, faintly but without much doubt, a "move of God" in the campaign that couldn't be explained in purely political terms. What everybody else saw as an effusion of national sentiment, stoked by the candidate's rare oratory talent as well as by the fact of his race, he could tell was a kind of intervention by the Lord into the affairs of a nation that needed His touch. The candidate, when president, would—he could feel it—usher in some new, unimaginable dispensation, an age in which miracles would come to be commonplace and signs and wonders would be the easy order of the day. "Something," he said, "is *shifting*, son." Why else, he asked, almost laughing, would I—a church boy with no special connections (he could tell)—be playing such a part in the proceedings? I was like Joseph among the Egyptians, he said. It was time, finally, for somebody like me, and like him—that equation was meant to flatter me—to be counted. We were vessels. Who knew what God would do.

Just as he was ending his monologue—I was concentrating so hard on what he had to say that I could barely hear the noise of the party, and I hadn't noticed that the VIP reception was over and the candidate had come out onto the lawn—two things happened. First, the candidate came loping out of the house's back door and onto the grass. Through the glass, he'd looked as he always had. That familiar speech possessed his body, took his physical self through its paces of confidence and exhortation. He'd give a kind of skimming summary of recent news—the better to make those present feel that they were getting a one-time-only improvisation, an experience, however quick and transactional, of real closeness. Then he'd connect each item that he mentioned to one of his longstanding themes: how we needed a fresh infusion of "will" as much as we needed new ideas; how the unending skirmishes between the parties had to be transcended by enlightened goodwill, not won by blunt force (this kind of shit drove Beverly, ever the advocate for power, insane); how enough hope, tethered to action, could cause an earthquake in America, subtly shifting the country's borders and shape. He yelled at rallies, but with crowds like this one he did his uplift act with an unpushy calm. It made his listeners just as inspired as the speechgoers in the primary states, but also did them the favor of making them feel cool.

Now, though, watching him leave one speech and start to ready himself for another, I could see that he looked annoyed. His skin looked dry, and his features were sour. Ron was at one of his sides and Alexis at the other, but when he saw me, he made an impatient gesture with his finger, calling me over.

"Let's get this going," the candidate said, before I was able to greet him. If he recognized me, he wasn't letting on. "Everybody needs to sit so we can get this—" He made rushing gestures with his hands. He seemed tired. Over his shoulder I could see several agents in ill-fitting black suits and white shirts.

The second thing that happened was that Beverly emerged from the crowd, walking toward us. She saw that I'd seen her and started smiling, wider than I'd ever seen her smile. She was wearing a short, pale sundress that swished around her thighs. She trained her eyes on mine—a look that bolted my feet to the grass where I stood—then at the candidate.

"That speech," she said. "That fucking speech needs a renovation."

Ron, surely protective over his party, made a throaty sound and looked ready to curse Beverly out. But the candidate, suddenly energized, started to laugh. He looked at me again, more friendly this time. "Whatever this woman tells you is a crock of shit," he said before he walked off, toward the tables, trailed by the men in bulging suits.

WHEN THE CANDIDATE WAS GONE, I stood with Beverly outside Ron Clarence's house. I told her where my hotel was—how impossible it had been to sleep—and she laughed. "Not tonight," she said. Before I could ask just what she meant, a driver came for her in a shining black car not unlike the one that toted the candidate around when he came to New York. She grabbed my hand and pulled me down into the backseat. Los Angeles looked different later in the day; its bluish light had gotten a chance to settle. The throbbing in my head began to wane. I looked up at the thin, digressive trunks of the palm trees on either side of the road. The overlapping tiles of the carrot-colored Spanish roofs. The mountains, far out there, rippling like the details of a torso. Shrubs stood out on them, green on sandy brown, like the isolated curls of a nappy head.

"I hate this city," Beverly said. She hadn't let go of my hand. Her cool skin mellowed out mine.

In her hotel room in the Beverly Hilton—endlessly tidier than Regina's place in New Hampshire; I surprised myself by making the comparison—just as naturally as all of our talk, without parsing or pretext or interpretation, Beverly kissed me. One of her hands slid slowly across the line between my stomach and my chest; her fingers lodged themselves in the space between two buttons of my shirt. Her yellow dress felt slippery under my fingers, but the leg beneath it felt springy and soft, gently pressurized, full. Neither of us spoke. Gently she undid the two buttons near her hand, then, outward from there, each of the others. I knew that I was acting too, was also making this happen, but I felt happily taken, subject to a strong force. On the bed, atop the dully gold blanket, tightly made, she undid my pants insouciantly, then grabbed me by the wrists and let her weight fall onto me. I squirmed free with one hand, quickly enough to pull the dress over her head. She pinned the wrist against the bed again, kissed me again, and soon started to speak, as easily as ever, into my ear. She told me what to do next.

IV

# 13

ABOUT A WEEK BEFORE MY DAUGHTER WAS BORN, A PROPHET VIS-
ited my church. Or, well, we called these people prophets: itin-
erant Pentecostal psychics, charismatic vagabonds purporting
to speak in the name of the Lord. This one had skin like a sun-
scorched penny, and his left eye rolled indiscriminately around
his head, liberated from the harsh focus of its twin, searching
like a satellite for the heretofore hidden will of God. Yes, the future belonged to God, but it was somehow also on permanent
loan to melodramatic guys like this, who, sometimes for hours
on end, would roam the sanctuary, call people out from the
crowd like sweepstakes winners, and tell them tidbits of tomorrow's news—soliciting tears, wild dances, sprinted laps around
the sanctuary, eventually money in the basket near the altar. I
sat in my customary seat—way up front, right next to an aisle,
feeling hot and slightly sick. The bottoms of my thighs stuck to
my dress pants on the plush seat. I couldn't concentrate on any
future but the one staring me down.

The baby was late—the due date had passed almost two
weeks earlier—and my pastor (despite his forced good cheer,

indicating faith, and his gasped assurances that God could, God *would* effect in his body total healing, a resurrection like the one that had been granted to Brother Charles) was very plainly about to die. Already naturally skinny, now he floated in his suits. Already fair-skinned, now he was almost white. He had little eyes, and the lids now looked loose, like a baggy sweater ready to overwhelm a body. His head had begun its transformation into a skull. He couldn't preach anymore.

The prophet—who foretold sudden fortunes, impending marriages, new cars, free mansions, saved sons, artistic and oc-cupational breakthroughs, drastic erasures of debt, answers to unknown and inarticulable prayers—was here, I assumed, to tell the pastor once again that he would live. He was a fre-quent guest speaker at the church. If every promise he made on God's behalf had been true, almost everyone I knew would be rich, and none dead. The offerings he raised were always big. I wanted to ask him where he'd learned to prophesy.

He delivered a rambling, emotionally manipulative, un-deniably effective sermon about the Roman centurion who came to Jesus on the street and begged the Lord to heal his sick servant. Jesus, always in a hurry toward the heart of his mission but somehow also always willing to swerve away from his course, offers to make the trip to the man's house. But the centurion—citing his experience with the expediencies of the chain of command—insists that all Christ has to do is give the order, however far the distance between the servant's near corpse and the Savior's healing intent, and the rejuvenation will start to take place. "Speak the word only," the centurion says. Save yourself a trip. Jesus likes this display of long-range faith. He obliges, and the servant—miles away—is on the mend. The centurion's famous phrase—"Lord, I am not worthy that thou

shouldest come under my roof"—shows up at the most solemn
moment of the Catholic Mass. Just as Jesus can remote-control
the work of bodily regeneration, so too can he speak the solemn mysteries—bread into body, wine into blood—into being.

The prophet, holleringly Holiness to the core, made no
such Eucharistic associations. He ignored, too, one of my favorite things about the New Testament: Jesus, the God-man,
fully aware of his miraculous power and of its cosmic implications, often seems surprisingly open to input on his methods. *Here*, some mortal says, *why don't you try it like* this? If Jesus
likes your tone, he'll give your way a whirl. Instead the prophet
worked and worked the obvious angle: at just a word, our God
could heal real people like you. Like your pastor. Starting cool
and ending hot, with much anecdotal and practical and speculative digression in between, he pulled the story apart, yielding
the only question that mattered in his mind. That soldier's uncommon, space-obliterating faith—was yours as total?

He got the crowd whipped up that way, talking about the
consequences of belief and the possibility of total repair, that
thin string between the present and things to come. Could
you believe, could you scream, could you cry enough to alter
the unfathomable mind of God? Soon he broke off from the
sermon—with these types, sermons were only pretexts, intro-
ductions to the real meat of more mystical forms of speech—
and began to eye his audience, prospecting opportunities for
prophecy. A cry went up. Who doesn't want a promise? I can
admit, not without some embarrassment that has grown over
the years, that I cried too. I shouted. I leapt.

The prophet gave the expected "Word" to our pastor: if all
of us would only pray and believe, he could live. Then, when
he took the handful of steps down from the pulpit, he made an

odd beeline toward me. Maybe it was the confusion so apparent on my face that beckoned him. The obvious strain in the
cries that I made along with the rest of the congregation. One
of his eyes bored through my forehead with a terrible intensity.
The other bobbed upward toward the balcony above my head.
I wanted to run, but instead I lifted my hands.

He was fast too; soon he had one hand on my belly and the
other on my forehead, absorbing its sweat and steaming grease.
This was the proper position for prophecy. For whatever spiritual or cultural reason, it depended on a physical connection.
This was quite opposite, I thought, from the Jesus of the Bible,
who could make such impossible things happen at a distance.
No matter. I tried to rein in my attention. I was twenty. I hadn't
yet met any possible president—nothing had assured me yet
that I could have an encounter more meaningful than this.

Usually a performer like this would've grabbed a microphone, so that the crowd, like a magician's, could be dazzled
and galvanized by his projections. But curiously, he whispered
his prophecy, such as it was, directly into my ear. "Your miracle," he said, and by this I thought—hopefully interpreting on
the fly, I couldn't help it—he meant my child, "is coming this
week."

When looking for clues into the sources of my own passivity, my odd relationship to effort, I think of scenes like this
one. Let's face it in all its strangeness: I was raised in an atmosphere of magic, christened into unrealism, made to feel
most at home amid excruciating cognitive dissonance, the kind
that never resolved. I believed and didn't believe and felt the
strain. The people I knew were and weren't *real,* in the sense
of authenticity. They did what they shouldn't do without jet-
tisoning the orthodoxies that should've made them ashamed.

God knows how. But I guess that's all of us. One of my favorite singers at our church is dead now. It doesn't matter why. Back then, though, he was slim and intense-looking, handsome and funny. For some reason, he liked me even when he was an adult and I was young. Downstairs from the sanctuary, in the dining hall where we ate between services, I'd sheepishly slide him a Snapple, and he—knowing what I wanted—would sing aloud the ingredients on the back of the bottle, riffing and wailing and running, showing me that his facility with sound had nothing, strictly, to do with content. Only vowels and plosives and sibilant hisses mattered: *Look, Davey, how one room in the house of a phrase or a word can open out into another.* He was funny, and smart in a way that he downplayed. He made circles—quicksilver clarifications—in the air with his hands when he spoke. He never said he was gay. I never saw him wince, even once, when a slur was shouted from the pulpit. Slurs *were* shouted—I wouldn't say often, but it wasn't never either.

One time, walking west on Christopher Street—then a bazaar of sex shops and bars, high boots and bare thighs, the first trans women, tall and haughty, I'd ever seen—I saw the singer holding hands and talking intensely with a man I didn't recognize. An instinct took over in my body and, I think, in his. We sailed past each other easily, too easily, not speaking despite our friendship. The next Sunday we carried on our talk and song without reference to the Village. Only God knew how! Sometimes I felt far too literal.

In the days after the prophet's visit I kept an eye out for a fulfillment of his word. Not without some self-indicting shame. Anybody could take me anywhere.

———

A MEMORY LIKE THAT ONE could keep me distracted for days, even here, near the hot center of the quickly moving campaign. Now I let it waft around in my mind—more as a set of sensual associations (noise, touch, holy anticipation) than as a sequence of events—as I sat in a tasteful living room in Darien, Connecticut. Fall had come but the heat had clung. I could see the leaves outside from the table where I sat: they were gently yellowing, easing their way toward colors still more brilliant. The house belonged to Scott Smith, a satisfied-looking lawyer whose career had ferried him back and forth between government and the private sector like a small boat of great tactical importance. He'd been counsel at a bevy of defense-related agencies during Democratic presidencies, and when his party was in exile, he scudded back to his high seat—partner of long tenure—at Skadden.

I looked away from the window and watched Scott as he sat at the head of the table, fussing showily with the page of notes he'd soon use to introduce his honored guest. Scott was fit in the way of someone who, at great expense of will and cash, had a decade or so ago lost a lot of weight. Thin, rounded shoulders, tough quads showing through the pants of his austere suit, a slight pooching around the hips and at the waist. He'd organized events for us and chaired a nationwide group of lawyers who supported the candidate. He treated his work on the campaign like a second job: he kept his own spreadsheets and had made one of his law assistants keep it. He'd raised more money by himself than the tag team of Beverly and Blackshear. Whenever he emailed the office, he got my name wrong. A different way every time. Sometimes even my gender. The note he'd sent setting the small invite list for this lunch had been addressed to "Denise." We'd met and spoken—always briefly, to be fair—many times.

But, yes, the invite list was very small: Scott himself, of course, as well as his wife, Patricia. They had the same slim noses and puckered mouths like unripe flowers. Her sleeveless dress was midnight blue and gracefully shapeless. We staffers were there, seated—uncommon occurrence—at the Smiths' long table like guests. Beverly was there, looking quiet and content, a hint of a mocking smile on her face. Wilson Taylor, the municipal guru, was there, chewing loudly and charming the table with grumpy stories about John Lindsay, the former New York mayor, whom he'd loved but also considered a "stiff putz." Unfortunately, he said, the candidate reminded him of Lindsay: "More than a little bit! It's how he holds that fucking high-class chin." More fortunately, though, the accident of black skin and his talent at class camouflage made the candidate's ivory tower comportment "sort of, I dunno, exotic? Like: some kind of mixture of things? God, who knows, but I think on his best days it works."

"Right," Beverly said. "Right." She looked over at me, her gaze equally mocking and suggestive. She felt more than she said, but—I could tell—didn't think her own affectionate complaints about the candidate were worth articulating, just this once. The look was an offer of intimacy that I greedily accepted; it assured me that later, after the meeting, she'd take me somewhere, perhaps home.

Then, ominously, ginning up a suspense only a cynic can muster in his audience, Wilson said, "We'll see."

Wilson was pulling, he knew, against a strong undertow of confidence. Shortly after the convention, the candidate had pulled out to a formidable lead. The others around the table—a handful of donors who'd already maxed out their contributions and who might later be juiced for new contacts—listened to ~~Wilson and vaguely~~ nodded because they too wanted to seem tough, but the looseness at their shoulders was evident. ~~Bev-~~ erly's earlier confidence had now spread—everybody seemed to think that we would win. The candidate's ease at making himself seem coextensive with the more encouraging currents in the country's history—or maybe this was truer: making himself seem like an apology for, and a redemption from, all that had so recently gone so wildly wrong—had created a kind of providential force field around his person. His inevitability was the inevitability of the future. This wasn't a fundraiser; the guests were here to have their deep hopes, prophesied on cable news, confirmed.

Smith's guest of honor was the tall, intense campaign manager. I'd seen him from time to time after witnessing his outburst—"drag her out to the desert"—in New Hampshire. He'd never looked my way. More and more often, armed with a PowerPoint presentation full of polling data, he made rounds like these for groups of a chosen few. The lunch was an "Insiders' Briefing"—he insisted that we call it that, and that we make the Smiths call it that when they sent out their invitations—where he could show off a shaped-up version of the most recent internal numbers and speak more freely than he usually did. Over the summer and into the fall, he'd become an almost daily prime-time guest on the cable shows. This was a new source of surprise and curiosity for me, how the senior aides—people who'd been profiled in short, mostly positive news pieces back at the beginning of the campaign but were otherwise recognizable only if, like I had, you'd seen them tagging along with the candidate for all these months—were, by slow degrees, becoming small-bore celebrities of a kind: gossip fodder for political junkies and wise-guy insiders.

Now the campaign manager, formerly a terse sourpuss, wore a semi-constant smile, testing the sun-dyed paper of his skin. It said he understood his new status. And you could feel the power of that status working among the guests at Smith's lunch. Anybody could find a flyer and finagle a photograph with the candidate by now. All their friends had been there, done that, put the picture on the mantel or on a desk at the office. Here was a tasteful room behind yet another veil, all creams and white with a steadily cooling breeze beyond the clean-silled windows. You had to squint to see the brocade in the Smiths' curtains and on the plush backs of their couches. Like power, it was invisible to those who couldn't afford to be so close.

The campaign manager was astounding evidence of the candidate's power, already accruing before Election Day—it had become distributive; he could send a friend, dispatch a surrogate, and the star-blinded effect would still set in. Only say the word. As the campaign manager pointed toward his first slide, projected onto a screen that had descended noiselessly from a seam in the Smiths' ceiling, readying to offer us access to the fate of the "battleground states," we all leaned forward in our seats.

IN THOSE DAYS BACK BEFORE my daughter was born, I'd given myself over again to music. The usual erratic kismet: a guy I knew from college was now playing keys for a handful of bands. One of the singers he worked with needed a backup vocalist who could "sound gospel." When I sang, the only way I could "sound" was "gospel." I'd stopped singing classical after leaving college and my deeper upbringing had reclaimed my voice like moss overgrowing the sides of an old house, slowly mulching it into consonance with nature. I had a whirring vibrato and a weakness for downward riffs. I listened for and tried to author unnerving phrases, took major passages and made them minor, papered over my modest range with an oboe's congealed falsetto. For a moment there, I was good. I wrote my own songs, but my fear masquerading as perfectionism stopped me from performing them.

Instead I followed Rachel, the singer, and Patrick, the kid from school, from venue to venue downtown, singing in dark haphazard places that romanced me with their run-down simplicity: Arlene's Grocery, the Living Room, the famous, brick-walled Bitter End, and my favorite: an insanely small room, always humid with sweat, called Rockwood Music Hall. It was the size of a nice bathroom; the stage took up half the space.

I liked doing backups. The primary responsibility of the gig was singing harmony—a close third below the melody and sometimes a floating excursion into falsetto an octave above. Singing hymns all the time makes those maneuvers second nature. The first real, unstabilizing encounter with art that I can remember is lying on a floor, listening to some song I can't recall over the stereo, marveling at the mystery of three voices as one voice. Harmony felt good, still feels good. The voices in tandem or pointed dissonance shudder through my body like waves through a tuning fork. The meddlesome aspects of consciousness—even memory—dissolve. Rachel had a fine, clear, high voice, easy to match in movement and tone. I sat on a stool, studiedly casual, shoulders in a stoop, just off to her left or right as she stood singing. I didn't really like her songs, especially their lyrics, but I was there to produce sound. I didn't mind.

The other part of the job, subtler and more difficult, more satisfying as art, was creating snatches of countermelody or repeating a melodic theme while Rachel introduced a new one. It was a way to make symphonic an otherwise simple, poppy song, turning its snatches of melody into ideas that could be restated, distended, complicated, made to ring like bells through time and sit like marks of color on the surface of the mind.

Color: that was it—you could turn sound gradient, subjective and emotional like hue. I liked to listen to one melodic idea against another, just as a color theorist might arrange and overlap swatches. Singing onstage, trying to juice feeling from the onlooking drunks in our sparse audiences, searching for ways to recast Rachel's songs and make them speak a language resonant to me, this is what I was trying to be: a colorist, almost imperceptibly influential. I was rarely paid. I thought my work, such as it was, went over most people's heads. Even the ones who sought me out and said they'd enjoyed me and bought me beers, despite my age, after our sets.


MAYBE HALFWAY THROUGH THE CAMPAIGN manager's presentation, Wilson cut in. We'd sat through, already, a painstaking, self-congratulatory recapitulation of the primary campaign, from Iowa to Super Tuesday and all the way through the great, final skirmishes in April. These tactical triumphs still lit him up, you could tell, although he was smart enough to affect a job's-not-done terseness about it. But after that outpouring of lingering affection, he had eventually transitioned to a consideration of the big, obvious general election states— Pennsylvania, Ohio, and Florida—plus the somewhat more exotic "gettables," as he called them: Virginia, North Carolina,

Nevada, Iowa, Colorado. This was a "change" election, he kept on saying, one whose outcome would be determined less by measurable elements like "the economy" than by the barely submerged spiritual longings of the country. On the screen now was a map of North Carolina, which he was convinced we could win. Did we know how many college graduates had recently settled in the state? All we had to do was find them and "turn them out." He meant to the polls, but the phrase made me think of the sexual initiate who gets one good life-changing taste of something new.

As the Carolina talk went on, Wilson, in his way, began to grumble. You could hear him vocalizing his dissent before a word emerged: a musical croaking in the upper regions of his chest, bursting with vivid, aggravated color into his throat and out his mouth.

"I mean, come oooooonnn," he said after so much introductory music-making. "I mean, your lips to FDR's ears, don't get me wrong—I hope along with you."

The campaign manager's lofty, satisfied look became, by gradual, visible measures, a glare.

"But—just, I'm sorry, please allow me some conjecture here," Wilson said, "but does it cast a cloud over your analysis *at all* that a Democrat hasn't won North Carolina since, what, Carter? Isn't that true?" Nobody else at the table felt, just then, like chiming in. "Even Clinton couldn't do it—either time!— and he was the greatest southern drag act I've ever seen. Funny how that accent isn't all that strong anymore, by the way. I just want to register that observation among friends." Wilson was beaming. "But anyway, so, fueled solely by the, I don't *know*, man, by the power of, what, *abstract desire? spiritual strivings?*, we're going to upend the political gravity of the past thirty years? Just pray and hope and turn these *kids* out to vote and click and turn the color blue? I mean—"

"I really like where you're going with this," the campaign manager said, recognizing in Wilson a person who would never stop the momentum of his own speech except by outside interruption.

Often, Beverly took on the role that Wilson was playing— the hard-ass pessimist. But now she sat back, watched the volley but didn't offer her own racket. Knowing her, she wasn't tired or bored; something about her passivity suggested a new kind of strength. Again, she offered only the most rote contribution.

"I think we don't need North Carolina either way," she said, still looking at me, meaning the utterance as an offer of peace.

AFTER ONE OF THOSE NIGHTS while I was out singing, the baby was born. I'd been in the back room of a bar on Avenue B— bright fluorescents even past midnight, an upright piano with gummy keys and an over-citrusy sound. We'd sung Rachel's songs for maybe twenty swaying people, ten of them friends of hers we always saw. The gig was middling, but we were all more or less satisfied. We said our goodbyes out in the November cold and dark, and went our separate ways home.

My cab went up the FDR, speeding perilously past the blurring red and white lights across the river and at the sides of the highway. The lights, as they passed, lit up the edge of my driver's cheek at lulling intervals. I looked out the back window and I could see the Brooklyn Bridge, its cables taut like the strings and frets of an impossible guitar. Just as my head hit the pillow at home and I was almost asleep, I got a text from the dancer. She was on her way to Mount Sinai, and soon so was I. I thought faintly of the prophet. He'd given me his "word" a week and a half ago now—technically incorrect but close enough to give me pause. If he'd been talking about this at all, that is. If he could be said to have been talking about anything, really. No other miracle that I could discern had occurred.

The birth, the next afternoon, took place almost outside the stream of memory, in the same hazy, soundless dimension as grief. The dancer shat and bled and here came the baby, my daughter, an alien to narrative, so far unstoried, covered in blood that smelled like a roomful of copper coins.

WILSON REFUSED TO BE SATISFIED by the campaign manager's assurances, but the initially tense, soon playful struggle between the two, over North Carolina and much else, became the afternoon's true entertainment and purpose. Beverly looked on like a benign referee, drunk on her own impeccable objectivity. At first I'd worried that the prim Smiths would be mortified by Wilson's interruptions, but by the time all the guests had gone and we staffers were helping straighten up, Scott kept saying how "utterly refreshing" it was "to have a real honest-to-God exchange of ideas." This "salon atmosphere," as he called it, was a forecast, he said, of American life under the candidate's enlightened administration. "We'll be able to *talk* again," Smith said dreamily. He thought the event was a total success. Fine by us.

Just as we were leaving, Wilson sent me and Beverly an email whose entire content was a subject line: "FUCKING PUTZ."

On the next day, a Monday, the stock market crashed. I

knew because I heard it over the radio in a cab, taking the long way from the top of the park. By now I'd met many people who made their money in the wide field called "finance." Bankers, traders, buyers-out and buyers-in, surfers of swelling numbers I couldn't begin to comprehend. Once or twice Beverly or Earnest had tried to explain to me the particulars of their businesses. My head cottoned up instantly and turned to static. Now, though, I understood well enough that my new acquaintances were in danger. All day donors called the office, some just to commiserate, others—sensing an opportunity of a kind—offering their services as informal advisers on the economy to the campaign and the candidate. "He's going to need some real help," I could hear someone saying over the phone to Jill.

We usually worked in silence, more or less, except for the murmur of one or two of us on the phone. Now we had the TV on, scrambling to understand. The biggest crash ever. Each variation of the phrase sounded faker than the last. Perhaps there'd be another Depression. It all had—please forgive me—something to do with housing, and something to do with the terminus of a euphoric optimism that rhymed with—or had it even helped to produce?—the atmosphere around the candidate. That's all I could glean.

Toward the end of the afternoon, Blackshear called. It was funny: I still didn't feel that I knew him well. But I did have a grasp of the textures of his voice, what his tones meant, how his inflections told the story of his mood. So I knew now, when he said "Mr. Hammond!" with a slightly mocking formality, that he was in a mood so excellent, given the circumstances, that he had managed to surprise even himself.

"You seeing this?" he said. He just wanted to talk. "Well,

I guess of course you are. How could you not. Everybody is. It's all anybody I know is talking about. About twenty different people have called me talking about people they know with stories about people *they* know who may or may not have already committed suicide. A couple others under constant surveillance. People with money caught up in those sour-lemon baby mansions—junk: real shit—who thought it over and decided they just couldn't face their wives at home. At least that's the story. Incredible!" He was ecstatic. The southern-adjacent populist was now nowhere evident in his voice. He sounded like an Ivy college kid between classes, loping from one end of campus to the next, briskly transmitting the news.

"And Lehman," he said. "Lehman! Don't get me fucking started on Lehman. Good riddance, I say. Pack of savages, they always were." He went silent for a second, thinking. "I don't want to sound like that. I mean, if you or one of your people are affected by this in any way—"

I stopped him. Usually I tried not to interrupt, but just then—just the possibility that this disruption could possibly have anything to do with me—I could name the strange feeling that had been growing in my stomach all day.

It didn't affect me at all, I told him, truthfully as far as I knew. Nobody I'd known before the campaign had invested in stocks beyond the kind you pick up here or there through some predatory broker. Very few of them owned a home of any kind—certainly nobody in my family did. Those digits declining rapidly meant, really, nothing to me. The feeling—for which, sure, I was slightly ashamed—was a kind of illicit glee at being beyond the clutches of the economy in this one quite limited way. It couldn't take away what it hadn't given me. My debit account looked like it always had.

"I figured," Blackshear said with a spacious airiness in his voice, like great winds on a plain. "Maybe that's why I thought to call you. My kind of stuff won't drop as fast as the rest, but there's still a fucked-up day coming, don't get me wrong. I'll make a way. I won't be jumping from any windows, I'll tell you that.

"I do wish I could have back my . . . what is it, now? A million? Somewhere in there?"

I didn't answer—the breath had suddenly left my chest. But I knew instantly what he meant. All those dozens of his employees and friends, coming dutifully in my direction, directly to the phone in the office on Park or my email in New Hampshire, or through Beverly, reciting their card numbers to me like complex incantations—he'd given each of them the money they'd donated. He hadn't "raised" the money—most of which was credited to Beverly anyway, had kept her in the game of the campaign's inner-ish circle as a creditable presence—so much as razed it from the fertile ground of his own wealth.

Or maybe the metaphor was animal, not agricultural: he'd sent the donations forward, toward the campaign, like firm arms—first to greet, soon to smother. I couldn't tell whether this was a sly admission or the slip of someone who'd never known the rules. Maybe he thought I'd known this all along. Why I decided not to tell Jill I still can't say. My feet sweated in my cheap shoes and my head faintly buzzed.

THAT NIGHT, EXHAUSTED, MY BACK and sides aching as if I'd exercised, not knowing quite what to do but, on a deeper level, knowing already that I'd do nothing, I went to Harlem to pick my daughter up from her mother. The dancer lived in the 140s, not far from the short, decisive bridge to the Bronx. Here, "uptown"—an all-purpose moniker that spanned boroughs, signaling above all a distance, physical and social, from the world into which I suddenly felt christened—applied more precisely than even "Harlem."

Off the train, walking west, I passed the Chinese spot on Lenox and fought a quick urge to cross the street and order from Jimbo's, the fried chicken and burger and mini sweet potato pie joint that speckled Harlem all over with its blue awnings. The burgers at Jimbo's were salty, flavorful, kind of unbelievably fresh-tasting, best expressed under the cover of too much ketchup.

But I kept walking, past an always busy gas station in the middle of the block, past the broad storefront where Al Sharpton dragged every candidate for office within sniffing distance of New York, making them deliver semi-sermonic appeals to the devoted legions of his membership—savvy citizens trained by the reverend himself who knew how to wave signs in the direction of the TV cameras from New York 1 and make themselves seem even more numerous than they were. Everybody had their problems with Sharpton, but I liked him because he made Harlem seem like a stronghold again. Without knowing what they were doing, big-time politicians, guided by Sharpton, paid substitutive reverence to the milieu of Hughes and Jessie Fauset. Not to mention so many nameless people that I knew. All our family friends were from Harlem or thought of it as a home. Before Harlem, their families had migrated from all points south.

At the corner, in front of a supermarket whose triangular plastic flags in red, white, and blue, heralding a GRAND OPEN-

ING, had been fluttering in the grit-flecked wind for at least ten years, a few older men had set up a wood-plank table on blue milk crates and were now playing dominoes. Oldies poured out of a small stereo near the curb. Around the corner and up some yellowing tenement stairs were the dancer and the baby.

These days the dancer and I almost never spoke. I came to collect the baby every other weekend, and on a few weeknights in between. The dancer, wearing a big shapeless white T-shirt and black tights, her small, flat feet bare, opened the door of her mother's apartment on a shallow fifth-floor landing. The place had the syrupy-sweet smell of unsorted laundry out in the open. Over her shoulder I could see piles of clothes—hers, her mother's, the baby's: an intergenerational mess. In a corner was another pile, an improbable tower of consumer goods—broken stereos, obsolete blenders, plush headphones. The baby, now not so much of a baby, almost three, but still "the baby" in my inner language, was dressed in jeans and a brown-and-pink checked coat and tan boots. Her hair was in curlicued braids, patterned beautifully, and clipped in round white flower-shaped barrettes. She had big cheeks and receding eyes like her mother's and lips shaped like mine, skin complected like mine, a mien initially shy like mine had been when I was a child. Every time I saw her, my chest gently tightened.

None of my usual mental habits worked in the presence of the baby. Not that I didn't try: the Christ child in the manger, Moses as an infant sent skidding down the river toward his fate, Isaac prepared as a sacrifice to God. Who else? That slain baby in *Beloved*, gone spectral and strange, embodied in blood. The child fought over by those two ancient mothers, one true and one counterfeit, until King Solomon gave the perverted decree to slice it in half, crown to crotch.

Babies show up in stories and in the Scriptures to stoke crises in the lives of their parents, I thought. They all bleed on some altar, offered up to causes outside themselves. And, sure, maybe in some prophetic corner of my mind I'd foreseen— back when I'd dumped the pregnant dancer, refused to go down the disappointingly squalid path that constancy would have entailed—that a sliced existence like the one the baby had now would be the cost of my escape into . . . into what, exactly, I couldn't have known. I thought it all but couldn't feel it. My stomach hurt.

Without a word, the dancer passed me the baby's bag.

# 14

I SPENT SO MANY NIGHTS AT BEVERLY'S APARTMENT, SUBTLY SWEAT-ing into her sheets. Out the window in her sparsely furnished bedroom, you could see Central Park from its southern edge on up. First, on Fifty-ninth Street, the row of remorseful-looking carriage horses and their riders, and slow swarms of East Asian and Western European tourists. Then, as you cast your eyes upward, the many congregations of trees, their growing distance suggesting Harlem. A body laid out flat, viewed from somewhere just beneath the toes.

With the lights off, both of us drowsing toward sleep, Beverly would sometimes ask to hear stories about my life. Her own reticence didn't make her less curious, or less quietly demanding. My biography, she sometimes seemed to be saying, was a fundament of the exchange that was our relationship. One night, not long after the meeting at the Smiths', I told her about the weird summer—1995—that had followed my first school year back in New York. I was ten, freshly mourning my father but not much outwardly altered by the change in my life—or so, at least, I thought. I spent the summer getting to know my mother's family, whom I'd grown up only hearing about. Mom was changed, that I could see. Moments before the funeral, in an upper room of the little church at which Uncle Jim had introduced my parents, she'd grabbed me and cried out, "This is all a bad dream!" Some church ladies had pulled her away and fanned at her face, and I'd wondered if, by *dream*, she'd meant my father's death or all of life. After that day she toggled between static quiet and unstoppable movement.

With what sometimes seemed to be the last of her strength, she'd take me on the long journey to the neighborhood she'd grown up in, Throgs Neck, that distant phalange hanging forgotten off the side of the Bronx, pointing into the Long Island Sound as if implicating it in a crime.

In the city's tabloids all that summer was the story of a construction worker who'd plopped, mid-shift, into the water beneath the Throgs Neck Bridge, on which he'd been doing routine repair work. The widow wouldn't chalk it up to suicide, even though one of his buddies, who'd been dangling just next to him, only a few airborne feet away, had said he'd seen the man purposely unbuckle the harness keeping him connected to the bridge. They'd been hanging from ropes like skyscraper window washers gone Olympic. No, the widow said, lacking evidence but abundant in passion that seemed convincing to the reporters at the *Post* and *Daily News*. No, there'd been something wrong with the equipment. Perhaps her husband's rope had been tampered with. Perhaps this was a murder. The months of speculation in the middle pages of the papers and on News 12, the local TV station, made for a season of parochial fame for the neighborhood. Usually it failed to figure into cultural narratives about New York. (Nobody ever settled for sure what had happened to the man. He'd probably killed himself, just like his friend said.)

Mostly the neighborhood was far. From Washington Heights, where we lived back then, it was an all but impossible commute. Train downtown, train uptown, another train to a high elevated station, from which you could see Boston Road giving way to a rust-and-red vista of the Bronx. From there we took a bus that swept across Tremont Avenue, past Westchester Square and the high school my aunts and uncles had attended long ago—and, near the school, a White Castle I always pined for but was only ever able to stop at once, when someone we knew was hospitalized nearby. We rode past wide, low-slung supermarkets and storefronts whose businesses were only erratically open, past a flower shop that signaled to me that we were finally nearby. At the corner where the florist's was, the bus would turn and head toward the huge park that cradled the projects in a wide, soft scoop. There were two public housing developments—Throggs Neck Houses, where my grandmother lived, and Randall Houses. Both were full of blacks and Puerto Ricans almost exclusively. Up the steep hill of Dewey Avenue, back on Tremont, were businesses owned and mostly run by middle-class Irish and Italians. The bars were for cops. Once I went into one, hoping to get a dollar split for quarters, and knew immediately, by the way the action in the place stopped, that I'd made some kind of mistake.

The bus dropped us across the street from the small courtyard outside my grandmother's building, right in front of the supersized bodega that much of the neighborhood used as a market. My grandmother's three-bedroom apartment was the center of our family's life. She'd raised seven children there, and now it was a way station, home to four or five people at a time—two of my aunts with their kids lived there in '95—and a visiting perch for scores more. My cousins would sleep over and we'd all bunk in the living room, seven or eight to the floor, with piled blankets as pallets. During the day we'd roam the projects and sometimes wander up the hill to Tremont—we called it, simply, "the Avenue"—where we'd rent videos and buy candy.

I spent that first summer following after the eldest of my cousins, Johnny, who, when I was ten, was seventeen and, for no reason I could figure out, let me go along with him wherever he went. I sat with him in the living room of a two-story home across from Nana's where one of his least parent-harried friends lived, as he and his buddies passed around a limp, ill-shaped blunt; Johnny fended the guys off as they offered me a puff, as you might try to get a pug to lap up liquor off the floor. I went with him to the apartments of countless girls, all high school juniors like him, and listened at their bedroom doors as they fooled around. I went with him most often to the apartment of his best friend, a Puerto Rican kid named Angel, who lived just across the hall from Nana, and whose mother used to wrap their whole front door like a gigantic gift on Christmas.

Angel had dark charcoal eyebrows and long lashes, a straight, thin nose, and a pink, changeable mouth that, when not occupied in laughter, was usually set in a humorous sneer. He was nice to me because Johnny was nice to me; both warned me that I'd one day be forced to toughen up. By "teaching me to fight," they mostly meant halfheartedly beating me up. Johnny would get me in a figure-four leg lock, or a cross-face chicken wing, or just a straightforwardly fatal headlock, and then—freezing the excruciating hold—murmur sweetly to me why he'd been able to catch me like this, and how I could possibly, *maybe* wriggle free. Angel liked to punch me in the sternum and give spontaneous lectures on pressure points. I remember thinking that these boys were my two fathers.

I followed Johnny and Angel on bikes around the projects. They rode like heedless geniuses—headphones on, hands dangling, bodies minimalistically dancing in their seats. I gripped the handlebars too tightly and sometimes fell on sharp curves. Because I was always lagging several blocks behind the older boys, they seldom saw me spill. I learned to bleed privately: my first lesson in dignity.

None of us listened, that summer, to much besides Method Man. Johnny, though, saved a bit of his obsession for Robert Miles, an obscure Italian he'd learned of from the European techno magazines he sometimes bought on solitary forays into the city. The other magazines Johnny bought, inexplicably, were about consumer electronics. He harbored opinions about widescreen TVs and subwoofers, turntables and home shredders, CPUs and DSLRs—stuff he didn't own but that tickled his taste. His main viewpoint was that the biggest brands were dreck, popular only because they were slightly easier for idiots to use. When, much later, the iPhone came around, he treated it with total contempt. Angel had a similarly speculative connoisseurship when it came to cars. When he snuck into Manhattan it was to go to car shows at the Javits Center. In his mind there was a big, multilevel garage, an automotive heaven, all his; he could tell you which sports car, tricked out just so, went into each spot.

One night that August, I told Beverly, Johnny and I were across the hall, sitting on Angel's bed and listening to the Wu-Tang Clan. His mother was gone for the night—she was a nurse and worked odd hours. We passed back and forth a Black & Mild that Angel had stolen from a pharmacy up the hill. Angel and Johnny were talking about their beef with the kids from Randall Houses, just next door. No outsider would ever be

able to distinguish the two developments, or even think to—
they were one almost totally continuous expanse of three- and
four- and five-story red-brown brick buildings, separated only
by the petty rivalries that sprouted up between the young people who lived in them. Once, the boys let me follow them across
the way, to a side street near the border between the developments, where two groups of kids—one from Throggs Neck, the
other from Randall—had a long, drawn-out sidewalk brawl,
organized as if it were a lesser branch of youth sports. They
told me to hide behind a garbage can a ways off from the
melee—from there I watched them body-slam each other onto
the concrete; draw blood by punches to the mouth; smash tin
garbage cans over each other's heads like wrestlers outside the
ring. The fighting had been occasioned by a series of slights in
the halls of Christopher Columbus High School, where almost
every kid from both projects went to school. When it was done,
the combatants had simply walked away, bloody and wincing
but also somehow calm.

Now, in Angel's room, the boys were planning another, less
direct campaign of revenge. "Your mom's gone," Johnny was
saying. Smoke poured out of his flat Doberman's nose. "And
the fruit's all right there. Like, mad fruit. She won't know."
Angel's mother was known for her huge freezers full of color-
ful fruits—pomegranates, cantaloupes, mangoes, kiwis, bread-
fruits, June plums and plums, oranges and nectarines, white
peaches and forests full of bright green plantains. She cooked
furiously, made cakes and pies and tarts. The first person I
knew who "juiced" and made daily smoothies was neither a
health guru nor a gentrifying yuppie but this roly-poly Puerto
Rican, not an inch taller than four-eleven, who always asked
me, when I was over, how "Mamie"—my grandmother—was

feeling that day, and would I want to take her over a slice of cake and a few peaches. She never let a piece of fruit spoil—it all sat frozen until she could put it to use.

Johnny liked to joke that the freezer was a trove of potentially deadly weaponry. Now he saw how to have some fun with it. "I don't know, son," Angel said. His mother was small but could punch. Still, he was helpless at the thought of jokey violence, and the trouble that followed it. His most treasured memories were of time spent in the guidance counselor's office, after probably sucker-punching some kid he barely knew while passing him in the hall. He was less a sadist than a brutal entertainer. Soon we were stuffing hard fruits into black bodega bags and running outside, across the courtyard and down the block, into Randall and up the stairs of an unlocked building randomly chosen, out onto the roof.

The plan, hatched by Johnny and refined by Angel, was just to throw the fruit down, not hitting anybody, but—here was Angel's interposition—coming dangerously close a couple of times if we could. Simple, indiscriminate, intra-neighborhood guerrilla action. It didn't matter whether the people we scared were the kids from school or not; they'd feel the ripple, be only a degree or two removed. The projects were small.

I was thrilled to be along, and quiet because I was terrified of being noticed and dismissed. Still, just before we started the fusillade, Johnny looked over at me and said, "If you tell your mother about this, I'll kill you." I nodded and, as a gesture of solidarity, threw the first melon.

It was dark and the streetlights were weakly on, making a violet-yellow wash on the ground, subtly iridescent. We could hear loose shouts and the noises of dying basketball games, but it was mostly quiet: if you listened closely you could hear

the static of the Sound. Then came the crashes from our fruit.
The frozen globes broke on the pavement like glass, in thud-
ding then tinkling bursts. I looked over the lip of the roof and
saw the fruit's flesh splayed out like open guts, still bright with
its fresh color. Rich reds, pale greens, freakish and startling yellows. The ground—still hot from the afternoon, melting the
fruit quickly—looked like a battlefield.

Then, too, came screams in bunches. "Fuck!" "Shit."
"What they doing in these projects now?!" "This how people
get hurt." "Lord Jesus!" As far as we knew, nobody had been hit,
but a commotion was growing more quickly than we'd imagined. The voices early on were women's, and mostly sounded
older. Between volleys, as we opened new bags and restocked
our arms, we huddled near the roof's edge and giggled helplessly, in trills. Angel sometimes rose to his full height, beating
his chest and yelling like Kong, shouting "Fuck Randall!" at
nobody in particular.

After a few minutes, the scattered voices downstairs became a chorus—more male and more organized. Someone
said, "Fuck what?" We started to laugh less, and the bags were
almost empty.

The same voice, a clear, strong baritone, shouted, "Ay!"
Then, awfully, we heard a single gunshot, the real article. "Get
the fuck down from off that roof," the voice said.

I felt the distance in age between the three of us col-
lapse—we all, like children, immediately and instinctively followed the voice, even though to go downstairs meant to draw
closer to it, and to the gun. Angel was the first down the stairs
and out the building's front door. We heard a fist hit the skin
between his nose and his left eye. A big man, over thirty, yoked
him quickly up by the neck.

"I don't know what the fuck y'all are thinking," the man said. His voice was the baritone we'd heard calling out. He kept his hands around Angel's neck as he bobbed back into consciousness and his nose bled freely. "But I don't usually fight with my hands," he said, finally releasing Angel and showing us the gun. "Don't let me see you little niggas again."

Before his soliloquy was done—now it rings in my ears as something unreal, like a snatch from an early draft of a screenplay about urban chaos—we were already running, scrambling among project buildings as through a wilderness, across our courtyard stealthily as if spotlit, up into our building breathlessly. Angel went into his apartment without saying goodbye. Johnny and I went inside, where his sisters were up listening to music, and our Nana—who stalked the house quietly and cooked at all hours—was standing by the stove, fretting a gravy at the bottom of her favorite pan with a fork. My mother and Johnny's father were there with her in the kitchen—its walls had forever been a glowing spearmint green—laughing and joking about a girl they'd known in their old neighborhood, the South Bronx, on Fox Street. The family had lived there before their short stay in a homeless shelter, and then, finally, this place in Throgs Neck. Our parents were two of seven, although by now their eldest sister had already died. The next eldest, just a year older than my mom, was now sick and would go soon. These two in the kitchen were a kind of pair among their siblings—relatively quieter, the two darkest-skinned, both of them uncommonly religious. My mom had let choirs sweep her into deeper Christian observance. Johnny's dad had, in his youth, found Five-Percent Islam—the sect whose language Wu-Tang had turned into a patois—among his friends in the street. Darryl was his given name, but for many decades now he'd gone by Salaam.

We listened to them reminisce about this girl, named Niecy—she'd pronounced everything wrong by way of some auditory dyslexia well into her late teens—until Nana was done cooking. Johnny and I stood at the threshold as they talked, suppressing our heaviest breaths and pretending at extreme normalcy, relieved that they didn't seem to notice that something had gone wrong. The dinner we all ate a few minutes before midnight was smothered chicken and white rice with long, thin, crisp, gently greasy green beans on the side.

# 15

THE CITY TWITCHED FITFULLY THAT FALL, ITS MOOD MIXED. THE financial crisis, concocted in the high buildings here, had now slipped New York's borders—there were stories in the papers about worried workers out West picking through their ravaged 401(k) accounts, and other stories about central bankers in Europe, watching the sickness spread and starting to panic. News of the troubles sounded like an accusation leveled at Manhattan. All conference calls among the campaign's donors devolved into gossip about who had lost what, and who might be saved by the rescue package—dollars tossed back into the coffers of banks—being flown so unturbulently through a usually rancorous Congress. On the bill's necessity the candidate and his crotchety opponent agreed with only a few nitpicked qualifications. What swift motion! The billionaire mayor, a sourpuss with a simian mouth and a working-class accent, made a pronouncement: So much money trouble, navigable only under the guiding of his knotty, spotted hands, meant that he should have a third term in office. An inconvenient law said to stop at two. But again, such strange speed: the city council quickened to revise the law—just this once. An honest emergency, tooth and claw, in an already overadrenalized town. The streets in midtown were shrinelike, quiet.

The televisions in hotel lobbies and restaurants—always on and tuned to the news, murmuring over the soft clanking of forks at business breakfasts—sometimes let slip, via the tight-jawed generals on their screens, that the seven-year-old fighting in the hills of Pakistan and Afghanistan wasn't going according to plan. From the very beginning, part of the candidate's appeal had been his early opposition to the war in Iraq. Now, though, foreign policy was a drag easily dropped, total in its eclipsement by the "crisis." War whispered and the economy spoke up. The streets felt empty, yes, but the lights in the windows were always on. And so the candidate made one final adjustment. Now there was no hint in his aspect of freshness or youth—he could afford, for the moment, to set those spent commodities aside. Instead he put on sobriety as he attended televised meetings and gave hushed speeches. The opponent was older by several decades and was well known by the press; the race was to seem mature enough to withstand a meltdown. The candidate—formerly so verbose—clipped his phrases and used clichés like an aging movie cowboy. In contrast to the opponent, who had ostentatiously halted the normal workings of his campaign to train his focus on forestalling a recession, our guy could "walk and chew gum," could manage all at once the rival necessities of politics and disaster. Once sleek, now tough. It seemed to be working.


ONE EVENING NOT LONG BEFORE Election Day, the candidate up by several points, the night warm, I walked down Broadway, toward the West Fifties, for an event. I passed the AMC where, as a kid, I'd snuck into movies one after the other, spending whole Saturdays on illicit screenings, and, a block south, the multilevel Barnes & Noble where, after the same logic, I'd started and finished books about photography and music, Sufism and sex, and slipped them back, unpaid for, onto their shelves. The old Upper West Side was a series of free rides. I watched old women on the street, walking in free strides, wearing shades and long, patterned jackets of peacocking color. The old men fared worse. Bent harshly at their waists, gripping walkers, moving too slowly to safely cross the street, they were more often than not accompanied by West Indian or Central American aides who smiled and softly chatted.

Soon I turned east, less out of necessity than because I wanted to smell the waning fragrance of the park. I stopped at the foot of the natural history museum's wide stairway, looking up at the statue of Teddy Roosevelt, which I'd always guiltily liked. Roosevelt was seated proudly on a muscular horse, looking over at the park and at the Upper East Side beyond it. Flanking the horse, on either side, on foot, were a Native American in braids and a headdress and a shirtless black man, as ripped as the horse, wearing some kind of robelike skirt. The gazes of these men of color were just as kingly and steady as Roosevelt's, and the skin of all three, plus the horse, had a lost penny's green patina. Facial phenotypes and stereotypical dress were the only ways to suss out race. Maybe I liked the statue because it showed how oppressed entities, the indigenous and the enslaved, and even domesticated animals—those ambivalent emissaries to civilization from "nature"—had carried into being the empire over which Teddy had so sportingly and cruelly ruled.

With the Spanish-speaking islands subdued and the nation
on the move, great monuments and obelisks going up in Washington, invisible influence spreading across the stirred oceans,
even a man as rich and game as Teddy couldn't survey the new
terrain without a pair of ghosts at his sides and beneath his
feet. The candidate's appeal, I thought, had something to do
with the fact that people—white people for sure, but not only
them—identified him with those earthbound figures, wise and
otherworldly in their subjugation. Now the lowly conscience
of the world could also be a kind of king. The idea was that,
despite the pomp of elevation, his feet would stay fastened—as
if long ago sculpted—to the ground. Having watched him,
though, I knew that he had no such hope. He wanted to mount
the horse and enjoy a higher view, to see the park and its planning from above, not squint through the small openings between branches. You couldn't rule from the ground, not in our
world; he knew that. But he knew, too, that the illusion couldn't
hurt.

The event was more a small rally than a formal affair—
a chance for the modest, minimally consequential field office in
New York to enlist volunteers who would take vans to the real
battlegrounds in Pennsylvania and Ohio. Gatherings like this
one were happening all the time, all over the country, especially
now that the big day was close at hand. People I knew from
high school and college, who sent me long and often impas-
sioned notes about my involvement in the campaign, sometimes included pictures from one pep rally or another, happy
to be history. But for me—New Hampshire felt forever ago—
these non-monetary events were rare and exotic. I was just a
body on loan, holding a sign-in sheet on a clipboard near the
door, where the dying light shone in strangely.

We were in a former nightclub, a handful of steps below ground, with low ceilings and dull gray carpeting on the walls. Sound got stuck in the fibers and didn't bounce around: the acoustics were a sponge. Jostling past me, scribbling their names in undimmable attitudes of civic pride, were wiry middle-aged men, tough and lonely-looking customers who reminded me of Derrick in his trailer, and women with graying roots but gently dyed tips—pastel pink and sunset purple—wearing cropped jean jackets in bleached blue, and college kids humming with ambition, slumming in artfully distressed sweaters, and many odd-balls, attending alone, who seemed to have gathered the last of their public decorum to witness the final days of the campaign. One such guy, painfully skinny, smelling like wet paper, with a flamingo's odd, angular physical comportment, asymmetrical about the eyes, put his face perilously close to my ear and said, "I see you, black man" in a conspiratorial whisper. I thanked him and, statesmanlike as I could, said that I saw him too.

The featured speaker was Peter Yarrow, from Peter, Paul and Mary—of course he thought the candidate hip—with his white, wavelike mullet playing softly at his neck. His spread-out features and intense eyes conveyed an almost off-putting peace, an ocean of equanimity. He looked like he'd never set foot in a city. He walked in unaccompanied, a nylon-stringed guitar hanging from his back, and when he saw me standing there, acting official, a look of wonder spread across his face. I wanted to tell him about how I'd sung "Puff, the Magic Dragon" non-stop for about a month shortly after my third birthday, or about how unfathomable it was to me that someone—a person alive today—had brought "If I Had a Hammer" to fame. That song seemed permanent, a feature of the landscape of my life as natural as rock or sand. *Sing out a warning*—my God.

But Yarrow rushed up to me before I could speak.

"You work for the campaign?" he asked. I nodded yes, starstruck for the first time in more than a year. Yarrow looked me in the eyes, quiveringly sincere, and made a sighing sound. Then, as if compelled by an outside force, he quickly grabbed my neck and pulled me close to him, settling into a harrowingly static full-body hug.

"Oh *God*," he said. "*Finally*, a person of color!"

When I couldn't find words for a response, he kept going.

"You know, I've been back and forth across the country for this campaign"—*all over this land*, I thought—"and you'd be absolutely shocked by the demographics of the staff . . ."


WALKING BACK UPTOWN THAT NIGHT, I felt like Yarrow's peace had left its mark on me. I waded through the darkness of the evening, checking out faces, rarely looking to the right or left. Along the way, though, I caught a glimpse through the wide, steamed-up window of a brightly lit diner I'd often passed but never eaten at. There was a television hanging over the far corner of the place's small, beige, dingy bar, tuned to CNN. On the screen was a face that, surreally, looked like Earnest Blackshear's. The face—still and smiling, a stock headshot farmed from some website—looked, in fact, so much like Blackshear's that I found myself passing through the diner's doors, hovering with a vague energy near the bar, hoping nobody would try to seat me or take an order, so that I could hear what was being said on the broadcast. The face in the picture that looked like Blackshear's was Blackshear's. A deep, dimpling smile swept his calm plains of a face. He wore a dimpled tie. He seemed old—more like he looked in person than he did in other photographs—but also secure, untouchable.

*Earnest Blackshear,* the voice of a news anchor was saying, *a pioneering New York commodities trader, was indicted today on several charges of campaign finance fraud, connected with his involvement in—*

The small hairs at my ears and on my cheeks got hot and started to sting. As the anchor went on, Blackshear's photograph never left the screen. As the words—the allegations—accrued, his face, wily and strong, perpetually amused, by now so familiar, started to mean something new to me. Aspects of his comportment and personal style that had, for more than a year, seemed mysterious now seemed obvious in their origins, almost bland.

*—The U.S. attorney said in a statement that Blackshear funneled campaign donations through more than a thousand so-called straw donors, flagrantly violating campaign finance law and resulting in almost two and a half million dollars in illegal contributions to—*

The screen changed. Blackshear's face was gone, and the anchor's appeared: a generically pretty woman with dark brown hair and hilly eyebrows, her legs crossed beneath a glass desk. She spoke to the camera for a while, her eyes perfectly still despite her mouth's activity. Then a cutaway—another photograph.

*—Authorities are also reportedly conducting a parallel investigation into Beverly Whitlock, a bundler for the campaign who worked closely with Blackshear, our sources say, on all of his fundraising activities—*

The picture of Blackshear had been recent—could have been taken yesterday, showed the full measure of his longevity: his history and age—but the photograph of Beverly that now stood still on the screen was well outdated. It was the first photograph of her I'd ever seen: the old *Black Enterprise* cover with the towers behind her, bracketed by twin blues—the river and the sky. Her gray suit without wrinkles and her arms folded, her bright smile a sociology of merited satisfaction. Back then, the big news was that she'd found her black way, like a pioneer to the coasts, toward a bounty of white cash, the kind that arrived in untroubled handfuls and made its recipients instantly plausible, respectable, inevitable, clean. "Beverly Whitlock Seals $175 Million Deal." Now here she was, similarly situated, dangling over the raw edge of that barely settled continent.

When I'd told her about my worries about Blackshear, I'd wondered what she knew. Now I wondered what I'd known, whether, in my practiced informational speeches, I'd made the nuances of the law clear enough; whether—understanding . . . *something* . . . without that understanding yielding a harvest of language I could use—clarity had ever really been my goal. Maybe my demeanor had sent a signal saying, *Use me however you'd like to.* But I was nobody, I thought, already soothing myself. *Nobody* couldn't make something like this happen. I felt a rushing surge of pity for Beverly, up there helpless on the screen, first in my stomach then down toward my groin.

A waiter with a meaty face and ice-blue eyes came over and waved with a weary grace toward the stool I was standing next to. Taking the cue as a command, I sat and ordered a fried fish sandwich and fries.

—*The campaign made no response to these allegations, except to say that they would immediately refund each of the contributions in question*—

"DAVEY!" MY MOTHER SAID WHEN I got home. Her TV, like the one at the diner and the ones in hotel lobbies all over town, was fastened to the news. "Davey, what's . . . are you . . . in trouble?"

I hadn't been home so much. For months now, I'd slept at Beverly's, as a kind of live-in apprentice, or, otherwise, away at work. Nothing else in my life, I realized, had much figured in. I stayed at home every other weekend and on a weeknight here or there, when the baby was with me. I spoke to my mother with the awkwardness of a stranger. After her early raft of questions just after I'd gotten the job, Mom had been careful not to ask how things were going or how long I'd be keeping this weird schedule—she was almost ostentatious in restraint. She was proud of me, I knew.

Beverly was my mentor; she'd brung me to the party and was now my partner in the dance. All year I'd seen staffers pair off, subtly or unsubtly but never quite undetectably—having witnesses was a large part of the point—with the donors with whom they'd become closest. As an official matter, favoritism was frowned upon: each donor needed to know that their "access"—to our office; to information; to the candidate himself—had only to do with merit, with dollars cajoled out of colleagues and family and friends. It wouldn't do to have people ducking under the velvet ropes, ushered along by anything so chintzy and abstract as a friend. But in practice favorites flowered. Were encouraged, if I'm honest. "Everybody needs a rabbi," I was told more than once. And even the rabbis had rabbis. There was, for instance, the class of people like Beverly, who had money but not so much, who raised it in handfuls, and knew how to stay seen, and, often, traded on their previous relationships with the boss. FOC, they were often called. Friends of the Candidate. One measure—a huge measure, really—of success in the job was the odd and sometimes disconcerting degree to which you could turn these people into your own Friends. Just as Alexis had ridden in on Clarence's back, I had come in quite accidentally—it was accidental on my part, at least: I grew more convinced every day that she'd had her own more or less self-apparent intentions—on Beverly's. And Beverly, in turn, close to power but without a permanent grip on it, had sought out a spin in Blackshear's ride. Blackshear got his gas from the ground, God's ground, like a rig out at sea. He'd let it gush too profligately, let it slip across too many hands, and now . . .

A national campaign was a great unfathomable whale, with all kinds of subsidiary life flourishing on its skin and between its strands of baleen. You had to find a place and hold on. Each new degree of closeness to your host was a sign of industry, a kind of diligence.

I wanted to convey all of this to my mother. She didn't mean to say, "I told you so," but she did have the sad, wise look of an unheeded prophet, surveying the doom—inevitable in fact if not predictable in detail—that she'd foretold. All I could say, feebly, was "I don't know."

THE NEXT MORNING, JILL CALLED me into one of the office's mostly empty rooms. Open window, spare desk. My stomach had hurt all night and morning. I was sure I'd be interrogated, or fired, or worse: slowly insinuated, first by figure—a "young staffer" somehow in on the game—and then by name, into the news. I'd certainly expected Jill to be upset. But she looked happy—even excited. One of her tight but real professional smiles was printed like a kind sentence across her face. Not unlike the first day she'd heard of Blackshear.

"Well, fuck," she said appreciatively. She looked like she'd learned a good piece of gossip, not from the news but in a private conversation with a friend. Then she reached across the clean desk and touched my arm gently.

"Did you tag all those donors in the system? All of Earnest's?"

I had.

"Let's get a spreadsheet of all of 'em. We'll have to send those to Chicago today. Get those refunds started."

Every once in a while over the next few days, a fresh mention of Blackshear and Beverly would shiver across the screen of one of the televisions in the office. Nobody changed the channel. But the story was already fading, and my name never came up. And why would it? My nobodiness had saved me.

Beverly, now lost at sea, had been proven right. Money had completed its travel, over the course of the campaign, from true commodity to pure symbol. It had helped prove the candidate's virtue—nobody unfit for the presidency, too green to wield its powers, could have gathered resources with such clean efficiency. And that virtue, now proven, had won him the benefit of the doubt. Was a character witness. Researchers everywhere, in the media and, surely, among the staff ranks of our opponent's campaign, had searched public records for other fishy-seeming instances and found none. You could almost hear the journalistic sigh of relief; nobody had to smudge the nation's one hopeful thing. Each day, the names—Earnest Blackshear, Beverly Whitlock—were more softly spoken. Soon you didn't hear them so much at all. The waters in which the whale swam, florid with life-forms unthinkable up here on the surface, had closed over them, wouldn't be troubled by them again. They sank.

Believe me, I did ache for Beverly. Well, more precisely: I ached when I wasn't angry. Thinking over our talks—and, too, the playful jousts in bed that she'd so calmly guided me through—all I could remember was how well she'd soothed me. Everything around me was natural, obvious, part of a pattern you could pick out if only you had ears to hear. That was the message. And so perhaps she'd been lulling me to sleep. Or she, too, had been lulled—by the candidate or by Blackshear or by the sheer force of desire's current. In any case, whatever her motive or meaning, she'd walked me to the water's edge and almost forced me to drink.

Still, yes, I was sorry for her. She'd brought me. A few times, at my desk, I thought to email Thadd, or even send Beverly herself a short text. Then I thought of things I'd seen in movies—wires and phone taps and listening agents, tapes spooling in slow circles—and decided against it. It took me a week or two to stop speaking her name.

# 16

EARLY ON THE MORNING OF ELECTION DAY, I SAT HALF-DOZING ON
a flight to Chicago, where the candidate would give his speech,
win or lose. Howland was in the seat next to me, asleep with
his head on my shoulder. I slept fitfully, shedding my last few
doubts about the outcome of the election, tossing *what if* scenarios around in my mind in order to ward them off. *What if*
the polls had been bogus all along? *What if* they'd left unde-
tected some current of racism strong enough to help the war
hero win? *What if* we staffers had all flocked to the Midwest
just to experience a great disappointment en masse? *What
if,* I thought, these speculations running amok, Beverly soon
crossed the line between *investigation* and *indictment,* joining
Blackshear in the courthouse queue, and a sweep through her
email combed up my heretofore meaningless name? Each of
these I batted away, more or less easily, riding the line between
consciousness and sleep.

Chicago, for me, is a counterfactual city. I'd lived there as a
kid for six years. Sometimes on trips to headquarters I babbled

about those days to Howland. More often, I kept the remembrances to myself. Both journeys, on either side of my deep childhood, to and away from the Midwest, had been occasioned by my father. After one of his periodic disappearances—I was two, and my mother bewildered—he'd turned up in Chicago, with a new job playing music at a Catholic church. St. Benedict the African, it was called, where they bent the liturgy toward the tastes and cultural styles of former Baptists like my folks. *Lead Me, Guide Me,* a hymnal for black Catholics, was a second Bible in our home. Being buddy-buddy with the Jesuits (and presumably, in his prodigal's way, with God) paid off for Dad again. Most of his work back home had come at their pleasure. The food of the Eucharist became food for my family.

It was fairly easy and perversely fun to imagine what I'd have been like had things gone otherwise. Catholic schools all through high school and, likely, into college—Fordham? Georgetown? Notre Dame? And what next? What if I'd become a priest? Or taken more seriously my thoughts of being a writer, started some novel? I wondered how the Chicagoan version of myself would judge, if he could, the real version—unescapable me—that time and accident and history had actually produced.

Augie March: "I am an American, Chicago born." What I like about that opening is its confidence in place. So much else changes, so quickly. Time grinds. God hides. How nice at least to feel your feet on the ground. That's part of the charm of that nickname: City of the Big Shoulders. Typed out it looks like somebody's broad back. Immovable, sure, rooted. Somebody because somewhere. As a boy, I used to think of that name and imagine myself grown—I always hoped I'd be big, even fat.

What if security could nourish you to growth? Or teach your hands to fight? I thought I'd be a crusher. Professional wrestling was second only to basketball as my truest televisual love.

My mother tells a story about our first Fourth of July in Chicago. We were on our way home from a party at the home of one of my parents' new friends—some fellow parishioner or teacher—and, on the road, several people, in tandem, as if choreographed or urged by a radio signal, reached out of their car windows and started shooting real bullets—substitute fireworks—into the air. She'd thought the Bronx was tough before that. The anecdote sounds like something out of another of Bellow's books, the one about a dean at a Chicago university who's written a long lament about the city in one of America's glossiest, most respected, least read magazines. Then, too, the professor is involved, inanely, in a criminal case following the death of a student at his school—at the hands, he says, of a black pimp and a black prostitute, both infamous in the squalid corners of town. The case and the article get the man—whose name is Corde, and whose cord, I'm sorry to report, is sort of fraying as he sits waiting in Bucharest for the death of his wife's mother, and for more news about the trial—labeled a kook, which he more or less is. But, oh!, to belong enough to a place to get so disillusioned by it. To feel so disappointed, when disappointment—reactionary ardor—comes from love!

When my mother and I finally arrived in town, my dad had yet to make real arrangements. Like some skewed Holy Family, we three lived in a convent, among nuns. We stayed in a small room with one wall of exposed brick. There were two doors—one leading into the hallway, the other out into a little walled garden clothed in ivy. We got there for the first

time late at night. Most of what I remember of that place
(memories transplanted largely from photographs) is evenings.
I stood at the garden door, dressed in white, cheesing wildly,
on the night of my baptism, at five or six. Flash light from a
disposable camera further smeared my Vaselined face. Nights,
my father spooned me in his blue terry-cloth robe. We three
shared one bed. By the time we found our own place we'd all
become wards of one institution: the school that belonged to
the church where my dad played also hired him as a music
teacher, and hired my mom—a gifted teacher who has spent
the rest of her life perfecting her lectures on the Epistles and
the Psalms, who could have, in another life, been a politician or
a university professor—as a second-grade teacher. Of course I
went to the school too, a student to both my parents. We kids
would file into my father's music classroom, all mandatorily
shake his hand at the door—we two found it hilarious to pre-
tend that our relationship was all business, conducted only in
the classroom—and sing the same song everyday:

> *Good morning, good morning, good morning to you!*
> *Good morning, good morning, good morning to you!*
> *Our day is beginning—there's so much to do.*
> *Good morning, good morning, good morning to you!*

For a good twenty-five years I believed, not because I'd been
told outright but via some strange apophatic pre-logic—he
couldn't not have written it—that this was my father's origi-
nal composition, until one day recently when, watching reality
television, I saw a famous gospel singer singing it in harmony—
tight thirds—with her young daughter. Before I could think too

much about it, a muffled anger rose and tears formed at the edges of my eyes.

We sang another song, in a language whose name no one ever offered but we all knew to be "African"—as in "How's that African song go again?"; such things happened quite often in the eighties and nineties. It went:

> *Ashe'ooooooo!*
> *Ashe'o-Kwa!*
> *Ashe'ooooooo!*
> *Ashe'o-Kwa!*

Then, in seeming translation:

> *We lift up the name of God!*
> *We lift up the name of God!*

The language must have been some bastardized Swahili. The tune was pentatonic, exotic to my ears. Such was the sunny Afrocentrism of late-twentieth-century Chicago: when my father's choirs, school or church, sang programs at black schools, or for Kwanzaa concerts at community centers, he wore a black-and-white strip of kente cloth around his shoulders like a shawl.

I got lightly teased for having my folks as teachers—especially my dad, whom everybody knew. Some older kid whose face I still unaccountably remember—tall, thin, yellow-skinned, close-eyed, runny nose—used to pantomime the spankings he imagined I received: "Ashe'o!" *Whap!* "Ashe'o-Kwa!" *Whap whap!* It was one of the funnier jokes I'd heard at the

time, a lesson in subtly twisted specificity; the unspoken law
of the "snap contest," which said I couldn't laugh along at myself, made me suffer. My actual spankings were rare, unmusi-
cal, and, on the whole, as far as I could tell, richly deserved.

"I am an organic Chicagoan," Gwendolyn Brooks once
said under interview. I probably felt that way once. My mother,
never. Sunstruck by the move, she toted me from museum to
museum, probably hoping to cure her homesickness and anger
at my father—sublimated into intense watchfulness over my
manners and education—by way of knowledge and, sometimes, art. We two were always close. Her favorite museum
was the DuSable, a shrine to black art, where we looked up—
I can't count how many times—at an Archibald Motley painting. She liked to point out individual brushstrokes and narrate
their movements without the context of the larger picture. She
walked into laundromats just to smell the clothes.

MY FAMILY'S WHOLE LIFE IN Chicago was studded by visits from
New York—reminders of my parents' old life and mine. How
porous it all was: what could've been and whom I could've
known in New York had an ongoing correspondence with reality in Chicago, and sometimes the two realms ramified together. When I was five or six, a cousin came to live with us.
Whether I'd been primed for his arrival I can't remember. Late
one night, my father's sister's daughter showed up at our apartment on Cregier Avenue, where I had the first dream I can
remember: a snake eats a white princess. (The book of Genesis
and a thousand years of art history were already doing their
work on me.) My cousin Meena was probably eighteen or nineteen then; I'd never met her before. Through a crack in my

bedroom door I watched her enter our apartment and stood there thinking that she was the most beautiful person I'd ever seen: a head of huge, ropy braids, dangling earrings, matte dark skin, high, full eyebrows, a small mouth and small ears. She wore marbled blue jeans and a heavy-looking black leather jacket. Neither of my parents seemed surprised to see her— I peeked out from the dark of my bedroom and listened to them talk. I was supposed to be asleep.

With Meena was a little boy—yellow-skinned with brown, peasy hair. The three adults (to me Meena was an adult) talked for hours. I could hear melioration in my father's voice; exasperation in my mom's. Meena spoke sparingly, but when she piped up, she was loud and used a pattering honk that would ring pleasantly in my memory until, years later, I encountered it en masse in New York and could place it as a specimen of a type. No words came clearly through the door, only tones. Soon I snuck back to sleep.

In the morning, Meena was gone but the boy was still there: Thomas. For some reason, nobody ever called him Tommy. He was three then, bad as hell, ceaselessly active, and a Hoover for the attention I'd always, as an only child, taken for granted as my property. I'd often noodged my parents about wanting a sibling, but when Thomas showed up—he ended up staying with us for two years—I quickly understood my folly. Once, at Mass, he teased me about my crush on a girl, and, during the sign of peace, I grabbed him by the collar. Back at home we took a pair of whoopings from my mom, who—because my father, the kid's actual uncle, never helped out—was suddenly a bristling, frazzled mother of two instead of one. Another time, in his underwear, he ambushed me like a spider monkey— sharp nails and little kicks—and ended up sitting with his groin

atop my face. Embarrassed and furious, I bit. He yelped and
went running to my dad, whose face twisted and turned red—
now that I think back on it, he was weirdly and disproportion-
ately upset. Dad yanked me into a corner. I was to sit there for
a half hour, he said, "and really think about how disgusting
that is: somebody's penis in your mouth." I was so shocked by
his anger and furious with Thomas that I couldn't say I hadn't
put it there.

Worst, perhaps, was a nighttime drive with Dad, who, at
some point on the way home, slipped past a red light. I was
a righteous little boy, a tiny judge, and my dad's descent into
illegality galled me. Thomas, on the other hand, was thrilled.
When we reached home, I wouldn't touch or look at my
dad—he was now a kind of convict in my eyes. (Only later
in my life did love hunger surpass my pinched obsession with
justice.) Rebuffed by me, Dad reached for Thomas, for whom
transgression was all attraction. Thomas climbed gleefully onto
his shoulders, and the two, together, bopped from the curb into
the vestibule of our building. I trailed behind them, already
regretful.

I remember feeling a mixture of sorrow and relief when,
eventually, Meena visited again and Thomas disappeared.

The next visitor was my uncle Jim. He wasn't a real brother
to either of my parents, just a best friend they held in common.
He had moved to New York from South Carolina as a young
man, along with his big, close family. Addicted to music but
unable to play or sing, Jim started almost immediately to hop
from one church to the next, on long Sundays that doubled
as sightseeing tours of Harlem, checking out choirs. He was a
friend maker. Soon he knew all of his favorite soloists—he'd ac-
cost them with flattery after the service. He knew the choir di-

rectors too; he flattered them as well, but gradually also learned to level friendly critiques. Mightn't they take this number a bit more slowly, in order to showcase Sister Jackson's unbelievable legato? Your robes are good, but a little purple piping could heighten their dramatic effect. That march-in could use a bit more bop, don't you think? He had a high, thin, questioning voice, ever so slightly sibilant, and he spoke with a friendly authority. The directors who took his notes found their choirs growing gradually more popular, and their Sunday-morning pews more tightly packed. He took a few jobs directing but, wanting more freedom to experiment than any local pastor would provide, started his own choir. He called them the JAB Singers, after himself: James Anthony Brown. He'd seen my dad play and my mom sing and recruited them both. They met at a rehearsal. "I'm the only reason you're alive," he often said, teasing me. His two sisters and their five old aunts—all tall ladies with clear, reddish skin and lushly white hair—were my first babysitters. Against my mother's wishes they fed me catfish and red beans and rice and collards.

I never knew what brought him to Chicago, but he showed up one day and, like Thomas, stayed for more than a year. He watched daytime soaps and talk shows and let me watch along with him as he lobbed aesthetic observations.

"Now, Davey," he'd say. "That man there? All them moles? That is a seriously ugly dude." I'd crack up and he'd barely betray a smile. He treated me like a miniature adult and I loved him for it—when he made tea he made enough for us both, and we'd take out cards and play I Declare War until I could win a game or two.

When he left Chicago, he disappeared for a bit. Neither my parents nor his sisters could find him. Maybe he'd dissolved like a sugar crystal into the deeper and less urban Midwest. Maybe he'd kept on drifting and found the coast. Eventually, though, like everybody else I know, he washed up back in New York.

Our escape from Chicago was abrupt, too. All I knew was that Dad was sick. Six years after we showed up, by which time I could only think of myself as a Chicagoan, my father—poor father—sprouted lesions and started to die. My parents agreed, I guess, that it'd be better for him to do that in New York, where both of their families still lived. When we all ended up back in New York, my entire recallable life—save a few fragments: the plane ride away from Manhattan; church ladies in Harlem, bedoilied, hopping around like huge frogs and beating madly at tambourines—was, once we'd completed the hurried move, just an episode. "I used to live in Chicago" was now how, in New York, a city foreign to me (the dog shit everywhere I found astounding), I started conversations and tried to make friends. I idealized the place—made it an idol. If we hadn't left, my dad wouldn't've died. Or did I have that backward?

The last time I saw my father, he was lost among plastic tubes, breathing heavily with help from machines whose purpose I couldn't fathom. We three held hands and said the Our Father. He died in a small hospital downtown, where nuns stood watch over the political deaths of plague victims. I couldn't tell which kind of death his was—I was one of the last Americans, I sometimes felt, with unabashedly secretive parents. He died, we were New Yorkers, and the world kept rushing on. On the night of his funeral, I wrote a song.

# 17

OFF THE PLANE AND CHECKED INTO OUR SHARED HOTEL ROOM,
Howland and I found ourselves suddenly without much to do.
The ballots wouldn't start being counted for several hours. We
unpacked our bags and dumped the contents on our beds,
then, from Howland's laptop, played "American Boy," by the
British pop singer Estelle, featuring Kanye West. It was a me-
chanical song, more surface than soul, indicating a joy it didn't
really embody. The melody was fuzzy, bright, unremarkable in
its catchiness, but the rhythm pushed you forward, made you
dance. Lip-synching, we made Kanye-like bodily gestures and
fixed our jaws into facsimiles of his vulnerable scowl.

Both of us were exhausted, and the finish line was near—
we felt silly and directionless, in the mood for nervous fun.
After the song had looped three times and we were fairly out
of breath, Howland looked at me and spoke loudly and with
a jokey force. "He's definitely going to win," he said. "This is
practice for the party."

Around noon, we left the room. We were free until five or so,
when we fundraisers would herd the donors into a booze-bedecked

tent in Grant Park, just behind and to the side of the stage where, win or lose, after the votes were slowly counted, the candidate would address a huge crowd. We went downstairs, approached the big, horseshoe-shaped hotel bar, and started to drink.

I DAYDREAMED ABOUT BEVERLY CALLING. She'd skip hello and feign seriousness, in a low cello's voice tell me that she hadn't known what Blackshear was up to—hadn't known that Blackshear's success in getting his employees to give was a sheer matter of money handed out and urged forward. She'd make the whole passage of incident—arrival and success, celebration and swift stumble—seem inevitable, the first step in some mysterious but viciously logical plan. She'd say *right,* and a vapor would clear. I'd understand.

I could see her now, secret smile and complex eyes, skidding over waters that would drown some other swimmer. I felt sorry for her. The silence around her was like an unattended funeral. Surely she'd helped efface herself. Or figured out that for someone like her—now I could recognize her as *nobody*—self-effacement was the fast track to success. You were somebody else's friend, somebody else's classmate, an usher for somebody else's entry into the big game, and you might, after a while, have a name worth sounding out. Drinking, talking shit with Howland, pantomiming the motions of the day, I thought I could hear her voice. She'd reached past narrative, past symbols, waded through money—mostly Blackshear's—looking for . . . well, she would probably call it *power,* but I knew it was something else. More like fun.

———

A FEW HOURS BEFORE WE were all supposed to come together at Grant Park, I stole quietly away and caught a cab. Without planning to, I gave the driver the only Chicago address I could remember. We drove toward the South Side, the river sparkling to one side and the city to the other. As downtown and the tall buildings receded behind the car, the city became the one I'd known as a child. Weeds pushed up from ancient cracks in the sidewalk. People—uniformly black—walked with an easy purpose, attending to chores and herding children. They seemed less impressed than my friends by the heaviness of the day. Every few blocks I saw a school or church with a voting line wrapped around its sides, but otherwise the atmosphere—here away from the bazaar of donors at the hotel—felt strangely normal.

I hadn't seen the church for many years. There were wooden boards across the windows I remembered, and the faces of the stone statues peeking from the upper floors had started to crumble. A big willow tree, smaller than it had been in my memory, scraped the sidewalk. Across the street were one-story houses, alert peaks for little heads, in a neat row. Somewhere a lawn mower was going, but I couldn't see it. I got out of the cab and started to walk.

The church was quiet—the quiet of many years. Diocesan downsizing: I should've guessed. I felt stupid for coming, in search of some impossible catharsis. From behind one of the boards a thin branch, dense with leaves, was growing. I watched the wayward branch sway, loving its color, for many minutes, minutes I didn't count, before I turned and left.

A quick search on my phone showed me where the new church bearing the parish's name now stood. Not far. I walked through the nearly empty South Side streets, taking in their

green odor. The old church wasn't the only boarded-up place.
Townhouses with yellow trimmings, low-ceilinged multifamily
homes, many apartment buildings whose clean windows I'd
once seen: so many of them were now crumbling from dis-
use, domestic spaces gone Gothic. Great gaps in the sidewalk
opened up like hungry mouths.

The new church had a modern feel. Its small building was
circular and low to the ground, its walls mostly windows. Its
people—some of whom I'd maybe remember—worshipped in
what looked like a covert observatory, poking out of the surface
of the sea. The neighborhood could see in and they could see
out. Two kinds of witness—proselytizing by mere sight. The
door was open. As I walked up to sit in a pew near the altar,
at the rise, nobody looked my way. There were a few older
women lazing through rosaries, mumbling pleasantly in low
tones, and a roly-poly priest—I could clock him even without
his clerical garb—adjusting the ferns and birds-of-paradise at
either side of the sanctuary. I looked up at a big, pliant-looking
wooden fan whizzing above my head, then, after a moment,
closed my eyes.

I was thinking about Jean Baptiste Point du Sable, the black
trader after whom my mother's favorite museum was named.
He'd established himself at the mouth of the Chicago River,
making money there at the convergence of waters before the
city had been named. He'd come from Haiti, maybe. Married a
Native woman and made her Catholic. Maybe. Everything I'd
ever heard about him was a myth. On elementary school quiz-
zes in history I'd had to identify him as the founder of Chicago.
Whatever your circumstances, our teachers had said, you could
be proud of a black man like this, from whose foreign hands
your whole world, the whole heaving city around you, flowed. I

imagined du Sable now as a twin of the candidate: come from parts unknown to the Midwest, mimicking then mastering the rhythms of its deeper currents, making his name, staking out ground. The campaign was like a fur he'd won in a trade. Or it was like the river spread out at his feet, carrying so many hidden, dark-eyed life-forms under its ever-shifting surface. Or, I thought, it was one of those unfathomable creatures, known but unseen, moving with the flow, slipping guilefully, unpredictably, with supreme skill away from predators and toward its own prey, shaking off silt as it went.

I think du Sable occurred to me when I realized that I couldn't remember a single thing about the black saint after whom this church was named. A black Benedict. I thought he might be Italian, but the rest was lost to me. For now the trader was my patron, his commerce the holy figure through which I directed my prayer—a sudden prayer had started; this, I realized, was why I'd left the hotel—to God.

I muttered soundlessly, without much aim, rifling through idioms, reaching for new frequencies, searching for a melody, needlessly complicating snatches of the future president's phrases, which kept playing at my ears, and I felt myself repelled by politics and disgusted by everyday life, attracted again, too urgently, to the veiled God of my youth, if only because He still spoke words I couldn't comprehend.

IN THE BACKSEAT OF A long white shuttle bus from the hotel to the donor tent in Grant Park, our team sat side by side, all facing forward together, like a row of kids in church: me, Howland, Hannah, Ashley, Jill. Jill's face was white, and her reddish freckles were correspondingly hypervisible. Each looked like the marker for a capital on a map. She didn't speak, so neither did the rest of us.

The bus dropped us on an undistinguished patch of grass; in many places, maybe most places, the ground was more muddy brown than green. We took squelching steps from the van to the vast white tent. Underneath were hundreds of chairs arranged around televisions—what they were plugged into I never found out—and finger foods on contingent tables, and donors jetting around, hugging and sometimes kissing one another, intermittently looking at the screens, working themselves up into a Dionysian mood. I recognized lots of their faces, knew their businesses and, in some cases, their business. Every once in a while, one of them looked over approvingly at me. Almost uniformly, I'd never seen any of them so drunk. People who thought they were having private conversations were more or less yelling. I'd expected to hear at least an undercurrent of buzz about Blackshear, and certainly about Beverly, notionally a friend to so many of the donors on the bus. But they'd cast no shadow that I could see now. Nobody mentioned their names or showed the slightest sign of worry. Nobody thought we'd lose. It was a big country. The blood under the skin of their cheeks blared attractively pink. How did I feel? Well, what did I know? A few times, here or there, as I stood by a table slurping up snacks, I could feel myself getting upset. I'd been deceived after all. In a way. I couldn't muster indignation, as hard as I tried. Maybe I was the last to figure out that I had changed. Been helped. I didn't feel grateful, not really. But, then, too, here I was under the tent. Still *in* things. So I got my body and my thoughts under control, settled my stomach, felt my feet against the soft ground, and genuinely relaxed.

I looked up: the interior of the tent was taut, rising into

tight peaks and throwing parabolic shadows, often doubled—
darker, lighter, overlapping—onto itself. Bright lights, nearly fo-
rensic, were affixed to the poles that held it up. Its surface looked
soft. The wind picked up a time or two and ripples shuddered
harmlessly across the tent's hueless expanse.

When, just after eight, the vote totals started to come in, I
called Regina without thinking too much about it. She was one
of the campaign's best organizers—she'd always been, but now
everybody knew. This had landed her in Pennsylvania, where,
just this moment, at a union hall whose dank and musky particulars she tried to describe over the phone, she sat looking at
a TV, just like me.

"If we lose, do we disappear?" I asked.

"From what I hear: yes," she answered. "But this kind of
disappearance means you're free to work in local government
or write memos for some mediocre member of Congress."

Every time somebody on the news said something even
remotely positive—turnout seemed to be up in an area sure
to be good for the candidate; some reporter had witnessed a
sea of signs outside a polling location—a genteel whoop went
up under the tent. Over the phone I could hear that whoop's
wilder, working-class twin. The vote in Pennsylvania came in
quickly—the candidate had won it. Another doubled cheer
went up; Regina made a long, heaving sob that gently harmo-
nized, like a bowed double bass, the shrieks and howls of the
union types she'd organized. She couldn't stay on, she said; she
had to go celebrate. I could hear people near her calling out
her name. We assured each other that we'd talk soon and said
goodbye.

I sat in a chair near a screen, every once in a while saying
something lighthearted—crosscutting my mood—to Howland,

or to some other staffer or money-raiser I'd come to know. Really, though, as the mood in the tent grew even more assured, and the voices I could hear became burnished, brushed in gold, by their proximity—even stronger now—to the lead float on the American parade, I could feel a pressure rising and subsiding like surf in my chest.

Not long after I spoke with Regina, I saw Wilson futzing around with a canapé, looking unfrazzled by the magnitude of the night. I kept looking over at him, perhaps twenty yards from where I stood, hoping to glean some key to his calm. The longer I watched him, the more sloppily he ate. He could have been at home, eating over the sink. After more than a minute, he glanced back at me. He seemed unsurprised to see me staring. He shot me a quick, unironic thumbs-up, then kept up his grazing.

The news came over a set of huge speakers, just after I saw a banner with his face spread itself across the cable-news display—a sob rose in my chest and receded before it could culminate. At once, without being told, all of us walked away from the tent and waded out together into the heart of the crowd in the park. Victory synchronized our steps. Jill was pressed against one of my shoulders, Howland against the other.

Flanked by his wife and children, the candidate soon bounded onstage. He looked grave and classical, like some ancient ideal modernized and made to speak in preacherly tones. As I watched him give his acceptance speech, I found my mouth moving. I wasn't echoing his words but looking for formations of my own, some music I could use. I was different now; I knew that. I'd learned at a distance from the candidate, but more closely from the likes of Earnest and Wilson, and dozens of others whose names couldn't reach me then, a language of signs I hadn't known of before. Beverly most of all. *Right.* I could hear her somewhere out there, in the expanse she so expertly swam, talking her way away from trouble. Laughing lightly as if over the phone. Thanks to her I was now fluent. More fluent than I'd known before Blackshear's arrest. I wanted to be fazed, but I wasn't. And I couldn't admire the candidate—he was more than that now—or even sustain the same jazzy curiosity about him that I'd once nurtured, now that I could interpret the symbols he offered in such profusion.

He was a moving statue, made to stand in a great square and eke out noise. He mattered and didn't, just as my own history did and didn't. Just like the fathers I knew, who were *there*—they cast huge shadows and never sank—but were also ciphers, names that survived in our minds because of how deftly they evaded stable meaning.

I wondered too—here my mind sharpened and wouldn't let me skim—if I'd be this kind of silty half-entity for my own daughter. I knew that I wanted to be more than a Rorschach, more legible than a symbol, more vivid and musical, at least to the kid, than even the most laureled statue could ever be. I wanted to be real in a way that history wasn't, and realized, listening to the new president, that I didn't yet know how, couldn't fathom where to begin.

I pulled out my phone and opened the camera, stretched my arm unprayerfully toward the stage and took a picture.

# Acknowledgments

Beneath this book's surface is so much friendship, so much love. No gratitude I express here could ever be enough. Jessica Friedman, more friend than agent, you are *GE*'s watchful godmother, present and patient and insightful from the start. Thanks to David Ebershoff for your instant belief in, and understanding of, the merits of this project. So many others at Hogarth and Penguin Random House have helped it into being: Erin Richards, Jaylen Lopez, Windy Dorresteyn, Maddie Woda, Darryl Oliver, Matthew Martin, Bonnie Thompson, and Evan Camfield.

*The New Yorker* has been a home for my work, a source of constant encouragement and fun, and a laboratory for many of the ideas and techniques I put to use in this work. Endless affection for David Remnick, Henry Finder, Daniel Zalewski, Shauna Lyon, Valerie Steiker, Helen Shaw, David Krasnow, Ave Carillo, KalaLea, Alex Barasch, Rhiannon Corby, Steven Valentino, Naomi Fry, Alexandra Schwartz, and David Haglund— a true brother and friend and companion in thinking.

No writer makes it far without many sympathetic editors along the way. Thanks to Sol Park, Mickey Stanley, John Warner, Christopher Monks, Matt Buchanan, Jazmine Hughes, Willy Staley, Liz Helfgott, Matthew Sitman, Ben Williams, and many others.

The schools I've taught at have allowed me to test my thoughts against the daunting reality of a paying audience. Thanks to Brian Morton, Paige Ackerson-Kiely, and Amparo Rios at Sarah Lawrence; John Pilson, Gregory Crewdson, Elle Pérez, Lisa Kereszi, and A.L. Steiner at the Yale School of Art; and Christian Parker and Lauren Britt-Elmore at Columbia.

Speaking of schools—I've been taught so well over the years. Deborah Stanford, you lit a fire for literature that will never go out. Thanks, too, to Mami Fujisaki, Woody Howard, David Bain, Cates Baldridge, Eisa Ulen Richardson, and Michael Seth Stewart.

My main material is the language of people I like. Thanks to all of you—and to many more; I'm begging for forgiveness—for ringing in my ears: Jordan Thomas, Angela Flournoy, Ian Blair, Ming-Toy Waters, Ming-Toy Taylor, James Pepper, Aly Richards, Max Maisonrouge, Benjamin Yee, Jenny Yeager, Hildy Kuryk, Jennifer Gerst, Collier Schorr, Xin Wang, Sara Cwynar, Mary Gordon, Esther Fein, Zadie Smith, Darryl Pinckney, Daniel Mendelsohn, Alex Beatty, Andrew Marantz, Sarah Lustbader, Emily Nussbaum (to whom titling credit will always go), Clive Thompson, Garnette Cadogan, Thora Siemsen, Durga Chew-Bose, Jason Parham, Jay Caspian Kang, Max Read, Jonathan Shainin, Adam Shatz, Lydia Kiesling, Matthew Sitman, Dorothy Fortenberry, Dan Walden, Antwaun Sargent, Jasmine Sanders, Melvin Backman, Lovia Gyarkye, Matt Buchanan, Carina del Valle Schorske, Aminatou Sow, Doreen St. Felix, Alexis Okeowo, Kevin Young, Yashika Walker, Raygine DiAquoi, Shyla Kinhal, Ira Rigaud, Hannah Giles,

Juliana Stevenson, Laszlo De Simon, Davida Farhat, Corey Reed, Charles Reed, Chelsee Lisbon, Peter Nilsson, Alphesena Chung, Christopher Chung, and Allyson Chung.

Patty Lisbon, Joyce Robinson, Diana Thompson, Requithelia Allen, Elana King, Robyn Roberts: I can't really apologize for eavesdropping on your conversations for so many years. Somehow that listening helped make me.

RIP: Vinson Cunningham, Sr., Uncle Johnny Brown, Bishop Charles Reed, Mamie Edmond, and Karlim Edmonds.

José Leonor, Victoria Lowe, Christopher Mizell, Ikechi Ogbonna, Andrew Patterson, Timothy Stanley, and Dmitry Terekhov: Friendship like this . . . what can I say? I haven't ever deserved you. (This is not a ranking.)

Madisyn Cunningham, you are my inspiration and highest joy. Keep pushing. Iva Cunningham—Mommy—you have helped push me across every finish line in my life, including this one. You and me, always.

Renée, you are still everything to me. Thank you for all you did to protect and encourage and goad me—*Do your work!*—while I struggled through these pages. You made our life together a world of love, and I'm so grateful. Please be resting. I miss you.

## About the Author

VINSON CUNNINGHAM is a staff writer and a theater critic at *The New Yorker*. His essays, reviews, and profiles have appeared in *The New York Times Magazine, The New York Times Book Review, The Fader, Vulture, The Awl, Commonweal,* and *McSweeney's Internet Tendency*. A former staffer on Barack Obama's first presidential campaign and in his White House, Cunningham has taught at Sarah Lawrence College, the Yale School of Art, and Columbia University's School of the Arts. He lives in New York City.

To inquire about booking Vinson Cunningham for a speaking engagement, please contact the Penguin Random House Speakers Bureau at speakers@penguinrandomhouse.com.

vinson.nyc
X: @vcunningham
Instagram.com/vinsoncunningham

## About the Type

This book was set in Baskerville, a typeface designed by John Baskerville (1706–75), an amateur printer and typefounder, and cut for him by John Handy in 1750. The type became popular again when the Lanston Monotype Corporation of London revived the classic roman face in 1923. The Mergenthaler Linotype Company in England and the United States cut a version of Baskerville in 1931, making it one of the most widely used typefaces today.